"I refuse to get out of the car."

Dion scowled at her. "Look, Solange, you simply can't come with me."

"Why not? Are you going to get into trouble again?"

"No, this time, I won't be caught."

A chill washed over her. "What do you mean, you won't get caught? Dion, I've known you've been keeping something from me since the day we met. I don't know what it is, and you refuse to tell me. Fine. Keep your precious secret. But I'm not getting out of this car, so whatever you're up to, you're going to have to drag me along, too."

"Okay," he finally said with a hard edge to his voice. "But I'm warning you. You're about to get your first lesson in breaking and entering."

ABOUT THE AUTHOR

Tina Vasilos knows about Greek men from firsthand experience. "My husband's Greek," she explains. "In fact, he didn't even speak English when we first met. But we found a way around that, and now we've been married twenty years." Tina and her husband currently make their home in British Columbia, but they visit Greece frequently.

Books by Tina Vasilos

HARLEQUIN SUPERROMANCE
351—ECHOES ON THE WIND

HARLEQUIN INTRIGUE
68—UNWITTING ACCOMPLICE
101—WOLF'S PREY
132—PAST TENSE

Don't miss any of our special offers. Write to us at the following address for information on our newest releases.

Harlequin Reader Service
P.O. Box 1397, Buffalo, NY 14240
Canadian address: P.O. Box 603,
Fort Erie, Ont. L2A 5X3

Black Night, Amber Morning

TINA VASILOS

Harlequin Books

TORONTO • NEW YORK • LONDON
AMSTERDAM • PARIS • SYDNEY • HAMBURG
STOCKHOLM • ATHENS • TOKYO • MILAN

Published September 1991

ISBN 0-373-70467-4

BLACK NIGHT, AMBER MORNING

PROLOGUE

IF THEY SAW HIM, he was dead.

Anger and fear twisting in his gut, the boy shrank into the prickly, inadequate cover of shrubs lining the path. He held his breath, fearing they might hear it.

The officer came first, marching with the precise cadence learned in the military academy. The two prisoners followed him, their steps shuffling and uneven, as if their feet hurt. Behind them came two soldiers, prodding them on with an occasional, cruelly directed rifle butt.

The boy's breath rasped in his throat, and he bit back a gasp of rage as the smaller prisoner tripped and fell, collapsing like a bundle of rags.

Fitful moonlight bathed the scene as the other prisoner stooped over the woman and tugged at her. She moaned, struggling to rise. Pushing the man aside, one of the soldiers kicked the woman and forced her to her feet. The boy clenched his fist against his mouth to stop his own scream as the woman cried out in pain.

The prisoners stumbled up the hill, driven by guttural curses. Keeping his head low, the boy followed.

At the crest of the hill, buffeted by a light wind, he paused. Below him the city sprawled in a spangle of lights. The cone of Lykavettos, crowned by a white church etched in moonlight, rose against a faintly orange sky. A necklace of candles formed a looping garland as the Easter worshipers left the church and made their way home. On the mountain no one celebrated the resurrection. They only celebrated terror and death.

The boy turned away, forcing his reluctant feet down the path in the wake of the prisoners and their captors, hurrying to catch up, his eyes fixed on the beam of the flashlight held by the officer. The astringent odor of pine trees stung his nostrils, and he knew he wouldn't be seen in the dense shadows they laid on the path.

The group ahead had stopped in a clearing overlooking a heavily wooded ravine. Taking cover in a thicket of shrubs, the boy crept as close as he dared, oblivious to the thorns ripping at his hands and arms. The elusive scent of early poppies crushed beneath the soldiers' boots rose from the ground, sickening in its sweetness.

He crouched again, a peculiar fatalism gripping his emotions and mercifully rendering them numb. It was too late, too late. His parents were about to die, and there was nothing he or anyone else could do. He touched the packet hidden inside his shirt, reassured by the crackle of the airline ticket that rested there. After it was over, he would carry out his father's last wish.

Tomorrow he would be gone, away from the madness that held the country in a relentless vise. But tonight, tonight he had to witness the final, agonizing farewell.

The ominous click of cocked pistols pulled his attention back to the group at the edge of the ravine. His numbness receded, a searing anguish flooding his body, clawing at his heart. Two shots rang out, flat, harsh reports that didn't carry beyond the clearing, an execution carried out in secret with deadly efficiency.

The boy's body jerked spasmodically at the sound. "No!" he wanted to scream, but an instinct for self-preservation he couldn't override closed his throat. His own death would only prove that the oppressors had won. He had to live. He bit down on the inside of his cheek, welcoming the metallic taste of his own blood as tears scalded his face.

"A slide," the officer ordered. "Make sure they won't be found."

It was over. The boy's low-pitched moan was inaudible as a rumble more terrible than an earthquake he dimly remembered shook the night.

"Done." The officer's voice was cold, emotionless, as if he'd disposed of a minor inconvenience that hindered the smooth running of the military system. He turned and struck a match, holding it to his cigarette. In the brief flare the boy saw his hand. The smallest finger was peculiarly bent.

He frowned. Strange. Then its significance hit him. The man had an extra finger on his left hand. Impotent sorrow gave way to a grim elation. A distinctive mark. He would be able to identify the man when he met him again.

The soldiers left, one of them making some remark that caused the others to laugh, a macabre sound that lacerated the boy's raw emotions.

When the tramp of their boots had been swallowed by the night, the boy rose to his feet, creeping over to the rock slide. All traces of the night's murder had been obliterated. He stood for an instant, his lips moving in a prayer for their souls. Silently, grimly, he made the sign of the cross, his first two fingers and his thumb joined to touch his forehead, his chest, his right shoulder, his left, repeated three times.

Laying his palm over his heart, he lifted his tear-wet face to the sky. He clenched the other hand into a fist and raised it over his head. It didn't matter that he was only sixteen. He was the only one left in his family, suddenly projected into manhood by an act of barbarism too awful to contemplate.

Shaking his fist at the sky, he shouted, "I'll find him. I, Dion Parris, will find him. And I will make him pay."

CHAPTER ONE

SHE HEARD the first gossip before six when she met Grandma Amelia feeding her chickens under an amber sunrise.

"New man in town, Dr. Solange." The old woman smiled in a sly, knowing way, and winked one of her rheumy eyes. "They say he's from Canada. You'll have something in common."

Solange Richards hid a smile of her own. The people in the small town seemed to abhor the single state in anyone over twenty-five. She had been the victim of matchmaking schemes countless times in the past four years. "Maybe he has a wife and children in Canada," she said calmly.

Tucking her black scarf more firmly around her chin, Amelia shook her head. "He's your age, and he's single. Didn't old Costas know his father? He would have heard if Dion had married. Of course, it's been more than twenty years."

Solange let loose her smile as she wrapped her arm around Amelia's narrow shoulders and gave her a hug. "Exactly. I think it's a bit too early to arrange the wedding."

"You'll see," Amelia called after her as Solange continued down the street toward the open fields. "Dion was a beautiful child. He must be a handsome man."

Laughing, Solange waved her hand and broke into a run, her long blond ponytail swinging across her shoulders. Her feet kicked up puffs of dust as the sky changed from amber to pink and the sun rose in a blaze of gold. Sweat began to trickle down her back and chest, soaking her thin cotton tank top and shorts.

Solange threw back her head and inhaled deeply, the exhilaration of supreme good health flowing through her veins. A flurry of sparrows rose next to the path, sending a patch of scarlet poppies into an agitated dance.

It was May, the time of year she liked best, warmer than early spring but not yet settled into the heat of summer, the brief hiatus between Easter and the tourist season. Wildflowers and roses were at their best in May and early June, and the land lay quiet and fecund beneath the burden of maturing grain. Corn in a mile-long field already stood waist-high, its rich green maintained by colossal sprinklers that sent a cool mist drifting down the breeze.

She enjoyed running, but it had taken nearly a year for her neighbors to accept her morning exercise as normal. At first they had shaken their heads in amused pity. Traveling on foot in rural Greece meant that you were too poor to afford a car or bus fare.

Now they took it for granted, as they had taken her to their hearts. If she missed a day, someone was sure to stop by her flat or her office to see if she was ill.

Forty-five minutes later Solange jogged into the front door of the house where she rented a small flat on the upper floor. Voices in the kitchen told her the household was up, her landlady Demetra Candiles good-naturedly scolding her children as they prepared for school.

The heavier voice of Demetra's husband Vasili carried clearly up the stairwell. "Dion Parris is back in town? That will put the cat among the pigeons."

His teenage daughter Litsa spoke up. "They say he's as handsome as a film star."

"Yes," said Demetra. "Now maybe the doctor will notice something besides her microscope."

On the stairs Solange stifled a laugh. Microscope? Is that how they thought she passed the time between patients? It was true that she was engaged in research with her assistant Penny, but analyzing a few blood samples was hardly devoting her life to a microscope.

She continued up the stairs and slammed the door loudly as she went into her apartment. They might as well be aware she could have heard their conversation, though she knew it wouldn't stop them.

Stripping off her shorts and shirt, she stepped into the shower, welcoming the warm spray on her sweating body. Even this early in the morning the sun's heat was a force to be reckoned with. She loved it, though.

She had found Greece to be a land of contrasts—lush green fields set against stark mountains, the intense brilliance of day dying abruptly into the opaque black of night. The Greeks fought the elements of nature, drought and flood, heat and rocky soil, and when they overcame that, they fought each other.

In Greece there were no halfway measures. Every situation contained the seeds of high drama, passion. She understood passion—understood how to fight for something.

But she'd also found that extreme passion got one into trouble. And had learned to temper it. Her reputation for cool competence not only ruled her work but had spilled over into her personal life. She liked it that way.

She rinsed her hair and turned off the water. Wrapping a towel around her head, she dried her body, fluffing on powder from a plain white tin. Her hair, wet and dark as honey, curled around her face in tangled ringlets as she pulled off the towel and brushed it into place. Dry, it was pale amber, the color an unusual contrast to her easily tanned skin. The combination, along with her eyes, which were dark-lashed and brown instead of the blue people expected in blondes, gave a dramatic emphasis to her appearance that she didn't always find comfortable. Frowning at her image in the mirror, she twisted her hair into a knot at the back of her head.

Oh, she looked all right. She no longer had the inferiority complex that had turned her teen years into a hell of nonconformity. But she was hardly classically beautiful; her features were far too assertive for that.

Dion Parris was as handsome as a film star, was he? Well, he wouldn't be interested in her, then, no matter how her neighbors tried to push them together. On impulse she stuck out her tongue in a childish gesture of derision before turning away to dress for work.

APHRODITE, Solange's office nurse, had already opened the little clinic on the town square. Solange strode briskly through the reception room where several patients waited, greeting them with a cheerful *"Kali mera."*

"Morning, Aphrodite," she said as she entered her office. "How does it look?" As she spoke, she took a pink smock from the closet in the corner and put it on over her cotton skirt and blouse.

Aphrodite, a heavyset woman in her forties whose stolid serenity had proved an invaluable aid in treating nervous patients, handed her a clipboard. *"Kali mera,*

Solange. We've got a light day. Just the patients out there, and at ten a mother whose child has an earache."

Although most doctors' offices in Greece were run on the first-come, first-served basis, resulting in frequent lengthy waits for patients, Solange had instituted the appointment system. While it didn't work perfectly, it did allow her to plan her day.

The people of Korfalli were a sturdy lot, used to taking care of minor ailments on their own. That, of course, had its bad side; some patients let illness or injury go until it became serious or life-threatening before seeing the doctor. But on the whole, Solange's work was pleasant and rewarding. The townspeople liked her, and she liked them, even when she disagreed with them on treatment or medical philosophy.

Solange scanned the list, noting the names on it. All repeats, people she'd seen in the past weeks. An easy day.

"Okay, Aphrodite, call in the first one."

By eleven the outer room was empty. Aphrodite made coffee on the little gas hot plate in the corner of the office while Solange updated the files. She opened from eight to one, then again from seven to eight in the evening. The hours weren't long, with the substantial siesta break, but she was considered to be on call twelve or more hours a day. The work and the responsibility left her with little time for a social life but, since that was low on her list of priorities, it didn't matter.

Penny came in as Aphrodite set the tray of coffee cups on the desk. "Good morning," she said cheerfully, helping herself to a cookie. She was a pretty woman in her late twenties, with a small, slight body whose apparent fragility hid a tireless energy that Solange appreciated during winter flu epidemics. In jeans and a bright

T-shirt she looked more like a kid than a rising expert in the relation between diet, life-style and heart disease.

"Morning, Penny." Solange looked up from the files. "You didn't have to come in today. It's been slow."

"I just wanted to check out some test results," Penny said, moving to her own desk and gulping from the coffee Aphrodite set at her elbow. "Thanks, Aphrodite."

She sifted through files in the drawer, exclaiming triumphantly when she found the one she needed. Draining the cup, she set it back in the saucer with a clatter and headed for the door. "Solange, I'll let you know the results when I've analyzed the data."

"No rush. Where are you tomorrow?"

"I'm doing my rounds in the hills. I'll check on Mrs. Zogas if you want."

"Yes, I'd appreciate it, Penny. She was slightly toxic with her other pregnancy. I never could prove if that caused the miscarriage, but it's better to be on the safe side. If she shows any sign of swelling, ask her to come in."

Penny's straight black brows knit in a frown, and she pushed her glasses higher on her small nose. "If I can get her husband to agree."

"Oh, you won't have any trouble with him. He comes on like a bad-tempered bear, but he loves his wife."

"You could have fooled me."

Solange smiled. "I'm sure you'll handle it. By the way, will I see you at your aunt's tonight?"

Penny paused on her way to the door. "I've got a lot of work analyzing these tests. I'll see how it goes. See you."

Which probably meant no, Solange realized, frowning. After her estrangement from her parents, Penny was determined to assert her independence. The irony of it was that she had settled in Korfalli, where her uncle Peter Bulgaris was mayor. Which only proved that no Greek existed in a vacuum, and given the choice of living in a strange place or a town where he had relatives, a Greek would always choose the latter. The only pressure Penny hadn't bowed to was to live with her family. She had her own apartment in a new block on the edge of town.

Family relations were very complicated in this society, Solange had discovered, and rifts were often irreparable. Sighing, she turned back to the work on her desk.

Aphrodite seated herself in the chair opposite, pulling out her knitting. "Dion Parris came back," she said with a certain emphasis.

Solange sighed. "Yes, I know. Who is Dion Parris, anyway?"

Aphrodite's carefully plucked eyebrows rose. "You don't know? No one's told you?"

Abandoning her pretence of writing, Solange picked up the tiny cup and sipped the thick, syrupy brew. "No one's told me what? Oh, I know he's handsome and the perfect candidate to take the doctor away from her microscope, but who is he? Why all the fuss?"

"You've heard." Aphrodite blushed and busied herself with a stitch she'd inadvertently dropped.

"I've heard." Solange folded her hands on the desk and waited, her mouth turned up in amusement.

"Well, you're not married." Flustered, Aphrodite dropped another stitch. "It's not right for a woman to be alone. You should have considered Yannis Tsika's proposal last year." The nurse eyed Solange critically. "You're not getting any younger, and most of the men your age are married."

"I hardly think thirty-two means I'm ready for a pension," Solange said dryly. She'd had this conversation, or a version of it, with almost every woman in town at one time or another. "And there's always Penny. She's single, too."

Aphrodite pursed her lips. "She's even more hopeless than you are. Ever since she got away from the man her father wanted her to marry and alienated her family completely by going to medical school, she's had no use for men at all. Besides, just now she's too busy. Any man who wants her will have to catch her between projects."

"Well, I've been busy, too," Solange said in her own defense. "Come on, Aphrodi, who is Dion Parris?"

"A handsome man. A handsome, *single man*." Again Aphrodite stopped.

"Yes, I already know that. What else?"

Aphrodite used her spare knitting needle to scratch a spot at the back of her head. "His family lived here once, but they moved to Athens when he was a child more than twenty years ago. Let's see, Dion must be about thirty-five now."

Lowering her voice to a whisper, she leaned forward. "Something happened to them—we never heard exactly what except that it was political—and Dion was sent to live with relatives in Canada." Her voice resumed its normal pitch. "He's a professor at an important university there, and they say he's here to study the Sarakatsani. You know, those shepherds who used to travel all over the country, south in winter, north to the mountains in summer. Of course, now they've mostly settled in the towns." She pursed her lips. "Why anyone would be interested in them is beyond me."

"Oh, really?" Solange finished her coffee and set down the thimble-size cup. "I think the subject would be fascinating."

Would Dion Parris be equally fascinating? She told herself she didn't care, but curiosity nipped at her, a persistent nuisance that spoiled her concentration as she reapplied her attention to the files.

Aphrodite had the last word, however. "You're a beautiful woman, Dr. Solange. You need a man."

Solange couldn't help the laugh that tumbled from her lips. "Beautiful? Me? I'm too tall, too thin and my nose is too long."

"Nevertheless," Aphrodite said, her needles clicking, "you're beautiful. Never mind those cute girls in magazines with their turned-up noses and round cheeks. You've got character."

Character? That was something at least, Solange conceded with inward amusement. And character certainly wore better than prettiness as one grew older. Maybe it was just as well that God hadn't given her the snub nose she'd prayed for at fifteen.

Aphrodite rolled up her section of sweater and stuck the spare needle through the bundle of blue wool before stowing it in an embroidered knitting bag. She stood up, stretching, with a hand pressed to her lower back. "One o'clock. Looks like no one else is coming." Picking up her bag, she paused by Solange's desk. "Once he sees you, Dion Parris won't be able to help himself. He'll fall in love."

Before Solange could recover from this amazing statement and form a coherent reply, Aphrodite was out the door, closing it gently behind her.

Solange locked up shortly afterward. Swinging a string bag from her wrist, she walked by the shops, stopping to buy lamb chops at the butcher's and vegetables at the green grocer's. She good-naturedly fielded the comments that flew around her, the speculations on a future relationship between her and Dion Parris. She wondered if anyone was setting odds on how long it would take for them to be married, then dismissed the thought as ludicrous. They hadn't even met yet, for heaven's sake.

"If Dion Parris is anything like his father, you'll meet him before the day is over," the woman who sold her a carton of yogurt warned. "You're single, foreign and educated." She lifted her hand and touched Solange's cheek. "And all that fabulous blond hair as a bonus—he won't be able to resist you."

"Other men don't seem to have any problem resisting me," Solange said with a wry grin.

"Dion lived in Canada. He'll know how to handle a Canadian woman."

Solange laughed, but as she walked up the street toward home, her smile faded. What if the Canadian woman didn't want to be handled? Still, she had to admit, she was dying of curiosity to meet this paragon of manhood.

They'd probably hate each other on the spot.

THE MEETING CAME sooner than she expected.

At nine that evening Solange presented herself at the home of Peter and Anna Bulgaris, Penny's uncle and aunt, where she'd been invited for dinner. Anna, who knew everyone in town, had been one of Solange's first patients when she set up her practice. She'd been invaluable for public relations.

Solange had originally come to Greece as a volunteer member of a relief organization, treating the victims of

a devastating earthquake five years before. She had liked
Korfalli and its people. And she'd felt as if she knew it
from fading photos in the family album. Her parents
had lived there for the first year of their marriage. True,
it had grown and changed, but after the relief organization pulled out, she'd stayed on and opened her own
office. Now, after four years, she was well established,
both personally and professionally.

Anna greeted her at the door. "Solange, I'm so glad
you could make it. No babies due to take you away early,
are there?"

"Not at the moment." Solange smiled, allowing her
hostess to draw her into the living room where several
other couples sat or stood, all talking at once.

Coming from a rather reserved family, Solange had at
first been taken aback by the sheer volume that was a
necessary part of every gathering. But her neighbors
meant well, for all their exuberance, and their open-
hearted congeniality had helped pull Solange out of her
depression when she first arrived.

"Ah, here she is," Peter boomed as he mowed a path
through the small crowd. Solange dropped a kiss on his
cheek as he pulled her boisterously into his arms, his
ample belly making her feel as if she were hugging a pillow. "Lovely as ever, I see." He pretended to leer at her
ice-green silk dress, winking broadly at his wife as she
went to get Solange a drink.

Solange glanced around the room. "Penny didn't
make it."

Peter frowned briefly. "Said she was too busy."

Solange nodded. As she'd expected. Penny would use
almost any excuse to avoid social gatherings, especially
since the subject of marriage always cropped up.

"Never mind," Peter said. "She's promised to come for her birthday dinner next month." He kept his grip on Solange's arm as Anna handed her a glass of ouzo. Before she could take a sip, Peter had dragged her across the room.

"Solange, I'd like you to meet Dion Parris who has returned to our town to do research on the Sarakatsani. Dion, this is our good friend, Dr. Solange Richards."

"I'm happy to meet you at last," Dion said with a smile so captivating that Solange was barely aware of Peter leaving them. Dion's English was as unaccented as her own and, after months of hearing only Greek, his speech sounded strange to her ears.

"And I'm pleased to meet you," Solange answered.

She took the hand he offered. His long fingers wrapped themselves around hers briefly, then let go. But not before she noticed that there seemed to be a number of bandages crisscrossing his palm.

Concerned, she reached for his hand again, turning it over. His smile didn't waver as she eyed the blisters he'd clumsily bandaged. "How did you do that?"

"Digging. Clearing up the rubble so I could get into the house." He shrugged as if it were of little consequence. "I thought my hands were tough—I play tennis—but obviously they're not tough enough for real work." He curled his fingers into a fist, wincing slightly. "They'll heal."

"Better come by my office tomorrow. I've got some ointment that will speed the process."

He *was* beautiful, she thought, with clear olive skin, tanned but not leathery. His black hair showed a mind of its own, with loose curls already tumbling onto his forehead despite the neat cut. Beautiful didn't mean perfect, she realized. His nose was classically straight, but one of his upper teeth was just slightly out of line with the others, a flaw that enhanced the friendliness of his smile. And his firm jaw showed the faint shadow of heavy stubble, which he must have to shave twice a day.

Solange lifted her glass, ice cubes glistening in ouzo turned milky by the added water. "Welcome back to Korfalli. I suppose you consider it your ancestral home."

The smile slid away, turning his face momentarily somber. She caught a glimpse of sorrow in his eyes, a dark ghost walking through his consciousness before he pushed it into the background once more. Aphrodite had alluded to a mystery in his past. What was it? She could hardly ask him five minutes after they met, but the question remained at the edge of her mind.

His smile returned at once and the moment passed, leaving her wondering if she had imagined the ghost.

"I was a child when my family left," he said easily. "There's only the land and a ruined house." He took a sip from his own drink, a richly scented red wine. "It never was much of a house, and the last earthquake shook it up some. Maybe you know it. It's right at the west side of the town, with a large fig tree growing over it."

Her brows lifted. "You're living there?" She passed the house every day on her morning run. It was built of sun-dried brick, which was durable, but only if well maintained. This house had been abandoned for more than twenty years, defenseless against the ravages of earthquake and winter storm. "It looks ready to collapse."

Dion shrugged, his shoulders flexing under the thin white cotton shirt he wore. "The kitchen is in good condition, large enough that I can use it for an office, as well, and so is one of the other rooms that I use for a bedroom.'' His smile became whimsical. ''Of course, I have a baby fig tree growing in the living room, and no roof over that part of the house.''

''Fresh fruit close at hand come August.'' She glanced around at the other people in the room. Although the noise level had barely dropped, she was aware that they were gauging her reaction to Dion, and his to her. ''You realize this is a setup, don't you?'' she said with droll humor.

Gravely he nodded. ''Yes. I've been hearing about you all day. So we can either develop an instant antagonism and hate each other, or we can ignore the way this was arranged, pretend we wanted to meet and go from there.''

''Pretend we wanted to meet? To be honest,'' Solange admitted, ''I was eaten up with curiosity.''

Dion burst into spontaneous laughter. ''So was I. And you're not at all what I expected.''

''Oh? What did you expect?''

''Oh, Mother Teresa, or maybe a sort of Margaret Mead, you know, flat shoes, spectacles. Everyone talked about your microscope.''

''Mother Teresa? You flatter me.''

''According to the townspeople, it would be impossible to flatter you. Everyone I talked to sang your praises.''

She felt her cheeks grow warm. ''Well, I'm neither Catholic nor a nun,'' she said with a touch of acerbity.

His eyes, deep blue like glimpses of a twilight sky, narrowed. They toured her face, ran almost lazily down her body and back up again. His expression didn't alter, but she could have sworn that a fire began to smolder between the thick black lashes. A light sweat broke out on her skin, and she wondered if the temperature had risen in the room. Either that or Peter's home-brewed ouzo was more potent than usual.

"And Margaret Mead," she babbled to cover her confusion. "I heard that anthropology's your field, not mine."

"Close," he said. "I teach sociology in Vancouver at the University of British Columbia. I'm interested more in the culture of contemporary societies than in the origin and development of primitive tribes. I suppose you've heard I'm here to research a book on the nomadic tribes of Greece. No big mystery."

The undercurrents receded, and she wondered if she'd been away from the dating game too long. First eligible man she'd met in a long time and she was acting like a star-struck teenager. "Must be interesting."

Peter's voice resounded across the room, calling them to dinner. Relieved, Solange put down her glass, taking the arm Dion politely extended to her. "I like history myself," she said. "It would be hard to ignore in this country."

"Is that why you came?" He pulled out her chair and waited while she sat down before seating himself at her right side.

"I came as a volunteer after the last earthquake and decided to stay." Solange's standard explanation slid easily off her tongue. "You must find Greece has changed a lot since you lived here."

Again his eyes darkened, and a muscle tensed in his jaw. "Yeah, it's changed."

The first course was served, and their private conversation lapsed as the talk became general. The woman on her left kept Solange occupied, asking innumerable questions about an elderly relative who was Solange's patient, and demanding a lengthy explanation of an illness that was simply the result of old age. Solange welcomed the breathing space and was further relieved when Peter engaged Dion in conversation for most of the meal.

There was something about Dion that disturbed her, a quality of watchfulness, of cynicism, as if he assessed everyone and found no one who could quite measure up to a standard he'd set. His eyes, too often hooded by those long, almost feminine lashes, held shadows of grief or pain.

It was to be expected if his parents had died when he was at a young, impressionable age. And more so if they had died violently as Aphrodite had hinted. But surely a man of thirty-five would have come to terms with it. That he hadn't was a mystery. She was only guessing, of course, but couldn't shake off the feeling of unfinished business and an underlying secret, something dark and dangerous driving him.

Dangerous? She almost laughed aloud at her wild flight of imagination. He was just a man, an extremely appealing man, to be sure, but just a man.

And she had been alone too long.

"YOUR GREEK IS EXCELLENT," Dion commented later as they ate a delicious creamy rice pudding for dessert. "Did you find it hard to learn?"

Solange smiled. "Not really. My mother was a Greek-Canadian. It was the first language I heard."

"Are they still living?"

"Dad is. He remarried after my mother's death. He's been living in the Bahamas since he retired."

"You're not close."

An odd flatness in the words made her look at him. "No. We're not. I had a much closer relationship with my mother."

Dion put down his spoon, his smile appearing forced. "That's to be expected. Greek families are always close."

Solange laughed, the faint tension subsiding. "I've noticed. And it's not only families. It's the whole society. Everyone knows what everybody else is doing. I found it hard to get used to at first, but now I like it. Of course, the matchmaking can get a bit tiresome after a while."

"Just play along with it," Dion advised with a grin. "They'll think they've been successful and stay off our backs."

"As long as they don't shanghai us to the church."

Coffee was served, and several of the younger couples made excuses about children at home and left. Peter lit a cigar and leaned back in his chair as Anna cleared the last of the dessert dishes from the table. "It's nice to see you two hitting it off," he said, grinning broadly.

Solange and Dion exchanged glances. Solange could feel laughter bubbling up inside her, fueled by Dion's wink. "Why," she asked innocently, "didn't you think we would?"

"Of course you would," Peter said. On the desk in the corner the phone rang. "Excuse me." He picked up the receiver and spoke briefly into it, listening for a moment before hanging up.

"Solange, you're needed. A child had a bad fall. They're bringing him to your office."

Solange stood up, stooping to take her purse from the floor. "Whose child? Did they say?"

"I didn't catch that. Do you want a ride? I can get the car out."

"That won't be necessary," Dion cut in. "I'll take her."

CHAPTER TWO

As HE STEERED the car into the square, Dion glanced at Solange. Her face was set in tense lines, her hands clenched in her lap. The switch from beguiling woman to concerned doctor couldn't have been more sudden or complete.

He touched the brake, and she was out of the car before the vehicle stopped rolling. The injured child, a boy of about seven, was already there, waiting on the clinic steps with his anxious parents. His younger sister clung to the mother's skirt, staring with huge black eyes as she sucked a grubby thumb.

Unlocking the door, Solange flipped on the lights. "Come in." She led the way into the examining room, the family trailing behind her. Dion brought up the rear. Directing the father to a chair, she went over to the sink and scrubbed her hands with brisk efficiency.

Propping his shoulder against the door frame, Dion watched as she picked up the pink smock draped over her desk chair and pulled it on over her dress. She crouched down in front of the boy, gently examining the wound, a shallow gash on his forehead. Blood smeared his cheeks and nose but only seeped sluggishly from the wound. "Mmm, it's not too bad," she murmured reassuringly to the parents.

Dion pushed himself away from the door. Going to the sink, he ran warm water into a basin and carried it to the table. "You'll need an antiseptic, won't you? Where is it?"

She looked up, a quick movement of her head, as if she'd forgotten he was there. Her eyes, the clear, deep brown of a forest pool, reflected her smile of thanks. "On the counter next to the sink." She took the basin from his hands, adding to the water a measure of the pungent liquid from the bottle he handed her.

The child sat quietly on his father's knee, his small features set stoically. Only the trembling of his bottom lip betrayed his apprehension. Solange pulled a stool close and sat down, shining a small flashlight into first one eye, then the other. Nodding, she dipped a gauze pad into the water. "You're a brave boy. What's your name?"

"Yiorgi." He winced as the antiseptic stung, and bit his lip to keep from crying out.

"Yiorgi, eh? How did this happen?"

"I was chasing my kitten—ouch!—and I fell from a stone wall."

"Damn nuisance, cats," his father muttered under his breath, then hugged the boy closer as he whimpered in pain.

"It'll stop hurting in a minute, Yiorgi," Solange said quietly. "I don't even think it needs stitches. Just a bandage."

She dabbed an anesthetic cream onto a sterile gauze square and taped it securely over the wound. "There, that should do."

As if the bandage made it all better, the boy hopped from his father's lap. "Will I have to go to school tomorrow?"

Dion muffled his laugh by pretending to cough into his fist. Some things never changed; he'd used the same excuse to get out of school as a child.

Solange, her expression serious except for the twinkle in her eye, stroked her chin. "No," she said at last. "I think you can stay home. But you'll have to rest in bed, and you won't have a chance to show your bandage to your friends...."

Two tiny lines appeared between the child's eyes as he considered this. "If I feel okay, can I go?"

Solange patted his shoulder through the smudged T-shirt. "Of course you may."

She spoke briefly with the parents as the two children wandered about the room, stretching up to examine the counters and poking their heads into any cupboards that weren't locked. From past experience Solange knew she could count on her young patients' good behavior as long as their parents were present. Under the watchful eye of their mother they looked but didn't touch. "I don't see any signs of concussion, but keep an eye on him overnight. If he's difficult to wake or if he complains of nausea, come and get me. You know where I live."

"Of course, Dr. Solange." The father clasped her hand between his work-roughened palms. "Thank you so much." Groping in the pockets of his wool pants, he extracted a couple of thousand-drachma notes from a thick bundle and laid them on the counter.

He swung Yiorgi up onto his shoulder. The boy stretched his arm in an attempt to touch the ceiling, pain forgotten. Solange reached up and clasped his hand. "Good night, Yiorgi. And be careful," she admonished as they went out the door. "No more running after kittens. Come and see me after school tomorrow, and I'll change your bandage."

Turning toward the sink, she washed out the basin. Dion, standing by the window, followed her movements, the grace of her walk, the fluid strength apparent in her muscles as she rinsed out the towel she'd used and lifted the basin to a shelf. He tried to keep his interest objective, a man admiring a beautiful woman who seemed refreshingly unaware of her attraction. But her gentleness with the child and her kindness to the family had touched some emotional depth in him. He frowned, trying to regain his detachment. She might be useful to him, but anything beyond a superficial friendship would hinder his cause. This time there would be no slipups, no woman to distract him. He'd learned his lesson well.

"There were your first Sarakatsani," Solange said, hanging up her smock. She saw he was frowning, the humor of a moment before gone, and wondered what he was thinking. Once again, the sensation that those dark eyes hid secrets crept into her consciousness. "You won't find many that live a nomadic life anymore, I'm afraid."

"As long as they still remember the nomadic life, and the customs that were uniquely theirs," he said absently, as if his mind had wandered far away.

She felt him watching her as she walked across the room to her desk, his expression unreadable. Pulling open a drawer, she rummaged through it, coming up with a slender tube, a pharmacist's sample.

"Here you are, Dion. This will fix up your blisters and help to harden the skin, as well."

She went over to the window and stopped in front of him. "Let me see."

"It's only the right one. The other's okay."

Taking the extended hand, she turned it palm up, smiling a little at the array of bandages. "This is going to sting."

His own smile flashed briefly, and he straightened his back. "I'll try to keep my screams low so the neighbors won't hear."

"Would you like a bullet to bite on?" Taking the end of the top bandage, she gave a quick tug. They all came loose at once. The skin they had covered was red and sore, the broken blisters weeping a clear fluid. "I think you'd better come over to the sink. I'd like to rinse this with antiseptic."

He said nothing as she cleaned his hand, as stoic as the little boy had been. As she smoothed on the ointment, she couldn't help but notice the sinewed masculinity of his hands and wrists, the hard strength that made her own fingers seem soft and slender by comparison. They were capable hands that knew work, skilled in manual tasks, hands that would know how to touch a woman.

Startled at the thought that sent a rush of heat into her cheeks, she let go, saying briskly, "Use the ointment about four times a day. And try to keep the skin exposed. Don't do any digging for a couple of days so it has a chance to heal."

"I won't," he said, his voice low and husky. For a fleeting moment he'd wanted her to go on holding his hand, soothing the minor pain. For a moment he'd wanted her....

Insanity.

"Now that I can get into the house I'll work on my notes," he added, moving away toward the door. "As soon as the store delivers a table and chairs. Tomorrow, probably. They promised."

"Whose shop? Candiles's?"

"Yes. Are they reliable?"

"Very," Solange assured him. "Vasili is my landlady's husband."

Her landlady's husband. For an instant the term struck Dion as odd. Why not her landlord? But she was probably correct. The house in which Solange lived was likely the property of Mrs. Candiles, her dowry, which meant that any income from it was hers, as well. Not that women were inclined to spend any such income on themselves. It would be carefully put aside for future necessities, like their children's education.

Solange followed him out and locked the door. The night was warm, fragrant with the roses that bloomed profusely in every garden.

Dion couldn't keep his eyes off her as Solange tilted her face up to the sky where the Milky Way stretched in a misty banner. Lit by starlight and the inner serenity that was such a part of her, her strong features took on an ethereal beauty that drew him in spite of himself.

She inhaled deeply. "I love the nights here."

Another night, two shots, a quickly stifled scream. The image flashed through Dion's mind, stark and unsettling, cutting through his bemused contemplation of her. She lived in the present, taking pleasure in the simple things like soft nights and the well-being of her patients. She saw events as self-contained happenings, without imagining secret plots and complex repercussions. She had none of the dark, brooding Greek traits that kept the country passionately alive through tribulation but which prevented a real stability in times of peace.

Briefly he envied her. Intelligent and educated, devoted to a demanding profession, she still retained a core of innocence.

He shook himself. Such thoughts were dangerous to his mission. He couldn't let this woman, tempting though she was, interfere with the job he had come to do.

"Time we went home," he said abruptly.

Solange turned, surprised at the change from the easy mood they'd shared tending the boy's injury. Had he sensed her errant thoughts? No, it was impossible. But he looked suddenly grim, impatient, as if he'd remembered more important things he had to do.

Or recalled whatever problem it was that ate at him. That was his business, she told herself, not hers. But she couldn't help but wonder. Years of diagnosing patients had honed her intuition about moods and mental conflicts. For all his efforts to appear open and straightforward, even amused by the matchmaking efforts of the town, she sensed a tension in Dion's character.

Which should warn her to steer clear of an involvement with him. Her experience with some of her male colleagues in medical school and in her hospital work had effectively destroyed the naïveté she'd carried through from childhood. The incident in Montreal that had almost ended her career would never have happened if Dr. Robert Malcolm hadn't allowed his built-in prejudices against woman doctors to condemn her without a trial.

Not that Dion seemed to have anything against her profession. But he had shown himself to be a man who would be difficult to know, even while the force of his personality made him impossible to ignore.

"Do you want a ride?" he asked.

She heard the edge of impatience in his low voice. "I wouldn't want to trouble you. It's not far. I'll walk. Thanks, anyway."

He stared at her for an instant, his lips parting. But he only said, "Good night, then. I'll probably be seeing you around town."

Somehow she had the impression that wasn't what he'd intended to say at all. No matter. If he didn't want to fulfill the townspeople's romantic little scenario, it was all the same to her. She hadn't time in her life for a man of his unpredictable, mercurial moods. "I'm sure you will," she said coolly. "Good night, Dion."

DION SAT for a long moment in his car without starting it. He drummed his fingers on the steering wheel as he watched the doctor cross the square with long, confident strides and disappear into the darkness of a street beyond. She was a lovely woman, gentle, kind and understanding. Calm. Not driven, like Eleni had been.

Solange was a woman a man would want to come home to. She saw the good in people; evil was only hearsay to her, something written into novels and movies to create a plot. She didn't know what it was like to suffer, to see your family destroyed before your eyes. She didn't know what it was like to hate.

Leaning forward, he twisted the key in the ignition. He allowed the car to idle for a moment, then let up the clutch and headed for his house on the edge of town.

AT SUNRISE the next morning he sat on the veranda at the side of the house, clasping a mug of instant coffee between his hands. He hadn't bought much in the way of kitchen equipment yet, only a gas hot plate and a couple of pots and dishes. It was sufficient for simple meals and making coffee.

The steady drum of feet clad in running shoes came to his ears as he sipped the dark brew. Solange, out for her morning run. The townspeople had delighted in telling him about her odd Canadian habit, implying that he might like to join her.

Not him. Not on a run. He found running a profound bore, preferring his exercise in a more competitive manner, such as playing tennis. He looked at his hands, a rueful grin crossing his lips. He wouldn't be getting much exercise for a few days, although he had to admit her ministrations had already made his blisters less raw and painful.

Solange came into sight, unaware of his presence. Her sun-streaked golden blond hair swung over her shoulders, a tawny swath. Last night it had been confined in a chignon at the back of her head, throwing her distinctive features into prominence. With it loose she looked softer, the vulnerability she thought she kept hidden bared to his eyes.

Her legs were naked and tanned under the curved hem of her shorts, corded with long muscles in the thighs and calves. She was a tall woman, skinny, he supposed, her breasts barely bouncing under a white T-shirt. But despite her lanky body, there was an air of femininity about her. He'd seen it come to the fore when she'd dealt with the child last night, but it was always there, lying quietly beneath the assertiveness she brought to her work and relationships with people.

She went by without noticing him. He gripped the mug until a jab of pain through his hand reminded him of the blisters. He couldn't deny she attracted him. But did he dare allow himself to follow up on that attraction?

He sat there as the sun climbed into the sky, chasing fleecy scarves of amber and mauve ahead of it. It was like the first morning of creation, when the world was young and as innocent as Solange. He'd thought himself immune to beauty, but here in his homeland the poetic core in him was tapped even against his will.

His coffee grew cold, but still he waited. His mind told him one thing, his heart another. Would she come by again, or would she take another route? He tipped his chair forward. No, she was coming, her footsteps slower as she cooled down.

The yearning in his heart overruled his misgivings. "Hi, Solange."

Startled, she jerked to a stop, her head spinning toward the sound of Dion's greeting. He leaned with studied ease against one of the porch supports, one hand braced above his head. "Good morning, Dion. You're up early."

"Always. I don't need much sleep." He gestured with his hand. "Why don't you come in and I'll make you a coffee?"

Hesitating, she glanced at her watch. Last night, when they'd parted, she'd gotten the impression that he didn't care if he saw her again. Today he was inviting her into his house. What did he want? "Okay," she agreed. "But not for long. I have to shower and dress for work."

He could smell the astringency of sweat on her, underlaid with a suggestion of the perfume she'd worn last night. An earthy smell that appealed to some primitive instinct deep within him. The sudden heaviness in his groin took him by surprise. He wanted her, just like this, warm from her run, smelling of woman and healthy exertion.

Knock it off, Parris, he rebuked himself as he struck a match to the gas burner under the pot of water. You need her for information and cover, not for sex.

"You've lived here four years?" he asked to distract himself.

"Five, actually," she interjected.

"Whatever." He shrugged. "Don't you miss Canada, or simply just cities? They tell me you grew up in Montreal, that you used to practice in a large hospital there."

"My, the grapevine is busy." Solange smiled to hide her annoyance.

"It always is. Sugar and cream? I've got canned milk."

"Just sugar, thanks. I've learned to drink it black." She took the mug from his hand and led the way back to the porch. The inside of the house showed the need for a great deal of work, grimy floors that he had swept but not yet scrubbed, and once-whitewashed walls showing the dark mildew of innumerable winters without heat. "You might speak to my landlady, Demetra," Solange suggested. "She'll be able to find you someone to clean the house, or even to do painting and carpentry."

"I thought I'd do that myself," he said, dragging up a straight-back chair with a woven cane seat. "But a cleaning lady would be appreciated. I've just discovered I hate any housework beyond simple maintenance."

Solange sat down, tilting the chair back against the wall as Dion had done with his, and rested her feet on the porch rail. The slanting rays of the sun caressed her, at this time of day only pleasantly warm. A mellow glow of well-being filled her. Last night with its odd tensions was forgotten, over.

Not that she had any more insight into Dion's personality, but at least he was friendly. She hadn't expected anything but a cool, distant courtesy after his stiff parting from her at the clinic. Today it was easy to excuse him. Perhaps he'd been tired.

"So why did you leave Canada?"

"I wanted a change," she said. "I like it here. It feels like home. You must feel it, too."

"Korfalli hasn't been my home since I was eleven."

"Then why did you come here?"

He shrugged, reluctant to spin his tale, to drag her in. "To find my roots, I guess. Does that sound pretentious?"

"Not at all." The phrase didn't, nor did the need behind it. She could understand an immigrant's desire to rediscover his childhood haunts. But the tension that had come into his body as he spoke of his roots was puzzling, warning her of depths that she might not want to fathom, dark secrets that she saw he wasn't about to divulge. She must ask Aphrodite....

Abruptly she jumped up, setting the mug on the rail. "I have to go. If I'm late, Aphrodite will have a fit."

"You're the boss, aren't you?" His voice was cool and lazy as he settled his hands comfortably over his flat belly with his cup between them. "What do you do for holidays?"

"I have an assistant, Penny, who's doing research on heart disease under my supervision. She takes the office hours several days a week, and also if I have to be away. She's an excellent researcher, but sometimes not quite assertive enough with the patients. I don't like to be away much."

The heart research. Someone had mentioned it. Those who were part of the study lived in villages widely spread over an area that stretched almost from Lamia to Larissa. Yes, Solange's knowledge of the countryside and its people would be invaluable to him.

He let the chair drop, its front legs thumping on the chipped terrazzo floor. "Solange, I'd like to talk to you later. I've a favor to ask of you. How about if I buy you lunch?"

Her easy laughter rang in the clean air. "Why don't you come to my place instead? The restaurants are really only good in the evening. People here eat the midday meal at home."

"That's right. I'd forgotten. Your place? What time?"

"How about half past one? If there's a light patient load, I might get off before one. That'll give me a little time to cook."

He held up his hand. "Don't make anything fancy. Just what you usually have. See you then."

SHE WAS IN HER FLAT at half past twelve, poring over a ragged cookbook that had once been her mother's. What she usually had—a bowl of soup or a couple of slices of toast—would hardly satisfy a healthy man's appetite. She'd bought fish, the tiny ones that resembled smelt, in the market, along with tomatoes and fresh bread. But an inspired way of cooking the fish didn't present itself.

With a sigh she pulled the flour tin from the cupboard and, pouring some on a plate, began to roll the cleaned, salted fish in it, preparatory to frying them in olive oil.

"Delicious," Dion pronounced an hour later as they ate the simple meal. "My favorite meal when I was a child, and one you can't duplicate anywhere else."

"Thank you." Solange took the empty plates to the sink, returning with a pitcher filled with ice cubes clinking musically in amber liquid.

Dion's brows lifted. "Is that what I think it is?"

"Yes, iced tea. You can get tea in Greece, the ordinary kind," she said with a smile. "It's refreshing in the heat. I've even got Demetra and Litsa drinking it. They think it's exotic, foreign. Why don't we go into the living room?"

Her living room was small, with several lace-curtained windows overlooking the street that fronted the house. It was decorated in blue and white in a style Dion thought of as a Greek island motif, with a cool airiness that didn't travel well to more temperate countries. He knew. During a spell of loneliness after he'd completed university years ago, he'd tried it, but had only succeeded in feeling out of place in his apartment during Vancouver's rainy winters.

Solange gestured Dion to a chair upholstered in cream cotton while she curled up on the window seat, arranging a couple of cushions behind her back.

"You've made a home," Dion said. He rolled his glass between his palms, welcoming the damp, cool feel of it.

"Yes. Is that so strange?" Lifting one knee, she tucked her wide skirt between her legs and tilted her head back. He could see her throat muscles flexing as she drank deeply. He wondered what it would be like to kiss her, to breathe in the scent of her skin.

Forcing his mind off that dangerous path, he said, "No, I guess not. But don't you think of going back? You are Canadian, after all."

A shadow crossed her face. "Someday. Someday I'll go back. When I'm finished here."

"Finished what?"

She gestured with her hand, twin lines of concentration appearing between her dark brows. "Finished taking care of the people who've become my friends. I'll go when I'm ready to."

He leaned forward, his gaze sharpening. "Are you hiding?"

Solange gave a short laugh. "Hiding? Don't be absurd. Why would I be hiding? You must have noticed my degrees on the wall in my office. And I'm not running from a malpractice suit, I assure you."

"There are many ways of hiding, Solange." He should know; he was a living example of hiding. Waiting. Planning.

She stirred restlessly, shifting her legs. The skirt twisted, revealing a length of tanned thigh before she pulled it straight. Solange looked up and caught his eyes on her, the dark, intense blue that seemed to see right through her. Come on, she chided herself. He's just looking, no big deal. After all, he'd seen all of her legs this morning when she'd worn shorts.

"What was it you wanted to discuss with me?" she asked, rattled by the thoughts he aroused in her without even trying. It was time they got down to business.

"I'm looking for a man."

She frowned, puzzled. "A man? I thought you were studying the Sarakatsani."

"I am, but I'm also trying to trace distant members of my family with whom I lost touch since I went to Canada. This man may be able to help me."

"What's his name? How do you know he'll be able to help you?"

Dion set down his glass and laced his fingers together. Only the whiteness of the skin over his knuckles revealed his tension. He'd decided to keep his cover story simple, as close to the truth as possible without giving away his real objective. "His name is Lambros Pavlou.

At least, I think it is. And I thought he had died fourteen years ago.''

"What do you mean?"

"There was a fire. Bodies. One of them was supposedly his, although no one could be positive. I found out recently it wasn't.''

Solange shuddered. Of all accidents, fires were the worst. Sometimes it was a mercy when the victims died quickly. Bodies after a fire were hard to identify. She could understand mistakes being made. "Go on."

"It came up in a conversation I had with a Greek-American history prof who just joined the faculty of UBC where I teach. Stefan told me Pavlou may still be alive, retired, and that he was possibly living in this area."

Solange shook her head skeptically. "You'll have to tell me more than that. There are a lot of people here who are retired. Did this man ever live outside of Greece? We've got a few returned immigrants from Australia, Canada and the United States who live on their pensions."

"I'm not sure. I believe he might have been away for a while but probably in Europe."

"That's a tall order, Dion. I don't know how I can help you."

"You know most of the families here, don't you? And many in the surrounding areas for your heart study."

She nodded. "I guess so, although I'm not the only doctor in town."

"You still might know this man's family. They have a peculiarity that I understand is passed down through their genes. The man I'm looking for has an extra finger on his left hand."

CHAPTER THREE

SOLANGE WAS SILENT for a long moment, mentally reviewing the people she knew in Korfalli and those she came in contact with elsewhere. No one with that unusual characteristic came to mind. "Offhand, I don't know, but I can always ask Demetra. She's lived here all her life, and knows much more family history than I do. Is it urgent that you find this man?"

Urgent? Dion clenched his fists, then slowly released them. If he could find the man today, the waiting would be over. The payment would be exacted and the record cleared.

Aloud, hoping his voice didn't betray him as anger wrapped a tight band around his chest, he said, "Not urgent, but I'd like to talk to him, to find out if I do have any family left. You can understand."

"Yes." Turning her head, Solange stared out of the open window. Sounds drifted up from the street, workers going home for their midday meal. Demetra called to her youngest son Taki, and a door slammed downstairs. The family would be settling for their siesta, a habit Solange hadn't adopted except during high summer when the breathless heat made it impossible to stay awake.

"What about military records, Dion? Virtually every man in Greece has to serve two years. If he's retired, he would be at least sixty-five. That means he was drafted about forty-five years ago. It shouldn't be too difficult to track the man down in the records, especially if you go back five or more years before that, as well."

"I tried that already. His name is a common one."

"Yes, I suppose it is," Solange said. "It would take months unless you know the exact years he did his military service."

"I know when he was in the army." The odd note in his voice made her turn back to him. His face was set in harsh lines, frightening in their intensity. His eyes glittered blackly. Anger and hate. The emotions spun across the room to hit her with an almost tangible force.

She recoiled, and must have made a sound, for in an instant his expression smoothed out, and he was once more the easygoing man who'd shared her table and her food. "Dion...?"

He shook his head, inwardly cursing his lapse. "Sometimes I think of my parents and how little I knew them. It upsets me. If I could find someone who remembers them..."

Sorrow wasn't what she'd seen. She was sure of it. She felt oddly helpless, not knowing what to do. But she could hardly force him to release the bottled-up tension he held so rigidly inside. "You tried the military records and found nothing at all?" she said in an effort to restore her own equilibrium.

"Nothing. The records weren't available."

She'd heard that the government offices could be very officious, and difficult to deal with. "Oh? To you? Or to anyone?"

"To anyone. Some sort of bureaucratic foul-up." The clerk in the military records office hadn't even pretended courtesy, merely telling Dion that it was impossible. When Dion had asked for an explanation, the man had curtly informed him that he would have to take his questions to a higher official.

And this Dion wasn't prepared to do as yet, nor could he, without revealing his objective.

Solange swung her feet to the floor. "All I can promise is that I'll ask around. And you can do the same when you're interviewing the Sarakatsani."

He also rose to his feet, putting his hand on her shoulder. The faint scent of a mossy after-shave tickled her nose, making her think of a deep green wood lightly dappled by sun. "Thanks, Solange." He grinned briefly, although it was clear to Solange that his mind was elsewhere. "Next meal's on me, remember."

"Okay. But I expect you'll be getting lots of invitations to eat out. The town is full of eligible girls."

Dion grimaced. "I'm supposed to be happy about that? Don't forget, I spent my childhood here. All a man has to do is look at a girl and her father's there with the shotgun and the priest."

Solange laughed. "No, Dion, I think you'll find that's changed a bit. Now you have to at least kiss the girl before her father comes after you."

"Well, I've got work to do," he declared. "I won't have time for women."

THE DOOR HAD scarcely closed after him when Solange, her hands in soapy dishwater, heard a faint knock. Thinking Dion had forgotten something, she called, "Come in."

"Hi, Dr. Solange," a soft voice said behind her. It was Litsa Candiles, her landlady's daughter. "I'm not disturbing you, am I?" Her English was excellent, although today she spoke in Greek.

An omen? Solange wondered, smiling at her. Many of the students addressed her in English if it was a subject of little consequence. On matters of importance, especially those involving emotions, they would invariably fall back into Greek.

She took a tea towel from its hook and handed it to the girl. "I'm always glad to see you, Litsa. You're just in time to give me a hand. Doing dishes is boring alone."

"Mother doesn't know I'm here," Litsa confided as she picked up a handful of rinsed cutlery. Slender and of medium height with straight brown hair cut to just below her ears, Litsa was seventeen and in her last year of high school. A serious student whose work consistently scored at the top of her class, she was even more intense about her studies than many of her classmates. She was determined to go to university and had a good chance, Solange thought.

"She won't mind, will she?" Solange asked.

Litsa shook her head, her short nose crinkling as she smiled. "Not if I'm here." Opening a drawer, she dropped the silverware into the appropriate slots.

They worked in companionable silence for a moment. Solange was curious but willing to wait until Litsa told her what the problem was. A boy, perhaps? She was a pretty girl, with fresh, clear skin and rounded cheeks that were rapidly losing their baby fat, promising a womanly beauty. No, the problem wouldn't involve boys; Litsa had no time for dating.

"I've got iced tea," Solange offered as she gave the sink a final wipe. "Would you like some?"

"Yes, please."

They moved to the living room, Litsa taking the chair Dion had recently vacated. "Did you have a nice lunch with Kyrios Parris?'' Litsa asked casually with none of the avid curiosity her mother would have shown.

"Yes, I did. He must find it strange to be back here after all these years.'' Briefly she debated mentioning the six-fingered man to Litsa. No, that could wait. Her mother was more likely to know if such a person existed.

Litsa sighed. "He's so handsome. Some of my friends saw him in the square this morning. Helena said she nearly fainted when he said hello in that sexy, low voice. But, of course, you know Helena. She practically swoons at the sight of any man over sixteen.''

Yes, Solange knew about Helena. The girl had asked her about birth control only last month. Knowing that the parents would never approve, Solange had advised her to wait until she was a little older before indulging in sex, but if she really felt she couldn't refrain, to come and see her again. So far she hadn't, but Solange suspected it was only a matter of time.

"Helena is young. She'll change,'' Solange murmured, hoping it was true.

"Or get married before she's eighteen,'' Litsa declared with the sturdy practicality she'd inherited from her mother. "She'll probably do it, anyway. She's not planning to go to university, and her father will offer a good dowry.'' The girl laughed. "He'll have to. She has—'' her voice dropped ominously "—a reputation.''

The worst indictment, Solange knew. She sipped her iced tea, waiting for Litsa to broach the subject on her mind.

The girl fidgeted, setting her glass down and picking it up again, coughing lightly, then sniffing into a handkerchief, a pretty square of linen around which she had tatted a lace border. The practical part of her household dowry.

"Dr. Solange..." Her face was flushed, and she squirmed in the chair.

What was wrong? Becoming alarmed, Solange leaned forward in her seat. She couldn't be pregnant, could she? It was the only thing that Solange could think of, with this intelligent, almost prim girl, that some boy had sweet-talked her into something she was far from ready for.

"Yes, Litsa? It's all right," she said quietly. "You can talk to me."

"It's Kyra," Litsa blurted. "My best friend."

Solange knew Kyra, although they'd never spoken beyond a casual greeting in the town square. A tall, thin girl with yards of dark hair and straight black brows, Kyra gave the impression of shyness. From Litsa's occasional comments Solange knew that her apparent introspection hid an awesome intellect. Kyra was the only senior student whose marks rivaled Litsa's. They planned to share a flat in Athens in the fall, once they were accepted into the university.

"What about Kyra?" Solange prompted when Litsa didn't elaborate.

"It's just awful, Dr. Solange." Litsa's fingers mangled the handkerchief, and a tear crept down her cheek. "Her father is being completely unreasonable. He'll hardly let her go out anymore, ever since that old aunt of hers told him she saw Kyra talking to a boy. She was only talking. If she had anything to hide, she wouldn't be doing it in full view of the street in front of the school gates. But her father won't listen. The only time she's allowed out is Sunday evenings, and then she has to be with me or her mother."

"That's a compliment, isn't it? He trusts you." Solange said the words, but they were only words. She'd seen it before, a parent or grandparent who alienated a teenager, accusing the child of something and having it turn out to be a self-fulfilling prophecy. Closer to home, Penny had left her family to escape an untenable situation and she'd never gone back. It was sad, but Solange knew of no easy or workable solution.

"Only because my mother is always at the square, too. He thinks she keeps an eye on us." She hiccuped, wiping at the tears with an impatient gesture. "My mother trusts me. She doesn't have to watch me."

Another self-fulfilling prophecy, Solange supposed wryly. "You're almost adults. Soon you'll be on your own, responsible for yourselves."

"That's just it. If her father keeps up like this, he may stop her from going to university. And Kyra wants to go." She groaned. "She's so upset she's having trouble concentrating on her work. Just when we have to start studying for the university entrance exams. And it's upsetting me, too. If we don't pass, we'll have to wait a whole year to do them over. I'll just die."

There wasn't much danger of either of the girls failing with the marks they already had, but emotions could interfere with the finals, which were crucial. "What about your mother? Can she talk to Kyra's father? And what does her mother say about this?"

"Her mother can't say anything. She has a hard enough time with her in-laws without bringing up new problems. The gossipy aunt is Kyra's father's sister."

That was another problem inherent in extended families—in-law relationships were complicated. And to exacerbate the situation, elderly parents often lived with their adult children. Many families found it worked fine, a live-in mother's helper, someone to take the pressure off parents who worked or were otherwise engaged. But others found it a living hell when they couldn't make a single decision without in-law interference.

Solange frowned, biting her lower lip. "Yes, it would have to be handled very delicately. I don't know what to say, Litsa, except that perhaps if some time goes by he'll see he's wrong."

"Maybe." But Litsa looked doubtful.

"Are you coming to the baptism on Sunday?" Solange asked in an attempt to introduce a more cheerful topic.

A smile lit up Litsa's face. "I wouldn't miss it. Not if you're going to be the godmother."

"I can't seem to get out of it," Solange said with a rueful grin. "Not that I'd want to. It's quite an honor." She was godmother to half a dozen children in the town, all of them babies she'd delivered. There was no way a doctor could remain impersonally aloof from her patients in this society.

"The baby's cute, isn't he?"

"Yes, especially since he got his first two teeth. Poppy says he was worth the wait." Poppy was one of Solange's successes. Married six years without a child, the woman was over thirty. After carefully charting her fertile days as Solange had taught her, Poppy had conceived and, nine months ago, had produced a healthy boy. "What are they going to name him?" It was considered bad luck to call a child by his name before the baptism, and the proposed name was often kept secret until shortly before the ceremony.

"Sophocles, I think," Litsa said. "That's the name of Poppy's father-in-law." She got up and carried her empty glass to the sink, carefully rinsing it out. "I'd better go and do my homework.'' She made a face. ''That classics teacher always piles it on.''

''It'll be worse in university,'' Solange reminded her.

''I know, but I'll be on my own then.''

She was lucky her parents could afford to pay her living expenses. University tuition was free, but apartments in either Athens or Thessaloniki were no longer cheap. Many students had to take a full-time job just to support themselves.

The universal problem, Solange thought as Litsa left. Money and marks. Fortunately Litsa needn't worry about either. With her excellent academic record she would be accepted into the overcrowded university with no trouble, and her parents could afford her upkeep.

She dried the glasses they'd used, putting them away, her thoughts drifting to Dion. What was the demon that lived in him? Even from the limited time they'd spent together she was aware that he fought some powerful psychological battle within himself or had some deep problem he had to resolve.

Was that why he'd taken the sabbatical and come here to research the nomadic tribes that hardly existed anymore? Maybe he was running away, too, just as she had been when she arrived.

They were bound to see each other again, either by chance or when pushed together by some of their well-meaning neighbors. She had time to figure him out.

If she wanted to.

''YOU CAN'T LET THEM run your life.'' Penny's vehement declaration carried all the way across the fortunately deserted waiting room as Solange entered her office that evening.

To her surprise Litsa's friend Kyra sat on the chair beside Penny's desk, her shoulders slumped in dejection, her hands tightening around the book bag she held on her lap. As Solange closed the door, the girl looked up and light reflected off the glasses she wore. Far from detracting from her beauty, the dark, narrow rims emphasized her eyes and gave the elegant bone structure of her face a charming piquancy.

"Penny," Solange said mildly. "I could hear you outside."

Penny halted her agitated pacing. "Kyra's thinking of dropping out of school. What a waste that would be of a brain."

"What's the use if Father won't let me go to university?" Kyra rubbed at a tear on her cheek. "I break my head studying, and what good is it?"

"It's for your own satisfaction," Penny retorted. "And you'll be an adult soon, on your own. You can go then. But only if you've passed the exams."

"If I don't get married," Kyra whispered miserably.

"Married?" Penny almost shrieked. "Why would you do such a thing? Especially now when you have the future ahead of you." Her eyes narrowed in sudden speculation. "He hasn't arranged something already, has he?"

Solange held her breath as Kyra turned pale and hesitated for a long moment before speaking. "No, not yet. But he's talked about it."

Penny assumed a militant pose that caused Solange to see her in a new light. Aphrodite had said she wasn't assertive enough. Well, she should see her now, ready to do battle for this girl.

"Listen, Kyra, you have to pass the exams. Then I'll speak to your father, if I have to."

"So will I," Solange put in, her policy of noninterference forgotten.

Kyra looked from one to the other, hope lighting her eyes, only to die as she thought of the consequences. "That will upset him more. He'll kick me out, and then my mother will be alone."

"With your father and his parents," Penny said disgustedly. "That's hardly alone. Maybe you should take her with you."

"But she loves my father. And he's kind to her."

"Yes, when that witch of a mother of his isn't there." Penny sat down, rolling her chair to a position in front of Kyra. "Kyra, if you want to leave home, you'd manage. I'll take you in if necessary. But you can't throw away your future like this." She clasped the girl's hands between her own. "Believe me, I know. I left home and put myself through medical school."

Kyra's eyes grew wide. "I wish I had the courage, but—"

"No buts. You can do anything you want. My brother was supposed to go to medical school, but he didn't want to be a doctor, no matter how much our parents pushed him. I did, but they had my husband picked out. So I had no choice."

Solange was surprised at Penny's candor. Not many people knew her story, the total estrangement from her family. And her brother had defied them as well, by emigrating to Toronto and opening a restaurant. The success of the business made no difference; he had brought shame on the family. Sometimes Solange felt sorry for the parents who had managed by their stubbornness to alienate both their children.

She heard voices in the waiting room. "Penny, do you and Kyra want some privacy? I think we've got patients."

Kyra jumped up from the chair. "I have to go. I'm expected home."

"Well, think about what I said." Penny wore a frown that indicated her determination to take Kyra's battle on herself. "You're not alone."

A brief smile lit Kyra's face. "Thank you." She turned and ran out the door.

Penny sat down abruptly, her breath escaping in a whoosh. "What did I do?"

Solange grinned. "You did fine. I had no idea you could be so, so—"

"So fierce?" Penny grinned, too. "I didn't, either, but it just made me so mad. That girl needs to go to school. She'll just wither away if she doesn't."

Solange squeezed Penny's shoulder. "Don't worry. It'll work out. Now, do you want to take the first patient? I think they're about to start pounding on the door."

DION RUBBED the bridge of his nose and dropped his reading glasses onto the desk. Nearly a week had passed, and he'd made little progress in either of his endeavors. The Sarakatsani in Korfalli were strangely reluctant to discuss their past. In fact, some of them had laughed that he would find their old customs and movements of any interest.

"That was in the past," they would tell him. "Now we are settled. People accept us, at least most of them do. We don't want to rake up that time when we were thought of as little more than Gypsies."

Perhaps he should switch to a study of the Gypsies, he thought. That society, too, was changing dramatically. They still traveled during the summer, camping in tents, and their dress was as distinctive as ever. But pickup trucks had become their mode of transportation, the ubiquitous Datsuns and Toyotas, most of which were equipped with loudspeakers guaranteed to wake up all siesta sleepers as they drove by. And their tents were powered by generators to run television sets. Not only that, great numbers of Gypsies had settled in permanent houses near the central Thessalian towns of Karditsa and Trikalla.

He put down his pen. Perhaps at some time in the future he would be able to come back.

He'd managed to avoid invitations to dinner from the neighbors, pleading the pressure of work and earning himself pitying looks. Solange passed by his house on her morning run each day, but beyond calling a greeting on the few occasions he'd been on the porch, they hadn't spoken.

Picking up his empty coffee mug, he carried it to the primitive kitchen, setting it in the sink. He pulled open the fridge door. The compressor came on, wheezing asthmatically.

Shaking his head at the sound of it and wondering how long the machinery would stand up under the onslaught of summer heat, Dion extracted a bottle of beer. Clipping off the cap against the underside of the counter, he took a long swallow, closing his eyes in pleasure as the cold liquid slid down his throat.

Voices drifted in through the open window, along with the scent of the jasmine growing beside the house. A man and a woman.

Solange. Dion snapped out of his indolence and charged to the window, sticking his head over the sill.

She was just coming up the dusty street, her medical bag in her hand. The man with her lifted his hand to his brow in a farewell salute and turned in at a garden gate two houses down.

"Solange!" Dion called.

She turned, her eyes alert and curious. "Hi, Dion. How have you been?"

"Fine, thanks." Stupid, mundane reply. Now that he had her attention, he had no idea what he would say to her. He lifted the dark brown bottle. "Want a beer?"

Solange considered. It was almost lunchtime. She was on the way back from a house call to a bedridden elderly man but had no other appointments scheduled. Penny was at the office; she would lock up at one.

Solange pushed open the gate. "Why not?"

By the time she reached the steps, he'd come out on the porch. Pausing, she noted the expectant smile on his face, and she was glad she'd accepted his invitation.

He looked warm and rumpled, like a man who'd just gotten out of bed, his hair clinging damply to his temples. His shirt was unbuttoned over ragged shorts, revealing a lean but surprisingly sturdy chest matted with black hair. He smelled tart and woodsy, like a mossy spring deep in a forest, and she couldn't help the current of desire that surged through her. It had been a long time since she'd met a man who attracted her on this primal level.

When he pulled his shirt back to hook his hand in his pocket, she saw a scar just to the left of his navel, a pale, jagged line against his tan. Not appendix, she realized, struggling to hold on to a clinical detachment. Too small and too high.

"Your beer," he said, extending the bottle.

She blinked, pulling her scattered wits together and rebuking them sternly. "Thanks."

The cold beer cut through the dust in her throat and hit her empty stomach with a pleasant jolt. She grinned at Dion, hiding her idiotic lapse behind a jovial facade. Had he been purposely avoiding her? "You've been busy, I hear."

"Busy, but I'm getting nowhere fast. I'm thinking of digging up the back lot and planting something just to prove that I'm not indulging in a colossal waste of time."

"The people will get used to you, Dion," Solange said sympathetically. "Most of those you want to interview didn't know your parents. They've only settled in the town in the past ten years. They consider you a stranger. It takes time for them to open up."

Dion gave a grunt of frustration. "It's not as if I'm prying into their family secrets. I only want background—customs and so on. Nothing personal."

"I've a friend in Athens who might be able to give you some background information. I could write her a note and maybe you could see her. But she's not a Sarakatsani herself."

"Maybe later, if I can't get enough from the people themselves. I was hoping to use firsthand knowledge, real family histories and anecdotes."

Solange nodded. "Yes, I see what you mean." She thought for a moment. "I've been thinking about some families I know, part of Penny's research program. A few of them still live in the *kalivia,* the reed huts, at least in summer. I'll talk to them for you on my next rounds of the villages."

"I'd appreciate it, Solange. I'm sure once they see I'm harmless they'll be more cooperative." He took another swallow of his beer. "Did you find out anything about a six-fingered man?"

Solange shook her head. "Not a thing. My landlady, Demetra, has been away since the day we had lunch. Her mother was taken ill, and Demetra went to Volos to take care of her." Solange's mouth tilted in a mischievous smile. "Litsa, her daughter, is in charge of the household, and she's certainly proved she can delegate. She even has her father helping with the cooking."

"What?" Dion's bewildered look sent her into gales of laughter. "You've lost me."

She tipped back her head and ran a hand under her hair, lifting its weight from her neck. Little curly wisps sprang free to cling damply to her skin. "Vasili tends to be complacent since Demetra is so efficient. He's not used to being asked to pitch in. But Litsa couldn't do it all by herself. She has her university entrance exams in a couple of weeks and has to spend the time studying. You know how tough they are."

Dion rolled his eyes. "Do I ever! I passed them by the skin of my teeth, and then it turned out all the cramming and sleepless nights were for nothing when I went to Canada and easily got into college there." The familiar nagging guilt rose in him, but he forced it back. He couldn't tell her that his sleeplessness hadn't been caused by studying but by his worries over his parents' imprisonment. It was a wonder he'd passed at all.

"They say you were sixteen when you went to Canada. That's young for high school graduation."

"I attended a private school. We were allowed to progress at our own pace. Since I knew how short money was, I took two grades in one, the last year. I wrote the grad exams early, too. That's why I was finished at Easter."

"Must have been tough."

"Yeah, which only made the contrast greater when I got to Canada." He took a swallow of his beer. "Why are you here, Solange? It can't be for the money."

She turned her head and regarded him with a quizzical smile. "Why do you ask? I told you, I like it. No, it's not the money. I own the clinic, which turned out to be a good investment since the land it sits on has increased in value. But it just means I don't pay rent. As it is, I only make a comfortable living."

"Not nearly what you'd make in Canada."

"No," she admitted. "But there are other compensations. Peace, no hassles. And the people here are wonderful."

"Sure, but you must have had a reason for not going back when your volunteer work ended."

"It's a long story, Dion."

He smiled. "Try me."

She smiled back, tempted. But she resisted. She didn't know him very well, and even five years later she still felt the anger and humiliation, and the nagging guilt that she should have handled it differently. She didn't want him to judge her by that incident. "Not today, Dion," she said lightly.

"Someday?" he asked with an almost whimsical, coaxing note in his voice.

Her heart warmed further toward him. "Maybe someday." Draining her beer, she set down the bottle. "Why don't we drive into Volos for lunch? My treat," she added quickly when she sensed he was about to refuse.

Dion rose to his feet, stretching his arms over his head and lazily arching his back. "Well, if it's your treat..."

"I'll pick you up in half an hour." She looked pointedly at his shorts, faded almost threadbare on the seat and thighs. "I want to change first."

"You mean you want me to change first." His tone was light, and for the first time in several days his depression lifted. "All right, half an hour."

THE HIGHWAY TO VOLOS wound along the coast, giving marvelous vistas of sea and sky. Olive trees cloaked the mountain slopes north of the road, interspersed with occasional thickets of almond and fruit trees.

Solange drove her little Alfa-Romeo with hair-raising speed, slowing down only when they passed through a village where the highway patrol might be lurking with a radar trap. It was clear to Dion that she knew the road and the often erratic driving habits of the area.

"Did you find it hard to get used to?" Dion asked as they narrowly missed a collision with a beer truck overtaking a slower car in the oncoming lane.

Solange threw him a rueful look. "The first year I was terrified. But once you drive like they do, it gets easier. I've had no accidents except for a minor fender bender last year. But I've patched up the results of some other people's accidents."

In the old section of Volos traffic was heavier, requiring concentration. She threaded the Alfa through it, displaying a Grand Prix driver's skill and nonchalance.

With a flourish she pulled into a parking space on the waterfront where an island ferry was loading passengers and produce. On the marble steps of the nearby bank a crowd of blond German students waited for the Flying Dolphin, the hydrofoil that would take them to the islands of Skiathos and Scopelos.

They walked a little, scanning the menus posted outside the numerous restaurants. A fresh breeze off the water and the shade of massive canvas awnings provided a welcome respite from the heat. "How about pizza?" Solange suggested. "It's a touch of home. The owner of the place used to live in Toronto, but he only stayed long enough to make enough money to open this place here."

"You're the boss," Dion said with an easy grin. "Since you're paying."

"Yeah, that's right. Okay, pizza it is."

The pizza was very good. Against Dion's will, nostalgia washed over him, as strong as it was unexpected. In Canada he often felt he missed Greece, the heat, the dust, the pervasive scents of diesel fuel and roasted coffee, but here he suddenly felt nostalgia for his adopted country. He shook his head. The mind played funny tricks. His first years in Canada he'd struggled to earn enough for university tuition, working long hours at a boring job rebuilding automotive starters. Going out for pizza on Saturdays had been his only entertainment. His student days were hardly worth missing.

"What are you thinking?"

He started, realizing how long he'd been silent. "Nothing much. I don't think I've enjoyed a pizza this much in years."

She didn't say anything, just stared at him with that disconcertingly candid appraisal in her brown eyes. "You don't talk about yourself, do you? I've given you dozens of openings and you've volunteered nothing."

He could feel sweat breaking out on his palms as he fiddled with the water glass before him, making wet rings on the red tablecloth. "You know everything that's important."

Solange cast him a long look from under knit brows.
"Come on, Dion. You know that's a lie." She shrugged.
"But suit yourself. It's none of my business, anyway."

The waiter came over and removed their plates. The
tables around them were mostly deserted. Solange
glanced at her watch. Late enough in the day to go calling, especially at this time of year.

She jumped up, slapping down a couple of thousand-
drachma notes. "While we're here in Volos, why don't
we drop in on my landlady, Demetra? She knows every
family in the area. She'll tell us about the six-fingered
man, if anyone can."

Demetra was happy to see Solange, and openly curious about Dion. She introduced them to her mother, a
stooped old lady in black. "She's almost well again,"
Demetra told Solange. "You can tell Litsa I'll be home
sometime tomorrow."

Demetra herself was a tall woman, broad in bust, hip
and cheekbone, with a wholesome, no-nonsense look
about her. Dion found himself liking her, a judgment he
made about few people on sight. "I'm very happy to
meet you. Solange says you might be able to help me
trace an, uh, acquaintance of my family."

"I'll try," Demetra said. "Why don't we go into the
living room? Solange, would you give my mother a hand
with the coffee things in the kitchen? She's still a little
shaky."

"Of course," Solange said readily.

"Who is this person you're looking for?" Demetra
asked as soon as she and Dion entered the salon.

Dion hesitated, glancing around the room. Stiffly
furnished with Victorian pieces, a chamber of such severe formality couldn't be called a living room. People

could sit in it, but living? Even the television set was in the large kitchen.

"I believe his name is Lambros Pavlou. It's too common a name to help much, but he had six fingers on his left hand. The extra one is bent at an angle toward the little finger. I've heard that such traits are often hereditary."

Demetra frowned, and her eyes slid away. "Six fingers?" She smoothed her hair, picking out a pin and securing a stray wisp into the bun at the back of her head. "No one in Korfalli has that. If they did, I'd know. But a lot of people have left the town in the past twenty years, and new people have come in."

Dion shifted impatiently on the hard chair. Demetra was hedging. He'd swear to it. She knew something, but for some reason she didn't want to tell him. "Mrs. Candiles, please tell me if you know anything. It's important to me."

"This person is a relative?" Demetra asked.

"No." He barely controlled his horror at such a thought. "No, he's just somebody who knew my parents. I'd like to talk to him." *I'd like to wrap my hands around his neck and squeeze until he turns purple, until he's as dead as they are.*

Demetra regarded him steadily, her dark eyes troubled. "There was a man once..." She shook her head. "It was a long time ago. I don't know about the extra finger, but his first name was Lambros."

She suddenly leaned forward, her voice rough and urgent, distress written all over her face. "Dion, let it go. There must be someone else who knew your family that you can talk to. And I think you must be mistaken about this Pavlou. Your parents fought against the very thing this man represented. If he's the one I'm thinking of, he's evil, completely evil. We heard he'd died years ago, but later we heard there had been a mistake, that he's still alive.''

Much the same information he'd been given. Dion couldn't still the heavy thud of his heart. ''Where is he?''

''Right now?'' She swallowed, her hand going to her throat, fiddling with the collar of her dress. ''I don't know. But he'd better not come around to Korfalli again. Some people have long memories.''

Dion's heartbeat was choking him. ''What do you mean?'' he asked in a thick voice.

She closed her eyes, making a quick sign of the cross. ''Years ago he came around a number of times, recruiting young men for a special division of the army, telling them what a great future they would have working directly with high government officials.''

''The Colonels.'' Dion could hardly force the words out.

''It was before they came to power, but they must have been planning their coup. Some of the young men went with him. He was from Korfalli and they trusted him.'' She crossed herself again. ''And none of them ever came back.''

CHAPTER FOUR

"IS SOMETHING WRONG?" Solange asked when they were halfway back to Korfalli.

Dion turned his head toward her, a muscle tensing in his jaw as he realized she'd repeated the question twice. "No, I'm fine," he said, aware that he sounded abstracted.

And well he might. Demetra knew something. And she'd admitted the man had once come from Korfalli. Without the evidence of the sixth finger he couldn't be sure that this was Lambros Pavlou, but the story fitted all the circumstances he knew. And Demetra was reluctant to talk about him. Was it really a lapse in memory, or was it fear? Her words had been a warning.

Apprehension knotted his stomach, fighting sickeningly with the food Demetra's mother had pressed on them. He barely noticed when Solange swerved the Alfa abruptly to avoid a tractor turning onto the highway out of a field road.

He would have to be even more circumspect now, especially if he went back to Athens to petition the military records office again. Someone must know where Pavlou lived now. But from what Demetra had said, he suspected his quest would only become more difficult. The harder he pushed, the more obstacles would appear in his way. For all he knew, Pavlou himself had buried the information in a morass of government files. There was plenty in his past he wouldn't want exhumed.

No matter. Dion wasn't about to give up. He would force those bureaucrats to search for the supposedly missing files.

Unless he found the answers in Korfalli itself. Not for the first time the possibility gave him pause. Pavlou might turn out to be a friend or relative of someone he knew, someone who would be hurt.

He pushed the thought aside ruthlessly, refusing to dwell on it. If someone got hurt, so be it. He had been hurt, too, and survived. Only death was irrevocable.

There were questions he hadn't been able to ask after Solange and Demetra's mother had come back into the salon with a tray of coffee and biscuits. But Demetra hadn't appeared willing to talk more in any case. She'd maintained an uncharacteristic silence as they'd drunk the coffee and later consumed glasses of wine accompanied by stuffed grape leaves, cubes of cheese and great chunks of newly baked bread.

"I may have to go to Athens in the next few days," he said, pressing his hand against his roiling stomach. He swallowed hard, willing it to settle down.

Solange glanced at him before returning her attention to the road. "Was Demetra any help?" Busy in the kitchen with Demetra's mother, she hadn't heard their conversation. But when she entered the living room with the coffee, he'd looked tense and unsettled, like a man who had just heard a piece of distressing news. Even now he appeared on edge, his face pale and sheened with sweat, as if he felt ill. "You're not feeling well, are you? Do you want me to stop for a few minutes?"

"No, it's okay." He grimaced as a cramp shot through his belly. "Too much food so soon after lunch."

Approaching Nea Anhialos, they crossed a headland high above the dark blue sea. In the distance scattered villages were blurs of white against the gold-green fields. A strong breeze coming off a pine grove up the mountain buffeted the little car and stroked Dion's face. His nausea subsided.

He forgot it entirely as he watched the wind playing in Solange's long hair, whipping it back from her vibrant face. She had put the car's top down, and the sunlight beat strongly on his head and shoulders, real, clean, the antithesis of the dark secrets that obsessed him. An illusion of tranquility, but he seized it eagerly. For a little while he would pretend that he was any man out for a drive with a beautiful woman.

"Demetra gave me a lead. I need to check the army records again."

She turned her face toward him, and light flashed from the frame of her sunglasses. "The man doesn't live in Korfalli, then?"

Dion shifted on the seat, pulling at his seat belt and letting it snap back into place. "No. If this is the man, he hasn't been there for a long time." He debated telling Solange the rest but decided against it. It didn't concern her in any case.

Lost in his thoughts, which had again turned bleak, he hardly noticed the rest of the drive until Solange pulled up in the shade of the fig tree that sheltered his house. She switched off the engine and turned in the seat to face him.

"Dion, I was talking about your research to Demetra's mother. She gave me the name of a Sarakatsani family in a village toward Farsala who might be able to help you with your research. I think I may know them. The name sounds vaguely familiar." She smiled. "I still find many Greek names hard to spell and pronounce. If you want, I can take you to see them.''

To her surprise he didn't react, just kept his eyes fixed on the distant hills. She tapped her fingers on the steering wheel. "You could at least say thanks," she added tartly.

He looked at her, smiling briefly. "Thanks. We'll go as soon as I get back from Athens."

"You'll be here for the baptism on Sunday, won't you? I'm one of the godparents, and Demetra expects you to be there as well."

"Does she?" After their conversation, he might have thought the opposite. "Yes, I'll be back in time. It's been years since I've been to a baptism."

Too many years. He'd lived a solitary life. He sat there, reluctant to get out of the car, to leave Solange's company. The rays of the setting sun slanted through the canopy of leaves to touch her hair with gold highlights, her cheeks with amber. In the distance thunder rumbled, although they'd seen no clouds. The heat was close and humid, condensed in the nook between the tree trunk and the whitewashed wall of the house.

"Solange..."

She turned her head, and a drop of sweat made a slow track down her temple. Silently she looked at him, a half smile on her lips and a soft warmth in those clear eyes the color of brook water.

He couldn't get involved.

But the message in his brain died as logic fled. Unable to stop himself he leaned over and kissed the drop of sweat from her cheek, absorbing its salty tang along with the sweet jasmine scent of her skin. "Solange..."

"Yes?" Her voice was low, a throaty whisper. He felt her breath, moist as her skin, scented with the coffee they'd drunk earlier. Their mouths were an inch apart.

Solange closed the distance, parting her lips as their mouths touched. At the first tentative contact, electric sensation raced along her veins. Their meetings, the game of advance and retreat, the attraction that was so elusive she hadn't been sure it was real—all of it had led to this moment. His hand tangled in the damp hair at her nape as he drew her closer. The gearshift between them kept their bodies apart, but Solange reached out to place her palm on his cheek. Sighing at the rough-smooth feel of his skin, she accepted the probing of his tongue, meeting it with the touch of her own.

A snatch of song from the street brought them to reality. Although they were off the road, farmers going to their fields often used a shortcut behind the tree.

Breathless, they pulled apart. Temptation shivered between them. Desire. The banishment of loneliness.

But even as the need within her strengthened, Solange saw regret come into Dion's eyes, darkening them to indigo. "Dion, don't—" She stopped.

His mouth turned up at the corner, although his eyes remained somber. "Don't what? Don't say a word? Don't be sorry? No, I'm not sorry. But—"

He broke off, pushing open the car door.

Her eyes flashed as she half rose from the seat. "But what? You can't leave like this."

Turning back, he leaned over and stroked his finger lightly over her lower lip. "It's better, Solange. Safer. See you Sunday."

SAFER? The word haunted Solange for the rest of the week. What an odd thing to say. But didn't it go along with the sense she had that Dion's presence here had far more significance than he was letting on? It would be safer for her, as well, for her emotional well-being, if she honored the distance he seemed to want to keep between them.

She didn't see him again until Sunday afternoon when he walked into the church just as the priest was moving to the door for the child-naming ceremony. Out of the corner of her eye she watched him, noting the tired lines in his face, the dark circles under his eyes. His remoteness and preoccupation rivaled that of the saints depicted in the icons arrayed at the front of the church. Only his mouth, as he silently chanted the prayer, appeared soft and vulnerable. Heat curled in her at the memory of their kiss.

"What is the name of this child?"

She started guiltily as the loud call of the priest jerked her attention back to the ceremony. "Sophocles," the godfather intoned, and she echoed the name quietly.

Baptisms were simple, the least formal of the sacraments, festive occasions that celebrated new life. The church was chaotic with the neighborhood children crowding around Papa Anthony who broke off his chanting several times to remind them gently that they were in God's house.

The verger filled the large basin at the center of the church with warm water while Solange and Poppy undressed the wriggling infant. Little Sophocles liked baths and greeted the ritual cleansing with an enthusiasm entirely appropriate to the occasion. Even Papa Anthony, a man whose normal demeanor bordered on the morose, permitted himself a tiny smile when the baby objected strenuously to being pulled out of the basin.

Solange received him into the white towel she held, wrapping him securely as the priest administered oil and sweet-smelling myrrh to his ears, eyes and forehead. With a tiny pair of scissors Papa Anthony snipped off a lock of hair, which would be carefully preserved. The rising hymn of jubilation followed Solange as she carried the baby to the back of the church to be dressed in new and elaborate finery for the final moments of the ceremony.

As she buttoned his little blue jacket, he patted her hand and grinned at her, his two teeth gleaming like grains of rice set in rosy gums. Solange felt her heart turn over. A sudden recognition of time passing washed over her. Her arms tightened convulsively around the child. Would she ever have a child of her own?

Shaken, she jerked back to present awareness when young Sophocles protested with an annoyed grunt that changed to a sunny chortle as she carried him up the aisle for the closing blessing.

The ceremony completed, the crowd spilled out into the churchyard, exchanging congratulations, handshakes, hugs and cheerfully shouted greetings. Proudly displaying his newly named son on his broad shoulder, Poppy's husband handed out little bundles of blue sugared almonds and coins to the children.

Moving outside in the wake of the others, Solange blinked in the sunlight, smiling as yet another old man, an uncle or one of the grandfathers shook her hand before rejoining his friends.

"Hello, Solange," Dion greeted her in his low, deep voice. "I made it back."

"Hello, Dion," she said quietly. "Was your trip successful?"

His eyes ran over her, lighting up with appreciation at the way her blue dress flattered her coloring and slender body. "Not as successful as I would have liked. The army records are still unavailable, but I did find an interesting book on the Sarakatsani, which I managed to borrow from the folk art museum."

Actually, the four days he'd spent in Athens had been a total loss in time and energy. He had been sent from one office to another, an endless round of bureaucracy that had gotten him nowhere. Nobody seemed to care anymore that justice hadn't been realized for those who had died under the oppressive regime of the Colonels. In the end he'd been forced to conclude that the present government just wanted to sweep those seven bloody years of tyranny into oblivion, preferably even out of the history books.

Dion wished he could forget the past as easily. But he had set himself a mission, one he was determined to carry through. His parents had been innocent victims. Lambros Pavlou had to pay for their murders.

If only he could find the man. Pavlou was proving so elusive that Dion wondered at times if he was pursuing a ghost.

"The Sarakatsani family you mentioned," he said as he and Solange walked toward the coffee shop across the square where refreshments were being served. "Can you take me to see them?"

No matter what happened with his quest for Pavlou, Solange could still help him with his stated work. And he was glad he had that excuse to spend time with her.

He'd missed her while he was in Athens. She had already invaded an empty place inside him. She was sweet and caring, and aroused a yearning in him that he'd sublimated since his abrupt projection into manhood at sixteen.

"Of course I'll take you." Her quiet voice washed over him, warm as spring sunshine. "I said I would. Will Tuesday be all right? Penny takes the clinic then."

"How far is this village?"

"A forty-five-minute drive. Why?"

He pulled out a chair and waited until she was seated. "Demetra might know if the family has a telephone. We could make an appointment and save time. I don't want to keep you from your work longer than necessary."

"It'll be fine, Dion." She laid her hand on his arm, and he felt her warmth burning through his skin. "Penny needs more office experience. She gets too wrapped up in her research."

His brows lifted. "That's what they say about you."

She shook her head, smiling. "Not anymore. Not since you came. Oh, hello, Demetra," Solange said as her friend came over to them. "How's your mother?"

"Very well. I'm sorry, Solange. I've just been too busy to come and talk to you."

"No matter. I've been busy, too." Solange took two cups of coffee from the tray Demetra was passing around, helping herself to the chocolate biscuits that were almost a ritual after baptisms. "Demetra, the Sarakatsani family your mother mentioned, can we get in touch with them by phone?"

"Better than that, Dr. Solange," Demetra said with a twinkle in her olive-dark eyes. She waved at someone across the room. "Kyrie Vangeli, could you come here, please?"

Vangeli was a short, stocky man who wore baggy black trousers and a white homespun shirt. A bright red kerchief adorned his neck, a pirate's touch that complemented the black wool fisherman's cap perched at a rakish angle on his wiry gray curls.

"Demetra." Throwing his arms around her, he gave her a smacking kiss on the cheek that nearly caused her to drop the tray.

"Go on with you," she chided with mock severity. "What would Maria say?"

"She'd say I still have an eye for a good-looking woman." A boisterous laugh boomed out, compelling the others to join him.

"Vangeli," Demetra went on after the laughter subsided. "This is Dion Parris from Canada." The two men shook hands. "I think you've met Dr. Solange Richards, haven't you?"

"Of course. The doctor treated my wife last year."

Solange had thought his face familiar but now was able to place him. "Yes, I remember. How is she?"

"She's very well. Those blood pressure pills have done the trick."

"She's having it checked regularly?" Solange knew that many people in the villages thought that if they took medication, there was no need for any follow-up.

"Yes, the public health nurse checks it every Friday. It's too bad she couldn't come today, but our son is visiting from Germany."

"Vangeli," Demetra put in, "Kyrios Parris is researching a paper on the Sarakatsani, the old customs. He'd like to talk to you."

Vangeli's barrel chest swelled to awesome proportions as he drew back his shoulders in pride. A broad grin spread over his weathered face. "You'll come to the village. Maria had a box of old photographs that you'll find most interesting. How soon? Tomorrow?"

Dion, who hadn't been able to say a word until this point, grinned back. "Tuesday. Solange is driving me."

Vangeli clapped his hand on Dion's shoulder, hard enough to make him stagger. "Then you'll both come for the midday meal. What do you say, Doctor? Can the patients manage without you?"

"They have Penny."

"Yes, Penny." His grizzled brows drew together. "She comes to the village to take blood samples for her tests. Conscientious but too prim. She needs a good husband. Maybe I could ask around. There must be somebody."

"Penny's too busy right now," Solange said hastily. "But if the time comes . . ." She let the words trail off as Vangeli turned to Dion.

"Well, is it agreed? Some good lamb, a few beers. We'll have the afternoon to talk."

Dion was conscious of relief that someone finally seemed happy to talk to him. But a faint guilt that he was using Solange remained. "It's very nice of you," he said. "But don't go to any trouble."

Vangeli groped in his pockets for a cigarette. "Trouble, my boy? Don't you know that we're just looking for an excuse to roast a lamb? It's no trouble. It's our pleasure to make you welcome."

The old man tapped a cigarette from a battered pack and pressed it between his lips. Pulling out a match, he struck it on the edge of a thumbnail as thick as a goat's hoof. Smoke, pungent with sulfur, curled up between his fingers.

It was then that Dion noticed the hand that cupped the flame, touching it to the cigarette. Vangeli had six fingers.

The din of voices in the crowded coffee shop receded as the blood roared in his ears. He knew his face must have lost all its color. He felt cold, and a violent shudder racked him as he forced his eyes open again. Forced himself to think. Had his memory become distorted by time?

Vangeli? No, it couldn't be him. He was too heavy and too short. It didn't fit. After nearly twenty years a man might gain weight, but he didn't shrink six or more inches in stature.

He stared at the man's hand, and relief flooded him. Vangeli wasn't the man. The extra finger was on his right hand, not his left.

"Dion, are you all right?"

As if from a long distance, Solange's voice reached him. He sucked in his breath, marshaling his control. He tried to force a smile, failing dismally. "You're asking that a lot." Solange's eyes were fixed on him in close appraisal. He blinked a couple of times and shook his head to clear it. "I'm okay."

"You don't look okay. You look as if you'd seen a ghost."

He laughed harshly, humorlessly. "You might say that."

Their lapse into English was incomprehensible to their companions, Solange suddenly realized when Demetra asked with a puzzled frown, "What is it?"

"Nothing," Solange quickly answered. "It's very hot in here, and Dion's a little tired. He got in from Athens late last night."

"How did you know that?" Dion asked sotto voce when Demetra turned to reassure the woman next to her who was also staring in concern.

"Lucky guess." Taking his arm in a firm grip, she led him toward the door. "Shall we go?"

"See you Tuesday," Vangeli, oblivious to the undercurrents, called after them.

"He had six fingers on his hand, didn't he?" Solange asked. "But he's not the man you're looking for."

"No," Dion said, miserably wishing he'd been able to control his reaction. Solange was giving him the strangest looks, and in another minute she would demand an explanation. "The man I'm looking for has an extra finger on his left hand, not the right."

Outside, they met Litsa at the garden gate. "Oh, Dr. Solange, I'm so worried. I can't find little Dino anywhere. He was playing, and with the gate closed I thought he couldn't get out. But he's gone."

"Well, I don't think anyone's kidnapped him," Solange said. "One of the neighbors has probably seen him. Have you asked?"

"I was about to. My mother will kill me if she finds out I've lost him."

Solange's brow lifted. "Not Dino's mother?"

Litsa made a scornful sound. "Not her. Kiki seems to consider him a nuisance. Why did she even have him, especially so soon after they married?"

"Pressure, no doubt," Dion muttered.

Solange turned her head. "What was that?"

"Pressure, I said. Haven't you noticed that once a couple is married, they'd better have a baby right away or the whole town talks? I think they have children in self-defense."

"I guess so." Solange wasn't sure whether to laugh; he seemed deadly serious.

Most of the neighbors were still at the baptism celebrations, but with easy familiarity Litsa opened gates and even house doors, calling for the little boy whom she frequently baby-sat while his young mother worked, or played. They each took a side of the street, and it wasn't long before Litsa shouted, from Grandma Amelia's house, two doors past her own. Solange and Dion ran across the patio into the kitchen garden at the back.

The toddler sat on the ground, his bottom planted firmly in a patch of mud while he stirred another, wetter puddle with a stick. Around him lay the ruins of young cucumber plants.

"I'm making a garden," he announced with a cherubic smile.

"I can see that," Litsa said through gritted teeth. "Bad boy." She scooped him up, regardless of the red mud that stained her dress. "You could have been run over by a car, going on the road by yourself."

"We'll stay here and put the plants back," Solange said. "I don't think there's too much damage."

The soil was damp, the cucumbers newly planted. Solange and Dion had the uprooted plants set out again in neat rows by the time Grandma Amelia returned from the baptism celebration.

"The plants—it doesn't matter," she said, dismissing their apologies as she went to bring them soap and a towel for their dirty hands.

Their shoes were muddy, and Solange had splatters of dirt on her stockings. Luckily her dress had escaped the stains. She knew from past experience that the rust-colored earth was nearly impossible to wash out.

Picking up a stick, Dion scraped his shoes, then rinsed off the soles with a gentle spray from the garden hose. He turned toward Solange to see if she needed help. She had lifted the hem of her skirt to unfasten her stockings. Balancing gracefully on one foot, she stripped off the stocking and pushed it into her shoe. Dion caught only a flash of creamy thigh as she pulled off the other, but it was enough to dry his mouth.

He realized that while he'd noticed her legs, especially when she wore shorts, he hadn't really seen them. Clearly his preoccupation with his work had dulled his normal instincts, a state of affairs he wished had lasted longer.

Licking his lips, he held out the hose. "Shall I?"

"Wait!" But her protest was a second too late. He turned on the water. Shrieking as the icy spray hit her feet and ankles, she hiked up her skirt and jumped out of the way.

Dion immediately jerked the hose aside. "Sorry, I should have guessed it would be cold. Sit down." He gestured toward the low brick wall that surrounded the garden.

Taking her foot in his hands, he massaged warmth back into the chilled skin, picking off little bits of caked mud with his fingers. Her skin was soft, lightly tanned. The bones had an amazing delicacy, seeming too fragile to withstand the hard work she demanded of them, running every day.

Her pulse beat strongly in her ankle as his fingertips brushed over it. Slowly he stroked downward, ending at her toes, noting that her nails were painted a pale pink, a mere blush of color.

She wriggled in his clasp. "That one's warm enough. How about the other?"

He took the other, rubbing it gently between his palms. "Careful," she murmured. "I'm ticklish."

As if in a trance, he looked up. Her head was bent, her face exquisitely flushed. Sometime tonight they would be alone, and he would kiss her again. The yearning in him was as deep as pain. Did she feel it, too? Under his fingers her pulse sped up. "Solange—"

"Here you are, children." Amelia's cheerful voice shattered the moment more effectively than a thunderclap.

Avoiding each other's eyes, they washed their hands, and dried them on a towel.

Amelia glanced from one to the other, her eyes shrewd. "Better run along now. Demetra said to tell you the food is waiting. For both of you."

"Demetra didn't mention dinner to me," Dion muttered as they left.

"She invited me," Solange said. "So I guess you're invited, too. Don't worry. She's a very good cook."

"That wasn't worrying me." He hadn't wanted to get involved with the town social life unless it was necessary. It wouldn't be fair to the people who offered him friendship if ultimately he had to destroy one of them.

He pushed the thought to the back of his mind and took Solange's arm as she stumbled. "I guess I'm not used to bare feet anymore." She laughed as she quickly recovered.

She looked like a carefree child, her shoes and stockings in one hand along with the edge of her flared skirt that she held up to watch for rough spots in the path. *You're beautiful,* he wanted to tell her. *And I can't touch you.*

"Go on in." Solange gave him a push toward Demetra's section of the house. "I'll be down as soon as I wash my feet and find some other shoes."

Dion was acutely aware of her throughout the long, cheerfully noisy meal. She helped Demetra bring dishes from the kitchen, and he couldn't take his eyes off her legs. She hadn't bothered to put on stockings again, and he could only think of how her skin had felt. Warm, resilient. Responsive.

Her smile flashed constantly in her animated face. She looked happy, very much at home, while he felt like an outsider.

He'd always felt like an outsider. His plans to avenge his parents' deaths had given him a single-mindedness that didn't allow for easy friendships. He'd been alone forever, but hadn't noticed his loneliness until he'd met Solange.

And he'd be lonely again when he left. Lonely and empty. It was the price he had to pay for honor.

DION WANTED to get Solange off by herself, but everything seemed to conspire against it. At nine he found himself sitting at a table on the square, along with Demetra, Vasili, Poppy and her husband, as well as assorted other family friends. And to his own amazement he made no protest when someone handed him the baby Sophocles.

The child cuddled trustingly against him, babbling in his own incomprehensible language and favoring Dion with a gummy grin. Dion gently poked his round tummy, and the baby gurgled with laughter so infectious that Dion had to laugh, too. But his laughter was tinged with some other, indefinable emotion that made his eyes burn suddenly.

Would he ever hold his own child?

Solange leaned over and wiped the dribble off the baby's chin. "Teething again, are we?" she said affectionately, and was rewarded with a gabble of sounds. "Dion, if you want to walk for a bit, I'll take him."

Dion shook his head, hardly trusting himself to speak. "No, he's all right."

For the moment Solange and Dion might have been alone as the others engaged in a lively argument about politics, the universal bone of contention. They idly watched the square, the people walking back and forth, everyone dressed up. The rich wore the latest fashions, the poor carefully preserved clothing in classic styles, the young mostly in jeans and baggy shirts. Kyra and Litsa passed them, holding hands as friends often did, chattering to each other and shyly eyeing a group of boys seated on the fountain edge. Penny walked by with her aunt and uncle, keeping a sedate pace.

"Look at those guys trying to get Penny's attention," Solange said with a laugh. "And she's pretending not to see them."

Only the high flush on Penny's cheeks revealed that she heard the young men's comments. Peter turned his head and spoke to them, and they laughed. None of it was serious.

"She's going to find herself married one day whether she wants to or not," Dion said. "The more she plays hard to get, the more determined everyone is to match her up." He bounced the baby on his knee. "How is it that Sophocles here wasn't baptized earlier? He must be getting close to a year old."

Solange grinned at the baby, who patted her hand. "Baba?" he queried.

"Your Baba is talking, darling." She fingered the little blue bead pinned to the child's sweater to keep away the evil eye. "He's nine months. He was small when he was born and they didn't want to baptize him in the winter. You've seen how babies are pampered, especially first ones."

"Baba!" Sophocles called insistently. "Baba!"

"Yes, darling," Solange said soothingly. "You can go to your Baba." She lifted the child from Dion's arms and passed him across the table to his father, who immediately started a nonsensical conversation with him, politics abandoned.

The group began to break up soon after. Solange and Dion walked up and down the square a couple of times, pausing briefly to speak to Penny before heading home.

The streets were quiet, dark between the pools of light cast by the wide-spread lamps. Dion held Solange's hand as they walked, uncaring of the knowing smiles they received from the few people they passed. He was pretending again, a game that became increasingly seductive the more he allowed himself to indulge in it.

Solange felt his odd mood, the tension he thought he hid. She wanted to ask him a hundred questions but couldn't find the words to voice even one. He was a puzzle.

Yet she forgot her misgivings when he drew her into a shadowed corner and kissed her.

The first touch of his mouth to hers was gentle, but then he seemed to take fire, and the fire echoed in her own body and mind. He opened his mouth over hers, and she felt the tremor that shook his body. His kiss was fierce and hot, his lips never still, as if he couldn't get enough of her. His scent swirled around her, his mossy after-shave and the astringent smell of desire.

She pressed closer, driven by a need to absorb him, to know his very essence, to break down the wall he kept around himself. He wanted her. The physical evidence of his wanting surged against her, but she sensed he also wanted her on another level.

But he wouldn't follow through, not tonight. She shivered as he gentled his hold, freed her mouth and rested his chin against her temple.

"Dion, what is it?" She kept her voice to a whisper but wanted to shout at him, to beat down the barrier.

He shook his head, and she felt the feathery brush of his lashes on her cheek as his eyes closed. "Solange, I'm sorry. There's so much I can't tell you. I shouldn't be doing this. But I can't help it. You're not like any woman I've ever known."

Frustration with his maddening secretiveness made her tongue sharp. "And I suppose you've known enough of them to be an expert." She pulled abruptly away. "Good night, Dion. I'll see you Tuesday."

CHAPTER FIVE

THE ROAD TO Vangeli's village crossed a rolling plain, the gray ribbon of asphalt looping through fields of ripening wheat and intensely green corn, dipping into dry or running streams marked by trees and climbing up again to crest the low hills.

Solange drove quickly but with the sure control that had already won Dion's admiration.

"Not far now," she said, breaking the silence that had lain between them for most of the drive. She wrinkled her nose. "I think I can smell that lamb roasting."

Dion laughed. "I've been smelling sheep for the past five kilometers, and not roasting."

They rounded a curve and entered the outskirts of the village, passing a cemetery where tall cypresses guarded the dead. A bell tower thrust its height into the cloudless sky, dominating the huddle of terra-cotta-tiled houses and tiny shops. The men at the table outside the coffee shop stared curiously as they passed.

Reaching a fork in the road, Solange slowed the car. "Let me see now. Yes, I'm sure it's to the right."

"You've been here before," Dion said.

"I've been to the village several times, but to Vangeli's house only once, when his wife was sick the first time. Later he brought her to the clinic. But it was a long time ago, and she's been well ever since. I was asking Aphrodite about her. You're not going to believe it, but

Maria's had ten children, nine of them big strapping boys."

"That must have pleased her husband," Dion said dryly.

"Maybe they prefer boys, especially since girls need, or needed, a dowry, but I've never seen a single case of a family not loving whatever children they have, regardless of sex."

Dion couldn't help admiring her positive outlook. He agreed that the preference for male children wasn't as pronounced as outsiders seemed to view it, but he knew several families who hadn't much use for their daughters. Fortunately they were exceptions.

They had no trouble recognizing the house, which stood in a large garden filled with flowers and fruit trees. In the center of the courtyard a lamb turned on a spit, filling the air with the pungence of herbs and charcoal. School was over for the day, and several children milled around, taking turns rotating the meat so that it would cook evenly.

"They're here. They're here," a small boy yelled, dancing from one bare foot to the other in his excitement.

Before they were out of the car Vangeli and his wife, Maria, a small, thin woman who looked too frail to have mothered one child, never mind ten, called a greeting. Hurrying up the path, Vangeli threw open the gate and enveloped Solange in an exuberant embrace. "Welcome to our house, Dr. Solange."

The introductions that followed showed more enthusiasm than the niceties of social skills. To Dion's surprise, not only were some of the family members dressed in authentic Sarakatsani costumes, which he had previously seen only in the folk art museum, but Vangeli had arranged for a small orchestra. Two clarinets, a violin and a guitar blended to create music that was almost Oriental in its minor keys and dirgelike intonations.

"This," said Vangeli, draping an arm around Dion's shoulders, "is how we used to live. Except for the house, of course. In those days we lived in tents or reed shelters." He winked at Solange. "Get our doctor to take you around the countryside. Some of the reed shelters are still in use."

"Thanks, I will." Dion pulled out a spiral notebook and began to write down his impressions.

Solange joined the women, who were cutting up the lamb. She helped hand out the plates, loaded not only with the meat, but with large squares of spinach and cheese pie. There was much joking and laughter, especially when Maria pointed out a man she was sure would move Penny to abandon her determined spinsterhood.

He was good-looking, with an open, cheerful face, and not above giving Solange a sly wink when no one was watching. But Solange paid him scant attention. Her mind stayed with Dion, even though she barely spoke to him all afternoon. Her head was spinning with music, the colorful costumes and the exuberant conversation—what must he be feeling?

They stayed until well after sunset, joining in the dancing. Dion quickly picked up the steps almost forgotten from childhood, supporting Solange when she stumbled, causing the woman in the line next to her to burst into gales of laughter. When they finally said their goodbyes and thanks, the music and song followed them back to the car.

Tired and bedazzled, they drove slowly home under a moon that laid a silver swath of light across the fields. "It was fun, wasn't it?" Solange asked, covering a yawn.

"It was," Dion agreed. He saw her yawn again. "Do you want me to drive?"

"No, it's all right."

"Why?" he challenged with one of his infrequent flashes of humor. "Don't you trust me with your car?"

Solange laughed, downshifting as they crossed a narrow wooden bridge over a stream that gurgled like a child's laughter. "Why shouldn't I trust you?"

"Yeah, why not?" he said with forced cheer as he pushed reality back. He could enjoy this day and this night, couldn't he? He was no nearer to finding Pavlou than he had been days ago. In Vangeli's family six fingers wasn't inherited. Vangeli was the only one who showed the oddity, and had assured Dion that it was just that, an aberration. The old man had an excellent knowledge of inherited genes through his seventy years of raising sheep and goats. He understood how recessive and dominant traits were passed on. None of his children had the extra finger, and neither did any of theirs.

Solange stopped the car in front of Dion's house, turning off the engine. "Tell me what you learned today, Dion," she said quietly.

He looked at her. Her hair was loose, its tawny waves springing back from her face, disarranged by the breeze from the open car window. Her angular features were softened by the dim light, her eyes in shadow, mysterious, unreadable.

"What did you learn, Dion?" she said again when he didn't answer.

That moonlight becomes you. The line—was it from a song or a poem?—jumped into his mind. "So many things," he said, his voice husky. "I'll let you read what I've written once I organize it."

Her head tilted up. "Will you? Can't you just tell me what you think without editing it? Dion, why do you always hold back?"

The repressed anger in her tone shocked him. "Hold back?" But of course he did. How could he tell her he was contemplating an execution? She would never understand. She would make some practical remark such as killing Pavlou wouldn't bring back his parents. *If* she could still bring herself to speak to him once she learned the truth.

"Yes, you hold back. I know nothing about you, while you probably know everything about me, thanks at least in part to our neighbors."

"Not everything," he said in an attempt to defuse the argument he sensed was brewing. "I don't know why you stayed on here when you'd had a successful career in Canada."

"I got fired." She averted her face, but not before he saw the gleam of tears in her eyes. "Oh, not fired exactly. But I lost my privileges at the hospital where I sent most of my patients. Which is as good as being fired. Or as bad." She rubbed her cheek with her hand, hating the weakness that made her cry even now. She should have gotten over it long ago. "And it turned out I was right and they were wrong."

"Do you want to talk about it?"

"No."

"It might help."

"Why should it? No one can do anything about it."

"Does this suspending of privileges last forever?"

"In my case, no. I could go there tomorrow and have it all back. There was a similar incident a few weeks later and I was exonerated. I received a written apology and reinstatement if I wanted it."

She was conscious of his arm resting on the seat back behind her head. A slight move on his part and it would be around her shoulders. Impatiently she shook her head. Dion, in spite of his childhood in Korfalli, had a career in Canada, one he would go back to. The day in the village had been fun, but it was pointless to carry it further.

And hadn't he made it clear on Sunday night that he didn't want to get involved with her?

Dion lowered his arm around her shoulders and pulled her against him. "You're a good doctor, Solange," he said. "I don't see how anyone could think you might be negligent."

"None of us are perfect." She refused to relax, although the temptation to melt into him was almost overwhelming. Instead she straightened and turned the key in the ignition. "I have an early day tomorrow," she said pointedly.

One of Dion's straight black brows lifted. "Don't you every day? Solange, you work too hard."

"That's what Aphrodite tells me. I worked harder in Canada." She stepped on the clutch, putting the car in gear. "Good night, Dion."

He had no choice but to get out of the car. Closing the door, he stepped back. The tires crunched on the gravel road. "Wait."

Solange stamped on the brake. "What is it?"

Dion stuck his head through the open window, suddenly not knowing what to say, only knowing he didn't want her to leave yet. "Solange, I enjoyed the day. If I decide to go looking for the encampment Vangeli mentioned, will you go with me?"

Caution warred with the promise of adventure. The low throb of the engine formed a background to her tumbling thoughts. Finally she nodded. "Okay. If you let me know a day or two ahead of time."

His spontaneous grin erased the barrier he always seemed to maintain around his emotions. She bit her lip in frustration. Too bad these unguarded moments only lasted for an instant. "Great." He kissed his forefinger and pressed it briefly to the tip of her nose. "Good night, Solange."

HER CHAOTIC THOUGHTS about Dion kept her awake. By one she still hadn't slept, and it was almost a relief to hear a knock on the door. Shrugging into a robe, she went to it. The little boy she had patched up the night of the Bulgaris dinner stood on the landing, nervously shuffling his bare feet.

"Dr. Solange, my mother sent me to get you."

"Come in." She pulled him inside and closed the door. "It's my aunt," Yiorgi explained. "Katerina Zogas. My uncle phoned. He says she's having the baby and can you come?" The child bit on the edge of his thumbnail, his lip trembling. "My mother says he sounded scared."

Solange hugged the child, feeling the fragile bones under the striped T-shirt. "Wait here. I'll get dressed."

Running back to her room, she tossed down the robe and pulled on underwear, a shirt and jeans. "They're in the mountains, are they?" she called through the open door. "Your aunt didn't come down?"

"No, Dr. Solange. Uncle Spiro says she couldn't walk to where he had his truck, and he didn't like to leave her."

That meant she was in heavy labor, or ill from the toxemia that had plagued her first pregnancy, a pregnancy that had ended in miscarriage. Not that there had been any sign of difficulty when Penny had visited her last week, but blood pressure could rise within a matter of hours, and then the mother would be in serious trouble. Not to mention the longed-for infant.

Solange's thoughts raced as she tied her running shoes. She knew their mountain camp where they grazed a huge flock of sheep and goats in the summer, living in a primitive hut a half-hour hike from the last place a vehicle could go. They were one Sarakatsani family who hadn't adopted modern ways.

She pulled a sweater over her head, then took a blanket, wrapped in a sterile plastic bag, from the closet. Automatically she checked the contents of her medical bag. A hut without electricity or water wasn't the most convenient place to deliver a baby, but the woman's ancestors had managed for generations. Solange closed her eyes, uttering a wordless prayer.

Reaching into the closet, she took out a box of emergency supplies she used for field childbirth and carried the items into the living room. Yiorgi still waited, his eyelids heavy as he slumped in a chair. Solange smiled, used by now to the late hours even children kept in the summer. Of course, they made up the lost sleep during the afternoon siesta.

She handed him her bag and the blanket. "Could you carry these out to the car for me, please?"

He obeyed with alacrity, jogging down the stairs.

When she dropped him off at his house, she had a brief word with his mother. Spiro Zogas hadn't called again.

She drove slowly through the quiet town, passing in and out of pools of light from the street lamps. As she went by Dion's house, she saw a light on, dimly visible through the open front door. On impulse she stopped, jumping out of the car and bounding up the shallow step. He sat at the kitchen table, books and papers spread around him. His bare shoulders gleamed in the lamplight. The tangled state of his hair and the numerous crumpled sheets scattered on the floor spoke volumes. He hadn't been able to sleep or work.

She only had a moment to wonder why when he saw her and scraped the papers he was studying into a file folder, pushing it under a stack of books. "Hi, Solange. I thought you'd be in bed by now."

"I have to deliver a baby. Do you want to come? It's a shepherd family in the mountains."

"Sure." He rose, shrugging into his shirt.

The headlights tracked their path through the night, which was very dark now that the moon had set. Although he spoke little, Solange was grateful for Dion's company. He might distract Spiro, who was inclined to be overprotective of his wife and unfriendly toward anyone from town. He saw himself as one of the last of a fierce and independent breed of men. Townspeople were weak, almost decadent, not worthy of respect. He had no problem with her being a woman doctor; in fact, for his wife he preferred it. But there would always be a barrier between her kind and his, a barrier of class, education and background.

Both Solange and Dion were out of breath when they reached the hut. Half an hour of clambering up a rugged path along which thornbushes lurked to claw at the unwary was hardly a stroll in the park.

At least the couple lived in a substantial shelter rather than the more usual flimsy tent. The thick stone walls and slate roof of the hut blended into the landscape so thoroughly that except for the path ending at the door they might have missed it. A small sheepdog rose from the stoop and sniffed at their legs, barking once. In response, the flock confined to a corral nearby stirred and bleated plaintively.

"*Scasse!* Shut up." The dog ducked its head as the shepherd, broad as a castle gate against the flickering lamplight, loomed in the doorway. "Doctor, you're here." He held the canvas that covered the doorway aside for them to enter, lowering his other hand to scratch the dog's ears as it begged pardon for barking.

Solange noted with approval the cleanliness of the hut, the packed earth floor neatly swept, but she had expected nothing less. A fire burned in a stove made from an old oil barrel, snapping cheerfully against the night's chill.

On the brass bed in the corner of the surprisingly well-furnished room a woman lay, breathing easily, although sweat glistened on her face. As Solange approached, she smiled, only to grimace as a contraction tightened her distended belly. Spiro laid his huge, gnarled hand on his wife's forehead, smoothing back her damp hair with a poignant tenderness. "She's been like that for hours. The contractions don't seem to be getting any closer together, I didn't know what to do. With sheep it's so much easier."

Solange hid her smile as she bent over the woman, taking her pulse and checking her ankles for swelling. She breathed a silent thanks as everything seemed normal, no sign of toxicity, the fetal heartbeat strong. She patted Spiro on his brawny shoulder. "Don't worry. She'll be just fine."

The night passed slowly. Dion, sitting near the fire, dozed off in his chair, only to awaken when Katerina groaned as the labor progressed. Solange sat next to the bed, sponging Katerina's face, feeding her bits of ice, which she had brought in a thermos jug. Solange's expression was serene, her manner calm.

Dion's heart expanded uncomfortably in his chest, and his throat tightened. Damn it, he had to stop this. He couldn't let himself care. He couldn't let himself feel.

Abruptly he stood up, stalking to the door. The canvas swung closed behind him as he went out.

Solange watched him go, her eyes troubled, clearing as Spiro muttered an excuse and went out after Dion.

Just as well, she thought. They would be company for each other, and she didn't need them in the final stages.

The two men were carrying the buckets of fresh goat milk to the little hut when they heard the baby's cry. Spiro dropped one pail, spilling the milk over the path as he ran the last two yards. Dion followed more slowly, reluctant to intrude on the family.

The sight that met him made unaccustomed tears burn in his eyes. Katerina, her face rosy and peaceful, held a little dark-haired baby to her breast. A minute fist curled out of the blanket covering him as the infant sucked vigorously, then sighed and fell asleep.

Solange drew a blanket up to cover both of them, smoothing her palm over Katerina's tired face. "Sleep now. You deserve it."

The sun came up over the mountain, entering the room in a broad swath around the pulled-back canvas, flooding the bed with an amber radiance. Spiro's face reflected the same radiance as he ran his hand over his wife's hair, spreading it on the pillow. Tears ran down his weather-beaten cheeks, but he smiled like a man who had been given the greatest gift. "Thank God," he whispered. "And thank you, for my son."

Dion said little on the drive back. Squinting against the sun, Solange knew what he must be feeling. Childbirth was always a moving event, one most men never witnessed until they had their own children. She had seen the tears he'd blinked back, the emotion he couldn't hide.

"That's what makes it worthwhile, isn't it?" he said as he got out of the car at his house. "A healthy child. A new life."

Tears stung her own eyes. "Yes, it's a good feeling when it goes right. But not my doing. That simple shepherd who's never gone to school, can hardly read or write, knows that. He was thanking God, not me, for the child. And that's as it should be."

But often wasn't, Dion thought with sudden bleakness as he turned away.

He had only made it to the foot of the steps when Solange laid her hand on his arm. Her eyes were huge, dark with suppressed emotion, and the light of the sun harshly defined the lines of weariness on her face.

"Dion, why? Why are you like this?" Her voice was thick, husky with unshed tears. "Why are you afraid to feel?"

He took her into his arms and pressed her against him, his heart aching with an overwhelming sorrow. "You're wrong, you know. I'm not afraid to feel. I feel too much. Sometimes I feel like I'm about to explode."

"Tell me," she said, the words muffled by his shirt. Then the shirt was pushed aside and he felt her open mouth against his skin. He shuddered with the effort not to drag her inside and make love to her until they were both too spent to care about reality.

"You'll find out soon enough," he murmured. "And then it will all be over."

"Let me be the judge of that," Solange retorted, the harshness of her tone at odds with the softness of her mouth as she kissed him again. "Oh, Dion, you Greeks make such heavy weather of everything."

If she only knew, Dion thought. "You're tired," he said. "We're both tired." With a finger under her chin he lifted her face up to his and kissed her tenderly. "Go home and get some sleep."

Her heart heavy, Solange frowned as she turned toward the car. "And I suppose you'll be working. I never saw anyone who could get along on so little sleep."

"Working?" A comical look of surprise crossed his face. "You know, I completely forgot to take notes."

She stared at him, a slow smile breaking through her exhaustion and overwrought emotions. "I think we're making progress. You *can* feel."

SOLANGE SAW NOTHING of Dion for several days. Even after her morning run there was no sign of him on his veranda, no graceful male body draped over one of the sling chairs he'd acquired.

She missed him, although she was reluctant to admit it. Her office was quiet, Penny in Athens for a couple of days to correlate some of her data with a lab there. In the lazy days of early summer few illnesses threatened. The wheat harvest hadn't begun yet, though the grain was rippling more gold than green under the hot sun. Once the massive combines went into the fields, she could expect the usual minor, and occasionally major, injuries.

Thursday morning she was sitting at her desk, reading the monograph that had accompanied a new medication the pharmacist had mentioned to her. She was struggling to decipher an unfamiliar Greek term when footsteps sounded in the waiting room. Swinging her feet off the desk and lowering the front legs of her chair to the floor, she assumed a businesslike posture.

Dion, dressed in khaki shorts and a white singlet, filled the doorway. "Oh, you're here. I saw Aphrodite at the market and wondered if you'd closed the office."

Solange gestured toward a chair. "Sit down. We had no patients scheduled, so I told her to go and do her shopping." She picked up a pencil and flipped it idly between her fingers. "You've been busy, I take it?"

He shrugged, muscles flexing under his tanned skin. "Busy enough. I looked for you yesterday, but you weren't here."

"No, I had to take a patient to the hospital in Volos." Dion frowned. "Serious?"

"Old age, mainly. Arrhythmic heartbeat. It's a common ailment in people over ninety." Her tone was matter-of-fact, philosophical. "But this lady will probably come home again. She doesn't want to die in a hospital among strangers. She'll recover enough so that I'll have to release her."

"And then when she has the next spell, there won't be a machine nearby to save her life."

Solange lifted her eyes from their contemplation of the pencil in her hands. She couldn't tell what Dion was thinking. "God's will, as they say here. It's impossible to save them all."

His breath came out in a gust. "As long as you realize that. I knew a doctor in Athens who had studied in Houston. He came back with all sorts of grandiose ideas without understanding that many of the people here don't want that. All they want is a little dignity in their old age."

"And I want them to have it." She broke off, then asked curiously, "This isn't your first time back to Greece?"

Dion had only realized the slip after the words left his mouth. But, on the other hand, why keep it a secret? "No, I came back fourteen years ago and spent the summer here."

"A holiday?"

"Yes." He seemed to bite off the word. "A holiday." A holiday that had turned into a nightmare. He got to his feet and paced to the window, raking his hair back from his brow with fingers that shook. Suddenly the reason he'd come to see Solange didn't seem like such a good idea at all.

The letter he'd received that morning had shaken him. It had been signed by someone named Costas Mavrakis. Dion had never heard of him before, but the words written in a spidery, nearly illegible script had contained enough information to assure him of the letter's authenticity. Costas Mavrakis had been a sergeant in the army during the years of the Colonels. He'd known Dion's parents, Zoe and Nicholas. And the cryptic statement about a man the letter referred to only as Lambros had to be Pavlou.

That alone would have decided Dion to follow up on the letter. Few people knew he sought Lambros Pavlou.

The tone of the letter was ambiguous. Dion had been unable to tell whether the man had condoned his parents' death. Mavrakis obviously knew something, but he was being cagey, leading Dion to wonder whether he hoped to be paid for his information.

Dion's mouth tightened. If Mavrakis had any information he could use, he was quite willing to pay for it. If not—

Making sure his face was expressionless, he turned toward Solange, forcing a smile. "Solange, I'd like to have another try at the army records in Athens. And I was wondering if you would like to come with me and introduce me to your friend, the anthropologist you mentioned the day we met."

Solange thought quickly. There was nothing pressing as far as patients went. The old lady she'd taken to Volos would have to spend at least the weekend to complete the tests Solange had ordered. Aphrodite could take care of minor complaints or refer them to the Health Center, and Penny would be back Saturday. "Sure, I'd like that. I was just thinking about taking a day or two off to go to Athens and buy some books and magazines."

"Don't you read Greek?"

She made a face. "Not for pleasure. I can figure it out, but it takes concentration. And Volos doesn't have much variety in English-language books, though they carry all the major newspapers." She reached for the phone. "Let me give Mary a call to set up a time when we can meet her."

The telephone conversation was brief. Dion listened to the banter that told of an easy friendship, then Solange briskly arranged for a time that would be convenient. "No, you don't have to fix a meal."

He couldn't stop his involuntary smile. In Greece everyone fed you. It was an essential part of hospitality, one that sometimes became arduous, since it was rude to refuse even if you had just had a large meal.

Solange wore a resigned smile as she hung up. "Mary wants us for lunch tomorrow." Excitement sent an odd little shiver through her. Alone with Dion, out of the limelight in which the little town's society placed her.

The intensity that burned in his eyes told her Dion was thinking the same thing, though he quickly turned away, muttering something about the butcher shop closing soon.

He went out into the street, dismayed at the heat that surged through his blood as he'd met her eyes. He couldn't let it go further, not until he'd fulfilled his vow. Solange, despite her strong, no-nonsense manner, was a woman he could hurt. She hid her vulnerability, but it was there. And loneliness, too. Sure, she had friends, but deep inside her he recognized the same loneliness that dwelt in his own soul.

What was he going to do?

"THE SARAKATSANI have been fairly well assimilated into the general population by now," Mary Waterbury said in a precise Bostonian accent. She was a spare, angular woman of seventy with a mop of improbable red hair, who appeared determined to fight old age to her last breath. Her last breath was likely to be a painful one, Solange often admonished her; Mary smoked incessantly.

Their unlikely friendship had started when Solange arrived in Greece to work with the earthquake relief group. Mary had been the group's rep in charge of coordinating their efforts, and they'd been friends ever since.

Solange smiled as Mary pushed aside the used plates from their rather haphazard lunch. The plates would probably sit in the sink for the rest of the day, once they made it there. Housecleaning wasn't this anthropology professor's strong suit.

Pulling a battered pack of cigarettes from her jacket pocket, Mary lit one, sending a cloud of blue smoke toward the ceiling.

Dion set his elbows on the table, his face animated. "Is it true that the townspeople in many places resent their presence?"

"Maybe, maybe not. Depends where you are." Mary gestured with her cigarette, ashes scattering over her rough linen shirt. Absently she brushed them away, muttering under her breath. "Dion, the Greeks considered the Sarakatsani upstarts, almost invaders, who were after their land."

"But they bought the land legitimately," Dion said. "Nobody disputes that."

"Sure they did, but then when the land increased in value, they became rich. That's what the other Greeks resent the most, I'd say. Fact is, some historians say the Sarakatsani are the real Greeks, that they descended from the ancients, the contemporaries of Pericles."

"Is that true?" Solange asked, amazed.

Mary shrugged, spilling more ash. "It's as good a theory as any. Their traditional costumes show many of the same features as the clothing in paintings on classical jars. Now the Vlachs, also nomadic sheep- and goatherders, are another group entirely. They're likely of Romanian origin, or perhaps there's some truth in the story that they descended from the remnants of the Roman army left behind at Pharsalus around 48 B.C."

"Pharsalus?" Dion scribbled a note. "Is that the modern Farsala?"

"Yes. It's probably its only claim to fame—the Battle of Pharsalus. Interesting area, though, with a wide variety of people. Dion, you might consider doing something on the refugees who left Asia Minor in the early part of this century. There are a lot of them in the area, actually all over northwestern Greece."

"I'll look into it." Glancing at his watch, he rose to his feet. "I've got an appointment. Solange, you wanted to shop?"

"Stores are closed now," Mary put in. She patted Solange's arm. "Stay here and visit with me."

"I'd like that." Solange looked questioningly at Dion. "Can you pick me up later, say about five?"

"Sure." He hid his relief. If she had insisted on coming along, he didn't know what he would have done. He was supposed to call Mavrakis at three and arrange their meeting, and he wasn't at all sure how the interview would go, or even whether Mavrakis would help him.

The unexpected letter, the almost peremptory tone of the writing so at odds with the meandering formation of the letters, and the repetition of the meeting arrangements all combined to give him an apprehensive feeling about the whole thing. For all he knew, he might be walking into danger. Stefan's warning rang in his ears. There were people who would rather their involvement with the former military regime remained hidden forever. Mavrakis might be one of them. He couldn't risk having Solange along.

"See you later," he said as casually as he could on the way out.

"That young man has something on his mind," Mary declared with a toss of her head. "Something he's not talking about."

"You noticed, too, did you?" Solange began to stack the plates, using the activity to quiet the restless energy churning inside her. Dion was always secretive, but today, especially on the three-hour drive into the city, he had been as remote as the range of mountains that ringed the plain of Korfalli.

"He likes you, though," Mary called after her as she took the dishes into the kitchen.

"How could you tell?" Turning on the tap, Solange ran hot water into the sink, adding a splash of dish soap.

Mary came in with the rest of the dishes, a fresh cigarette dangling from her lips. "I can tell from the way his eyes followed you when you were helping me serve, the way he looked when he went out."

"The way he looked?" Solange gave an ironic laugh. "He looked determined. Mary, you're imagining things that aren't there. You're just as bad as the busybodies back in Korfalli."

"They've been on your case, have they?"

Solange rolled her eyes as she stacked washed plates in the drainer. "Constantly. But Dion, I don't know what's in his mind. Sometimes it seems as if he wants me. Then he backs off. Maybe he's just playing along with the game."

Mary gave the cutlery a perfunctory swipe with a towel before dropping them into the drawer. "Do you want him?"

Did she? Solange paused, her hands up to the wrists in suds. "I want him to be honest. I can't stand this...indecisiveness—the way he closes up. But maybe he's smart to keep his distance. He'll be leaving when he's finished. I won't be."

"Aren't you?" Mary's uneven brows shot up. "Are you really planning on staying here forever? Isn't it time you came to terms with what happened?"

"I have, Mary. As much as is possible. A child died. I'll never forget it, but I can go on." She placed the last cup on the drain rack and pulled the plug, watching the water gurgle into a whirlpool and disappear.

"Then why are you still hiding?" Reaching around her, Mary turned on the water, killing her cigarette with a sizzle in the wet sink and rinsing the butt away.

"I'm not." If it had been anybody but Mary, Solange would have resented the question. "Someday I'll go back."

"For Dion, would you?" Mary's eyes narrowed cunningly.

Solange threw up her hands. "Dion. Any woman who gets serious about him is asking for big trouble."

Mary led the way into the living room, lighting another cigarette as she sat down. "You may be right. It will take an exceptional woman to nab Dion Parris, and first she'd have to drive out that ghost that's sitting on his shoulder."

The afternoon passed quickly as they talked of mutual acquaintances who either lived in Greece or had left the country after their job was over. Mary kept up an extensive correspondence, an activity for which Solange had little time or interest.

Five o'clock came and went. By half past Solange was looking at her watch frequently. At six she had begun to pace the room. Something had happened. Dion wouldn't be this late without calling her.

Finally at six-twenty the phone rang. Mary picked it up, listening for a moment, her expression darkening.

"Maybe you'd better talk to her yourself," she said in an odd tone. She handed the receiver to Solange. "It's Dion."

"Dion, are you all right?" Her fingers gripped the phone, sudden sweat dampening her palms.

He gave a harsh laugh. "I don't know. Solange, can you come? I'm in jail."

CHAPTER SIX

WHEN HE LEFT MARY'S, Dion had almost an hour to drive to Amaroussi, the working-class suburb where Mavrakis lived. The distance, even allowing for searching out the street, would take only ten or fifteen minutes to cover from Kifissia.

The meeting was set for three o'clock—during siesta. An odd time to meet someone, but maybe not so odd if the person had something to hide. The narrow streets were nearly deserted as Dion drove slowly past closed shops and apartment buildings.

His uneasy feeling remained. He found the address without difficulty and debated knocking on the door and confronting the man at once. But Mavrakis's instructions had been to phone from the kiosk on the corner at exactly three.

The kiosk was open, Dion noted with relief. A positive sign. He cruised past, running his eyes up and down the street. Two-thirty.

Going a block farther, he parked the Renault under a mulberry tree. He locked the car and walked back, squinting against the brassy sunlight. The heat, concentrated between whitewashed buildings lining the treeless street, was heavy and oppressive. He swept his hair back as sweat dampened his temples.

Outside Mavrakis's building, Dion paused. The door stood open, and he looked inside, stepping forward to the row of brass mailboxes. Costas Mavrakis, apartment 3.

That would be the main floor. Dion moved a few steps down a hall smelling of herbed roasted lamb. His nostrils twitched. Someone had lunched well, better than he and Solange. They'd been served stewed beans, cheese and cold cuts.

A large red *A* marked out in spray paint marred the wall next to Mavrakis's door. Anarchy. A slogan currently popular with the more volatile political protesters.

Come to think of it, the Amaroussi district was an odd place for a former member of the Colonels' regime to be living. Long a stronghold of the Communist Party, it must have been a prime target during the turbulent years of the military dictatorship.

The floor creaked as Dion moved away from the door. At the same instant a door opened farther down the hall. A woman poked her head out, saw him and pulled back, slamming the door.

Puzzled, Dion stared at the dark varnished panel. Somewhere upstairs a baby began to cry, a plaintive wailing muted by distance.

A door at the end of the hall stood open, revealing an inner courtyard. Dion paused in the doorway, noting the potted plants, some well cared for, some drooping in the heat. Laundry hung from sagging lines fastened to corners of the building. Looking up, he could see more clotheslines, attached to narrow balconies that held the overflow from crowded apartments, oil stoves used for supplementary heating in winter, boxes of diapers and detergent, a child's tricycle.

He advanced into the courtyard, ducking under a brightly striped bed sheet and dodging a row of dripping swimsuits. A bantam hen with a clutch of chicks set up a racket in a wire cage in the corner. As he neared the window that must be Mavrakis's, a poodle began to yap from the balcony above.

Dion cursed and jumped back behind the striped sheet as a man shouted at the dog, his voice hoarse with sleep.

Mavrakis's flat was tiny, probably a studio, Dion guessed. Two windows, with a door in the middle. Did he live alone? Again he considered knocking on the door, but discarded the idea. For now he would go along with Mavrakis's instructions.

It was almost three. Dion walked back through the building, pausing in the front doorway. The street was quiet except for a radio playing rock music from the building next door.

The man who ran the kiosk was half asleep, his head tilted against the back wall at an awkward angle. He started violently when Dion spoke, his gaze skittering from left to right, then back again, avoiding Dion's eyes.

Nervous man, Dion thought dispassionately, but then some people were that way upon first awaking. Dropping a couple of coins into the plastic tray on the counter, Dion picked up the phone and dialed.

It barely rang once before it was answered. "This is Dion Parris. I'm at the kiosk."

"Yes." The voice was gruff and abrupt. "Wait." He hung up.

Dion put down the receiver and thanked the man, who silently gathered up the coins. He moved to the corner of the small wooden structure, scanning the deserted street. Sweat trickled down his back, pooling at his waist. Wait, the voice had said.

Five minutes ticked by. Seven. He heard a faint rumbling sound but paid no attention as he saw a figure come to the door of the apartment building.

The man was old and stooped. He hesitated, glancing furtively up and down the street. Dion didn't move. The hairs at the back of his neck prickled. He wasn't sure whether it was from excitement or apprehension or simply from the heat.

The old man came out, shading his eyes with one hand. He walked with a limp, using a cane to steady his uncertain balance.

Dion pushed himself away from the kiosk, stepping off the curb and skirting a parked car. The old man had reached the middle of the street, a scarecrow figure whose clothes hung on an emaciated body. He seemed to stagger slightly, and Dion hurried toward him.

With a shriek of tires spinning on the heat-softened pavement, a small white car shot out of the next street. Picking up speed as it raced down the gentle slope, it headed straight for the old man.

Dion leaped ahead, came close enough to touch the man's shirt, but he was too late. Like a bundle of rags, the man tumbled over the car's hood and fell in a broken heap to the road.

The car sped on down the hill, a white Renault. Dion squinted against the dazzle of sun reflecting from the back windshield, but the distance was already too great for him to read the license number.

"Damn!" For a moment he gave in to the anger surging up in him. Speeding on a residential street—there was no excuse for it even if the driver was some kid trying out the family car and expecting the streets to be deserted in the siesta hour. Hit and run. The old man had gotten in the way. An unfortunate accident.

Or was it? The anger drained away, to be replaced by cold calculation.

He turned, calling to the man in the kiosk. "Quickly, get an ambulance."

The kiosk was locked, its shutters lowered. Again he cursed in helpless frustration. The rumbling noise he'd heard had obviously been the man closing up.

Dion looked up at the surrounding buildings. Here and there a curtain flicked as if someone watched from within. The radio still played, but as he crouched down next to the crumpled figure on the road, it was abruptly shut off.

The man was dead, the eyes staring sightlessly at the hot cobalt sky, telling Dion there was no need for an ambulance. Dion gently ran his hand over the man's face, closing his eyes, before making the sign of the cross. "I'm sorry."

He picked up the man's left hand, limp and skeletal. Four fingers and a thumb. Definitely not his quarry.

Where were all the people? The silence was uncanny. Siesta or not, by this time there should have been a crowd of curious gapers on the street. No one appeared.

Slowly getting to his feet, he walked over to the apartment building, pounding on the first door he came to. The door opened a crack, held by a chain. He could see part of a woman's face, her one visible eye dark with terror.

"*Telephono?*" he asked, forcing his voice to be calm.

"*Ochi.*" The woman shook her head, and closed the door.

No telephone. Dion bit his lip in frustration. There was something strange going on. While it was true many people had no phones, he had the feeling he would get the same answer even if they did.

Well, there must be another kiosk in the neighborhood, or a pharmacy or local grocery open. He started toward the street again, then abruptly turned back and entered the courtyard. Unclipping a couple of clothespins, he took a sheet from the line.

The dead man still lay in the middle of the deserted road. Dion draped the sheet over him. With a final glance at the pathetic figure, he set off briskly to find a phone.

It took Solange only ten minutes to reach the Amaroussi police station in a taxi. To her relief Dion was no longer in jail, if indeed he had been.

As soon as she walked into the building, blinking in the gloom after the sunshine outside, a clerk directed her to the captain's office. He held the door for her and gestured her to a hard wooden bench at the side of a small room crowded with filing cabinets, a desk and a couple of chairs.

Dion sat at the opposite side of the desk from the shirtsleeved police officer. A name tag on the cluttered desk spelled out Captain Demos in both Greek and Latin characters. Overhead, a fan lazily churned the heat, and a fly hurled itself against the closed section of the window, buzzing irritably against its imprisonment.

"Dion, what happened?"

The captain, a thin man with glasses who looked more like an accountant than a policeman, frowned. "Miss, uh, Dr. Solange Richards?"

"Yes, I'm Dr. Richards. What's going on?"

"All in good time, Dr. Richards," Demos said with barely concealed impatience. He lifted his hand, palm up. "Please sit down."

She sat, perched on the edge of the bench, her fingers clenched around her purse strap. Dion, his face in profile to her, hadn't said a word, hadn't acknowledged her presence. His face was shuttered and remote, one cheekbone decorated with a dark smudge that looked like engine oil.

The captain wrote something on a legal pad before him, her name, no doubt. She realized that he'd addressed her in English and wondered if he was aware that she spoke Greek.

When he spoke again, to Dion, it was in Greek, with an inflection that seemed to indicate he'd asked the question before and that he'd keep asking it until he was satisfied with the answer. "You were standing by the kiosk, you say, when the car came along? Why were you there when the kiosk was closed?"

Dion raked his hand through his hair. Solange could see a drop of sweat oozing slowly down his cheek. His hair clung in damp curls to his nape and temples. He looked tired, and she wondered how long they'd held him before he'd made the call. How many questions? How many accusations?

"I've told you, the kiosk was open not ten minutes before. I used the phone to call Mavrakis. I don't know how the man left so fast. Why don't you ask people in the neighborhood? There was a radio playing in the apartment right across the street from the kiosk."

"We did that." Demos laid his glasses on the desk and wearily rubbed the bridge of his nose. "No one saw anything, except that it was a white Renault 5. Like the car you were driving."

"But I'd left it parked a block away. And I don't know how the headlight got broken. Besides, the car that hit Mavrakis had Greek plates. I saw that much, even though it was gone too fast for me to read the numbers. My car was leased in France, with red license plates."

A car had hit Mavrakis? A dozen questions raced around Solange's brain. Who was Mavrakis? She could only assume he was Dion's appointment. Did that mean he was dead?

"How well did you know Mavrakis?" Demos asked.

Dion shook his head. "I didn't know him at all. He wrote me a letter, asking me to call him." He groped in his pocket. "Here, see for yourself."

Putting his glasses back on, the captain unfolded the letter, scanning it quickly. He looked up, pursing his lips. "And what was this information he had for you?"

"I don't know. I was hoping it was about my parents who died nineteen years ago. I'm trying to find out if I have living relatives here in Greece."

Demos handed back the letter. "You've waited a long time to do that."

"Yes. It wasn't possible for me to take a leave of absence from my work before this," Dion lied glibly.

"You're a professor of sociology at the University of British Columbia. And you're researching the Sarakatsani, are you?"

"Yes, but I thought I'd also look up some relatives while I'm here. The only family I had in Canada, a distant cousin of my father's, died last year." He gestured with his hand. "You know how it is. Friends can never make up for family."

"I understand." Bending his head, Demos scribbled some additional notes. When he looked up, his eyes went straight to Solange.

Solange could barely restrain herself from squirming under that penetrating stare. But to her surprise he smiled. "How long have you known Mr. Parris?"

"About a month, sir." Somehow that sounded more substantial than a couple of weeks. "But he's well thought of in Korfalli where his parents come from."

"Am I under arrest?" Dion demanded in a tone that made Solange cringe against the hard back of the bench. Even if they had nothing against him, they might arrest him for insubordination.

Demos put down his glasses again. "I don't know. You left the scene of an accident—"

"I told you," Dion cut in, "I was looking for a phone."

"Your car has a damaged front. No one can confirm where you were at the time of the accident."

"I was on the street." He closed his eyes briefly, his mouth twisting in pain as he remembered his helpless horror. "I tried to reach him, to pull him out of the way, but the car came so fast."

A knock sounded on the door, and the clerk who'd directed Solange earlier walked in with a paper that he handed to the captain. "Thank you."

The man walked out. In the silence the fly droned monotonously, a counterpoint to the slight squeak the fan made on each revolution.

"I guess you're not under arrest, Mr. Parris," the captain said, looking up. "The bits of glass at the scene of the accident don't match those of your car. Besides, the damage to your car is slight, not consistent with the force of the impact."

Dion rose, his mouth set in a straight line. "Thank you," he said without the faintest sign of gratitude. "My car keys?"

"You can get them from the impound lot attendant behind the building."

"Come on, Solange. Let's get out of here." Anger and disappointment formed a hard knot in his gut. If he stayed here a moment longer, he would be sick.

"Oh, one thing. Who is the man Lambros our Mr. Mavrakis referred to in his letter?"

Dion turned. "It's personal."

"Personal or not, I have to know," Demos said in a mild tone that didn't fool Dion for a minute. "Besides, you're looking for someone and having difficulty finding him. Maybe I can help you."

Dion thought for a moment. "I'm looking for a man named Lambros Pavlou."

If he hadn't been watching closely, he wouldn't have noticed the captain's reaction. The man's eyes widened ever so slightly before he could put his glasses back in place. And a muscle tensed in his jaw. "The man you're seeking no longer exists," he said in a flat tone.

Dion took a step toward him. "What do you mean?"

"Just what I said. He doesn't exist."

"You mean he's dead?"

In answer, Demos got up and pulled open a filing cabinet drawer. Extracting a folder, he withdrew a sheet of yellowed paper, silently handing it to Dion.

A chill hollowed his stomach as he took in the words. Death Certificate of Lambros Pavlou, died fourteen years ago. He read further. Cause of death: fire. Distinguishing features: mole on right earlobe. No others were mentioned.

Dion looked up. "This isn't the man."

Demos took the paper and returned it to the file. He shrugged. "He called himself Lambros Pavlou. That's all I know."

"Still, this isn't the man." But it was likely that the real Lambros Pavlou wanted people to think the dead man was him. That meant Pavlou was probably using another name now.

Again the captain shrugged. "Goodbye, Mr. Parris."

They were almost at the door when Captain Demos spoke again. "Mr. Parris, if I were you, I'd be very careful. In fact, I'd forget about looking up relatives. Some things are better buried. Dig them up and they stink."

"Thanks," Dion said sardonically. "I'll remember that."

"Good. Don't forget to get your headlight repaired."

"WHERE ARE WE GOING?" Solange asked as Dion drove onto the main arterial road after picking up his car. He propelled the little Renault through the traffic with a hard, reckless disregard for safety or the rights of other drivers. "This isn't the way back to Mary's."

"We're not going to Mary's, though if you want, I can drop you off in the town center and you can get a taxi." He pulled in front of a slowing bus, then turned into a side street, tires squealing as he accelerated between rows of dwarf orange trees. "Maybe that's best."

He tramped on the brake under a sign that designated three parking spaces as a taxi stand, stopping so abruptly that Solange was thrown against her seat belt. "Ouch! Watch it," she muttered.

"You can get a taxi here." Dion stared straight ahead through the windshield, his fingers tensing impatiently on the gearshift.

"I don't need a taxi." She made no move to get out. Instead, she turned to face him. "There's no need for me to go back to Mary's. I told her I'd phone when I found out what was going on but that we wouldn't be back."

"Then I'll drop you at a hotel."

"What about you?"

"I'll join you later."

Evasive. He didn't meet her eyes. She knew he was hiding something. Something other than what he habitually hid.

"You're not going to get into more trouble, are you?"

His knuckles whitened. "No. This time I won't get caught."

A chill washed through her. "What do you mean, you won't get caught? Dion, whatever you're up to, I'm going with you."

"No use two of us—"

"You can't stop me," she interrupted, her jaw tightening. "I refuse to get out of the car."

Dion scowled, staring at the darkening street. One by one the standard lamps blinked on, shedding a meager illumination. Traffic swished or roared by, depending on its speed and the aggression of the driver.

He could drop her off at a hotel, get them both something to eat and then go off when she was asleep. But the delay nagged at him like a pit bull with a bone. If he waited too long, the police or Mavrakis's family would go to his apartment to clear up his affairs and remove his belongings. They might already be there, but he was betting the death would be ruled an accident and the follow-up wouldn't be activated until tomorrow.

"Okay," he said finally with a hard edge to his voice. "Come along. But don't blame me for the consequences."

"What consequences? Dion, you're not making any sense."

"Maybe not." He put the car into gear, switching on his remaining headlight before sending the vehicle into the stream of traffic. "I'm just warning you. You're about to get your first lesson in breaking and entering."

CHAPTER SEVEN

"THERE'S MORE to this than looking up family members, isn't there?" Solange's low-voiced question broke the silence that had lingered throughout the drive to Mavrakis's apartment.

"You insisted on coming along," Dion said, his eyes raking the street. Nearly ten o'clock, but children still played football, mothers gossiped on the apartment steps and men sat in front of the coffee shop on the corner. After sunset, when the day's heat had abated, came the time for leisure. "Trust me."

"Trust you? With what? How can I betray any secret when I don't know what it is?"

"It's better if you don't." He slowed the car as they came abreast of the building, crossing the spot where Mavrakis had died. There was no sign that violence had occurred in the hot afternoon, the pavement stained only with engine oil. The activity around the building, or rather the unnatural lack of it, indicated that it was unlikely that anyone had come to clean out the flat.

He kept on going, finally parking two blocks away in a small lot next to a supermarket. His Renault, despite its foreign license plate, would blend in with the other cars, especially in the dark. Turning off the engine, he laid his hand on Solange's as she unclipped her seat belt. "Wait. I want to make sure we haven't been followed."

Impulsive questions trembled on her lips, but she swallowed them back. Time enough later. Whatever he was caught up in, she was well and truly part of it. And she found curiosity outweighing caution as adrenaline pumped into her veins.

Moments passed. No cars turned into the parking lot, though several shoppers loading plastic bags into nearby cars cast them odd looks.

"Okay. Let's go."

Dion slowed his steps as they neared the apartment building. "I don't know if anyone will remember me from this afternoon."

Solange reached up and ruffled his hair, loosening it from its careful brushing. "Different shirt, no sunglasses. I suppose you were wearing them this afternoon?"

"Yeah. It was bright out." He had changed his shirt at the police station. The one he'd worn earlier had been stained with Mavrakis's blood, a fact the policeman who'd stopped him had pointed out with grim emphasis.

"There may be no one around." The clatter of dishes carried clearly through open windows and doors. "It's about supper time."

They were able to enter the building without incident. No one sat on the front stoop, nor was there anyone in the hall. The door to the courtyard still stood open, and deciding the back door was less risky than picking a lock in the hall, Dion led the way through it.

A single amber light bulb shone on the courtyard, but a fresh line of laundry, flowered sheets and rows of flannel diapers cast a shadow on Mavrakis's door.

Dion bent down, examining the lock. It was a simple thing, probably easy to pick, though he'd only seen people pick locks on TV.

"Maybe it's not locked." Solange reached around him and turned the doorknob. Without so much as a squeak the door swung open.

On the balcony above the poodle yapped briefly, subsiding with a growl as its owner spoke to it. Glancing upward, Dion gave Solange a little push, closing the door behind them. "I wanted to check it out first, especially in view of the unlocked door, but someone might see you out there."

"He probably never locked that door," Solange whispered back. "Probably didn't think it necessary."

"Or somebody's been here before us. Wait here."

They were in a tiny kitchen. Solange could make out the counter, a couple of cupboards on either side of the sink and the whitewashed plaster arch where a gas hot plate sat. Dion turned on the penlight he held, keeping his fingers half over the beam. Thin cotton curtains covered the window, flanked by heavier draperies.

Dion touched her shoulder. "I'll be back in a minute."

Solange waited, hardly breathing as he went through a doorway at one side of the room. The flat must contain only the kitchen and a sitting room that served as a bedroom at night, tiny quarters but sufficient for a bachelor.

Dion returned almost at once. "No one's been here." He pulled on a cord, drawing the heavy drapes. "With that light outside I don't think anyone will be able to tell if we turn on the lights in here."

He flipped a switch, and Solange snapped her eyes shut. But at once she realized there was no need to protect them from the glare. The bulb was of a low wattage that barely lit the corners of the small room. "How did he see to wash dishes?"

"He didn't, by the looks of things." Dion grimaced at the sight of a sink full of used plates and cups. A cupboard door that stood open showed only a single water glass on the shelf. "Probably used them until he ran out, then did them all at once."

The kitchen yielded little of interest. The trash container was full of cans, an unusual circumstance in Greece where most people shopped for fresh food every day. The cupboards contained almost nothing, although under the sink a cockroach scuttled out of sight when Dion opened the door and shone the penlight inside.

The adjoining bathroom was equally austere. Shaving gear and a bottle of cheap after-shave took up half a shelf in the medicine cabinet. A lone bottle of aspirin sat on another. The towels were mismatched and threadbare.

"He was poor." Solange couldn't keep the sympathy out of her voice.

"And old." Dion closed the bathroom door. "I wonder what he wanted to tell me."

She clenched her jaw, wishing he would level with her instead of asking for a nebulous trust. "About your long-lost relatives?"

He stiffened at her tone. "Whatever you think, Solange, I'm not lying about that. It does concern my relatives."

"Then why was he killed?"

"It could have been an accident."

"But you don't think so, do you?"

Dion shrugged. "I don't know what to think. Come on, maybe the sitting room will be more productive. At least there's some stuff lying around."

Solange looked around the small room, which also had a window overlooking the courtyard. Again heavy drapes hung alongside the white cotton curtains. Dion pulled them closed before turning on a floor lamp that stood next to an easy chair, the only comfortable piece of furniture in the room.

At one side stood a cot, a rumpled sheet thrown over the thin mattress. Solange shifted the pillow, finding only a pair of gray pyjamas stuffed untidily under it. "What do they put in these pillows? Feels like a sack of cement."

Dion was systematically rifling through the drawers of a rolltop desk next to the window. "Cotton, I think. Or wool. You're supposed to take it out and fluff up the fibers once a year to keep its resilience. Why don't you look through the bookcase?"

The bookcase held a variety of literature, a few books and a good many magazines. Solange whistled softly. "This guy was weird."

"Why?" Dion came over and looked at the magazine she held. "Bondage? S and M? Yeah, pretty weird. I wonder where he got them."

"Have you seen some of the stuff on the newsstands lately?"

Dion shook his head. "No time."

"Well, they've got comics for adults that you wouldn't believe. This guy seems to have been their biggest customer."

"Interesting," Dion agreed, raising his eyebrows at a particularly graphic scene.

"You should find it interesting. You're in sociology. Don't you study behavior?"

"Sure. But I think this stuff would be of more interest to a psychologist, one who specializes in aberrant sexual fantasies."

He looked about the room, a scowl of frustration marking his brow. "And none of it's very useful, I'm afraid. And there's nothing in the desk, which is odd. Didn't he have any friends or family? There are no photos, nothing personal at all."

"Did you look under the drawers?" Solange asked, restacking the magazines. "That's where people hide things in the movies."

"Yeah, I saw those movies, too. But obviously our Mr. Mavrakis didn't. There's nothing."

He pulled open the wardrobe that served as a closet. The shelf and the floor were stacked with what looked like back issues of every pornographic magazine published. But sifting through the stacks and shaking each one produced nothing.

Solange squatted back on her heels as Dion searched the pockets of a shabby black suit and two pairs of pants and three shirts that hung from the rod in the wardrobe. "What are we looking for, anyway, besides old photos?"

"Papers. Documents to indicate what he was doing fifteen or twenty years ago."

"Under the mattress." Solange jumped to her feet and flipped it up. All she found between the slatted spring and the thin pallet was dust and a couple of thousand-drachma notes.

"His contingency fund, I presume," Dion commented dryly.

"Not much of one." Solange dropped the mattress back into place over the money. "Where haven't we looked? Nobody is this unconnected. There has to be something."

She walked back into the bathroom. "Dion, I just found a dandy hiding place."

He joined her in the narrow space, following her gaze upward. The plaster ceiling, lowered over the tiny bathtub, was damp, with stained rings that showed years of leaks and drying. At the slightest touch white paint flaked off, sifting into the age-yellowed tub like snow. A door, of white-painted planks, was set into the section of wall that protruded over the tub.

"A chair. That's what we need." Solange waited while Dion fetched one. Stepping nimbly onto the rush seat, she unlatched the door, recoiling as the humid odor of rotting plaster rushed out and enveloped her.

"Damn, I can't see a thing. Do you have your flashlight?" The rust-pocked enamel of the water heater blocked most of the doorway. Even on tiptoe she couldn't see beyond it.

"Maybe you'd better let me look," Dion suggested. "I'm taller."

"Not by much." But she didn't relish poking around in the dampness that might provide a home for countless spiders and bugs. She hopped off the chair, using her hand to steady it as he climbed up.

The penlight provided minimal illumination, but he could see that the space was barely large enough to contain the appliance. A tap on its side indicated that it must be nearly empty. Beneath it lay a puddle of water that slowly seeped down into the wall next to the tub.

"Nothing here. It's too wet." He stepped off the chair and scanned the rest of the little room once more.

"Wait a minute." He closed the lid on the stained porcelain toilet and stood on it. Groping behind the old-fashioned tank that hung high on the wall above it, he gave a grunt of triumph.

A thick envelope sealed in a plastic shopping bag and fastened to the tank with rubber bands inconspicuously wrapped around the vertical pipe came loose with a snap. Dion held it up as he stepped to the floor. "Maybe this will tell us something."

They were heading back into the kitchen to work at the table when a commotion sounded from the hall. Solange froze by the door. Next to her Dion drew in a sharp breath as he listened intently.

The conversation was clearly audible. A man, who indicated obliquely that he was from the police, spoke with a woman who was probably the building manager. "I need to check Mr. Mavrakis's apartment for next of kin. There was nothing in his pocket except his identification card. We need to know who has to be notified of his death."

The woman was complaining about the irregularity of it, a policeman arriving this late at night, but a moment later the scrape of a key in the lock told Dion and Solange they were about to be discovered.

"Quick, out the back."

Solange lost no time in obeying Dion's whispered command.

They ducked under the clothesline and into the doorway leading back to the hall. If anyone was watching the courtyard, they were trapped.

Luck remained with them. Peeking around the doorway, they saw a man in an ordinary shirt and pants entering Mavrakis's apartment in the company of an old woman who held a jingling ring of keys.

toward the back seat. "We still have the
ok from the flat."

look at it later."

ut me you won't."

in resignation. "Okay, let's stop some-
hungry?"

But I could stand a soft drink."

d the commercial center of Kifissia, and
n front of a pastry shop still crowded with
pite the late hour. He chose a table under
t others had rejected because the birds that
vere a nuisance. This late they slept with
itter or two to indicate their presence.

of Cokes," Dion said to the waiter who
them. He looked at Solange. "Is that all

e, wrapped in white plastic, lay between
able. A mixture of emotions ran through
as he stared at it, reluctant to discover its
wasn't sure why. Perhaps it was Solange's
package might be innocuous, but its hid-
ated to some importance. If it was filled
ts referring to the Colonels' regime, he
tell Solange what he was really doing in

uld despise him. Or try to talk him out of
an.

't understand that the need to avenge his
st death had burned in him all these years.
t it go, even if it destroyed his soul.

were served, tall glasses clinking with ice.
them and the waiter left them alone.

"A cop?" Dion said in a stage whisper. "He's no
more a cop than I am." He took Solange's hand in his,
noting its chill. He glanced at her. Although she looked
a bit pale, her eyes were bright with the spirit of adventure. "Come on."

On silent feet they ran down the hall, gulping in air as
they emerged onto the street. "The lights," Solange
panted as Dion set a fast pace back to the car. "We forgot to turn off the lights."

"Maybe they won't notice. We left everything as it
was. They might think Mavrakis forgot them this afternoon."

"When no self-respecting, economy-minded Greek
would have had them on? Come on, Dion, you can't
believe that."

"Well, it can't be helped." Reaching the car, which
stood alone in the lot next to the now-shuttered supermarket, he unlocked the doors and tossed the package
into the back seat.

The engine started with a reassuring roar. "Fasten
your seat belt, Solange. We're going to do a little sur-
veillance. I want to know who our 'cop' is."

He parked down the hill from Mavrakis's building at
the end of the block, keeping an eye on the entrance in
the rearview mirror. They didn't have long to wait. The
man came out and got into a blue Ford Escort parked at
the curb near the kiosk.

"You're sure it's him?" Solange asked as he drove by
them and continued down the street.

"Of course. His hair's long enough to touch his collar—that's why I don't think he's a cop. They're usually
required to have neat haircuts." Dion put the Renault
into gear and pulled out, keeping a distance between
them and the Escort. The lack of traffic both simplified

and complicated tailing the car. The red taillights were easily visible a block ahead, but the man might also notice them following if he were paying attention. However, Dion doubted he would, for a while. He would have no reason to believe anyone was interested in Mavrakis now that he was dead.

On the other hand, the smashed headlight on his own car, which he had replaced at a service station, showed that someone must have been aware of his appointment with Mavrakis. The man ahead, perhaps?

Solange's thoughts must have been following the same track. "Who would have smashed your headlight to make it look as if you hit Mavrakis? Did anyone know you were coming here?"

"Not unless Mavrakis told them."

The Escort turned onto a main arterial road, merging with the quickly flowing traffic heading toward Kifissia and the outskirts of the city. Dion turned after it, closing the distance and keeping only one car between them. Less than a mile ahead the Escort again turned, taking the road toward Mount Penteli. Free of the stop-and-go traffic, it sped up.

On the twisting mountain road Dion kept a curve or two behind, knowing he would be able to see if the Escort turned off. Actually, here there were few houses as the road snaked between shrub-covered hills, interspersed with occasional pine forests.

The chase ended when the Escort stopped in front of the wrought-iron gates leading into a substantial estate. Obviously the man was expected, for the gates immediately swung open, probably by a remote control device. The Escort passed through, and the gates closed, a formidable barrier set in a high brick wall.

Dion slammed his fist
"Damn."

"What is it, Dion? Why
comes out?"

"Won't do any good."
compartment and pulled
turning on his penlight to s
in his jaw as he nodded gri
Tossing the items back int
restarted the car, turning it

"And what did you figu

"He's reporting to som
proach unless it's absolute
why the army records had
they were driving away fr
eral whose activities du
wouldn't stand close scrutii
soon as the general had g
in the country he would
search. What was surpr
hadn't been more direct
probably knows that the

Solange stared at him
mess."

"A trained observer v
been moved. And there v

"Does it matter?"

"Probably not. He wo
have been some kid look

"Petty theft is rare her
cinctly, as if she were the
second thought, maybe t
of the country for a goo

She g
package
"Yea
"Not
He si
place. A
"Not
"Fine.
They
Dion sto
customer
a tree, on
roosted i
only a sof
"A co
hurried o
right?"
"Sure.'
The pac
them on t
Dion's mii
contents.
presence.
ing place
with docu
would have
Greece.
And she
his revenge
She woul
parents' unj
He couldn't
The Coke
Dion paid f

Dion cast his eyes over the surrounding tables. The place was emptying as midnight passed. No one sat near them, nor did anyone show any interest in them. Not that he expected trouble. He was sure they hadn't been followed.

If someone didn't want him snooping into the past, they wouldn't need to tail him. Anyone in the Amaroussi police station could now be aware of his quest.

But not Solange, who regarded him with perplexed concern.

It was time. He picked up the package and pulled off the rubber band, slowly unrolling the bag. Inside was a large rubberized envelope of the kind the military used to transfer dispatches during a war. He unsnapped the flap, tipping the envelope to empty the contents on the table.

More envelopes. And photographs, small black-and-white prints with old-fashioned serrated edges. Dion picked up a flimsy sheet of paper folded into quarters and carefully spread it out. Army discharge.

Solange pointed to the photo stapled in the corner. "Is that Mavrakis?"

"Yes." He scanned the sheet. Costas Mavrakis had attained the rank of sergeant and had received honorable discharge in 1976, well after the demise of the Colonels' regime.

That didn't mean much. Even if he had been involved in arresting and executing political dissidents, with his relatively low rank, he could have said in his own defense that he'd only followed orders. Punishment after democracy was restored had mainly involved high-ranking officers, and even their punishment hadn't been severe in most cases. Sick from the years of injustice and oppression, the new government had deemed house arrest or exile as sufficient penalty.

He emptied out one of the envelopes. A dozen or so photos tumbled onto the table. He sifted through them, carefully examining each one before handing it to Solange. Of course, they wouldn't mean anything to her.

He was wrong. She picked up one of the pictures, larger than the others, of a group of soldiers standing next to a tank. "Dion, I've seen this picture before. In Korfalli."

He took it from her, turning it over to read the names on the back. Yannis, Yiorgos, Elias, Costas, another Yiorgos... Mavrakis had apparently only kept the pictures for his own use, for he hadn't included any last names. "Where in Korfalli?"

"On the wall in Grandma Amelia's house."

"Your grandmother?"

"No, that's just what everyone calls her. She's a widow whose only child was killed years ago. She's the surrogate grandmother for a lot of the village children. She's lonely and likes it when they drop in, always gives them cookies or chocolate."

"What happened to her child?"

"Elias? I'm not sure. Something about the army. It was years ago. Nobody talks about it."

"Elias?" Dion's brows shot up, and he grabbed the picture for another look. "Is it possible that he was one of the men in this photo? You're sure it's the same picture?"

"Yes, I'm sure. I've sat in her kitchen many times. She keeps it on the stand with the family icons. It's the same picture."

Dion scooped the papers back into the rubberized envelope. He could hardly believe it. After realizing the general was behind the stonewalling, he'd thought he'd hit a dead end. Now to find another lead— But it wasn't really miraculous when he considered it. His parents had originally come from Korfalli. So had Pavlou. Mavrakis must have had some connection with them, as well. There was a definite pattern to the events, and Korfalli lay at the center.

"I'll look at the rest of these later," he said. "When we get back to Korfalli, I have to talk to this Grandma Amelia."

CHAPTER EIGHT

GRANDMA AMELIA'S HOUSE smelled of mothballs and lavender cologne. Solange introduced Dion, and together they followed the old lady to the kitchen. Amelia's faded blue eyes twinkled as they sat down at the table. "You did meet. Didn't I tell you, Dr. Solange?" She winked roguishly. "He's quite a man, isn't he?"

Solange's mouth tilted up in a smile, which she directed at Dion. "Quite a man." Red color washed up his cheekbones, and the women laughed aloud at his embarrassment. "You should have expected this," she murmured as Amelia, still chuckling, turned on the gas to brew their coffee.

She knew he itched to look at the photo, to ask about the people in it, but his innate good manners overrode his curiosity. They would have to eat the candied quince Amelia handed to them, toast her politely with the accompanying ice water and then sip their coffee. After that, serious talk could start.

Amelia stirred the coffee in the little pot and brought it to a boil. "I remember you, Dion. You were just a toddler."

He frowned. "I should remember you, but it's just a blank."

"That's because, when you were a child, I lived in Athens where my husband worked. When we came back, your parents had left."

"But you must have known them quite well, Grandma Amelia," he said in as casual a tone as he could manage. Under his skin nerves were jumping.

"Yes, of course I did. Your father was Elias's hero." A look of sadness crossed her wrinkled face. "He wanted to go into journalism, too, when he finished his military service." She sighed heavily. "All of them dead now. So young."

"What happened to your son?"

Amelia lifted her coffee cup, sipping noisily from it. Out of her apron pocket she drew a handkerchief, which she used to wipe the tear from her cheek. "He was killed when a jeep overturned during army maneuvers in the mountains north of Goumenissa. It was a tragic, freak accident."

A chill ran up Dion's spine. There were too many accidents, too many witnesses who were turning up dead. Coincidence? Or perhaps a plan, part of a massive cover-up?

Amelia went to the icon case mounted on the wall. Unlocking it, she removed the framed photo. "This is my Elias," she said, pointing to a handsome young soldier whose beret was set at a jaunty angle.

So young. Amelia's earlier words echoed in Solange's head. Too young to die. But wasn't that always the case in wars? The young men died. The commanders, many of them old and hardened, survived, seemingly oblivious to the tragedy of it.

Only Elias hadn't died in a war....

Dion gripped the cheap plastic frame. Yes, it was the duplicate of the photo from Mavrakis's flat. "You wouldn't know who the other men are, would you?"

Amelia took the picture and deftly slid off the cardboard backing. "It's written on the back."

Elias had been more thorough than Mavrakis. He'd noted down both first and last names, as well as rank. Mavrakis had already been a sergeant. The others, including Elias, had been privates, except for the tall man who stood to one side. He was Lieutenant Angelo Hatsis.

"When was this taken?" Dion asked, his eyes narrowed as he tried to make out the face beneath the brim of the cap.

"In 1965," Amelia said. "Elias had his accident only a month later."

Disappointment rose bitterly in his throat. Too early. All the soldiers would have been out of the army by the time the Colonels took over, unless they had reenlisted. Still, Hatsis, an officer, was a possibility. He had to look at the military records again.

"Do you know what happened to any of these men?"

"Only Hatsis. He was very kind to me, came and told me personally when Elias died. He still sends me a card at Christmas and Easter."

Renewed excitement surged in him. "He does? Could you tell me where he lives?"

"I'd have to look it up. I know it's a village in Pelion."

Pelion? That was close, only past Volos. Depending on which village it was, it couldn't be more than three hours away by car. He leaned forward earnestly. "Grandma Amelia, this is very important to me. What village?"

Obviously puzzled by his intensity, she looked at him for a long moment before pulling open a kitchen drawer and removing a box that had once held chocolates. She piled the contents on the table. Most of the letters carried stamps from Australia.

Amelia sighed wistfully. "My sister emigrated years ago. She writes to me. I always wanted to visit her, but after my husband died, and then Elias, I couldn't bear to leave my home. Ah, here it is."

The envelope was postmarked Kissos. Dion's heartbeat sped up. "That's not far at all."

"Kissos?" Solange suddenly blurted out. "What's the name of this man?"

"Hatsis. Angelo Hatsis. Why, have you heard of him?"

She shook her head. "I don't think so. But my mother's family came from Kissos."

Dion went still, his mind frozen. Was it possible that the man he sought was related to Solange? Was she the one he would hurt? His throat tight, he couldn't speak.

"My father came to Greece as a tourist," Solange was saying. "He's French-Canadian. They met, and married against her family's wishes. Their name was Zorras, and she didn't talk about them often. But she used to tell me stories about her grandmother, who was quite a character. Of course, she died long before I was born, and my grandparents died in a flu epidemic about twenty years ago. I've been to Kissos, but the family seems to have died out."

Dion allowed himself to breathe freely again. Her family profile didn't fit. It was very unlikely any of them had been involved with the military regime. But Angelo Hatsis might prove a valuable lead. "I think," he said, "I'd like to go up to Kissos and talk to this Hatsis."

"He doesn't live right in Kissos," Amelia said. "Just off the road to Kissos there's another, tiny village—I don't even know if it has a name. That's where Angelo has his house."

"No matter." Dion gestured with his hand. "It's a two- to three-hour drive at most. We could still go today if we start now."

Solange looked at her watch. "Saturday's not the best day to visit people. Tomorrow would be better."

Dion looked at her, realizing she expected to go along. Was it wise to take her? He didn't know what he would learn from Hatsis, if anything. Could he risk it? Even though sooner or later Solange would discover his true mission, he wasn't sure he was ready for it yet.

"I can go by myself. I can use a map."

She smiled, an enigmatic smile that held both sweetness and determination. "With me along you won't need a map."

She wasn't sure why she felt the need to go with him. Perhaps it was that odd stillness that had come over him when she'd mentioned her mother's family coming from Kissos. Or it might have been the reserve in his manner since the episode with Mavrakis.

On the drive back from Athens at dawn this morning after an uncomfortable night in a hotel on one of the main Kifissia streets, he'd been as remote and silent as the craggy hills that bordered the highway. They might have been two strangers instead of a man and a woman who'd shared a tentative passion, whose hearts had seemed for fleeting moments to merge into one.

Mentally she shook herself. If she was smart, she would leave Dion to find his own ghosts and to settle them into their place. She had enough problems of her own.

But she admitted it was the very intensity of his strange quest that drew her. She needed to know what was behind it, even though at times he frightened her. This obsession with his parents' death couldn't be healthy. Perhaps that was why she felt she had to stay with him. Disturbed by the ambiguity and dark secretiveness she saw in him, she was more afraid to leave him to handle it alone.

"We'll go tomorrow," she repeated firmly.

"Okay, tomorrow," Dion agreed, surprising her with his acquiescence. But she wasn't about to risk his changing his mind by remarking on it.

She stood up, giving Amelia a fond hug. "You won't stay for lunch?" the old lady asked.

"I'm sorry. I have to check my office."

"Penny's doing fine." Amelia chuckled. "She's learning to be more assertive."

Solange's brows lifted. "Really? Maybe I should go away more often, then."

Grandma Amelia winked at Dion. "Yes, you should. You work too hard." She tilted her head. "Penny's in awe of you. Did you know that?"

"Oh." For a moment Solange didn't know what to say. She and Penny got along well; she'd assumed they were equals. Now she understood the odd moments when Penny had seemed to hang on her every word as she elaborated on some diagnosis or explained some treatment. "Coming, Dion?" She tucked her hand into the crook of his elbow and pulled him toward the door.

"Thank you, Grandma Amelia," he called back, ducking under the lintel.

"No thanks necessary, Dion. Come again."

"I will," he promised, and was surprised to realize he meant it. It had been his intention to remain aloof from the townspeople, but little by little he was beginning to be assimilated into the fabric of their society. After years of being a confirmed loner, he found the experience unexpectedly pleasant.

And disturbing.

PENNY HAD EVERYTHING under control. Solange had anticipated nothing less. The waiting room was cool and empty, and Penny sat at her own desk, updating her files.

"Solange, you're back." She jumped up and took a pile of books off Solange's desk, laying them on the floor beside her own. "I thought you'd stay over the weekend."

Solange smiled as she glanced around the office. "We finished our business and decided to come home. Everything looks great. You weren't rushed off your feet, were you?"

"Yesterday was busy, being market day. We had a steady stream of people for blood pressure checks. Nothing serious." She handed Solange a file. "I've updated the list."

"Good." Solange sat down and ran her eyes down the names. "I see Vangeli and Maria came in."

Penny pulled a face. "Yes, along with a cousin of his who just happened to be visiting from Thessaloniki, drives a Mercedes and is one of the leading heart surgeons in the medical center there. And he just happens to be single, widowed."

Solange heard the faint sarcasm and said, tongue in cheek, "Sounds like the perfect setup."

"That's exactly what it was." Penny slapped down a folder and picked up the next one. "A setup. You know how I feel about arranged marriages."

"So does everyone in Korfalli, and perhaps all of Thessaly," Solange said mildly.

Penny was silent for a moment, ruffling the pages of a thick textbook as she searched for some piece of information. "I'm having dinner with him tomorrow night."

The words hung in the room. Solange didn't know what to say about this major softening on Penny's part. Finally she murmured noncommittally, "I hope you have a good time."

"I probably won't," Penny declared tartly. "He'll probably turn out to be a self-centered oaf, like so many men."

"Don't judge him too soon."

"No, I won't." She scribbled something in the margin of her notebook, then looked up again. "By the way, Kyra, Litsa's friend—you've met her—came by last night and again this morning."

Solange had wondered about Kyra, since she hadn't heard anything about her in the past week or so. Of course, Litsa, her source of information, hadn't dropped in, either. "Oh? Did she say what she wanted?"

Penny shook her head. "Only that she had to talk to you." Her forehead creased in a frown, and she took off her glasses, peering critically at a speck on the lens. "I don't know why she didn't talk to me. She usually has in the past."

"Well, I suppose she'll be back." Solange took the stack of files from the out basket and put them in the cabinet. "I'd say that's enough for today. Let's lock up. The rest will wait for Monday."

MOST OF THE SHOPS were open until 2:30 on Saturdays. Solange stopped to buy some necessary groceries before going home. She had just started to unpack the bags on the kitchen table when there was a timid knock on the door. Thinking it might be Litsa, she called, "Come in."

Immediately she realized it wouldn't be her, since Litsa was spending every spare moment studying for the rigorous graduation exams. And the girl wouldn't have bothered to knock.

The knock sounded again, barely audible, as if the caller didn't want the other occupants of the house to know anyone was there.

Solange pulled open the door. Kyra stood on the landing, a melancholy expression on her face.

"Dr. Solange, are you busy?" she whispered, her eyes darting around the room.

"Not too busy to talk to you. I hear you were looking for me. I'm sorry I wasn't there."

The girl came into the room, pausing just inside the door, which she closed carefully behind her. "Litsa doesn't know I'm here."

Mystified, since the two girls were such close friends, Solange asked, "Don't you want her to know? She might think it odd that you came to the house without talking to her."

"She's studying. We've hardly had time to see each other."

"Is that what's bothering you?"

"No, no, of course not. I'm supposed to be studying, too, but what's the use?" With a cry of distress she covered her face with her hands.

"You mean your father hasn't backed down?" Solange bit her tongue against the hot anger that rose inside her. Kyra didn't need to hear a tirade, which might explain why she'd come to Solange instead of Penny, whose views on the subject of education were much more militant.

"It's worse than that."

Marriage. The word jumped into Solange's head and was immediately drowned by the heartbreaking sound of Kyra's sobs.

Gently Solange led the girl to the sofa, urged her to a seat and waited until the tears subsided. Kyra finally lifted her head, sniffing as she wiped her nose with a handkerchief.

"Dr. Solange, my father wants me to get married instead of going to university."

Solange nodded. "After what you said to Penny the other day, I can't say this comes as a surprise. Is he going to at least let you sit for the exams?"

"He'll let me write them." She hiccuped dismally. "Maybe he hopes I'll fail and then there won't be any point in arguing with him. He doesn't want me to go to Athens, alone to the city. He wants me to stay here."

"But you won't be alone," Solange pointed out. "You'll be sharing a place with Litsa. And you have relatives there, don't you?"

"Yes, but he won't hear of me leaving. He wants me safely married. He's even picked out my husband."

"I see." Solange perched on the edge of a chair. What could she say? What could she do? She tried not to interfere in family affairs, but this went too far. And when Penny heard— Wearily she closed her eyes. It didn't even bear thinking about. "And what does your mother say about this?"

"She agrees with whatever Father says. She would be happy to see me stay right here, where she can visit."

Although Solange was less outspoken on the subject than Penny, she didn't condone arranged marriages, either. Sure, many couples fell in love after marriage, but to Solange the arrangement smacked of coercion, the removal of a basic freedom. "What can I do?"

She'd always managed to give advice without disrupting family unity, but this time she couldn't see any other way. What could she tell the girl? To defy her father? She was a minor; children had to obey their parents. No one would take the child's side against the father unless there was blatant abuse, something Solange had rarely seen.

"Help me when I tell him. Dr. Solange, you're an outsider—no, not in a bad sense, but you can do things that other women would be ostracized for." She paused, as if to gather strength. Looking straight into Solange's eyes, her own dark and suddenly passionate behind her glasses, she said without a trace of ambivalence, "I can't marry the man my father wants me to."

"Then tell him."

"When I do, he'll kill me." This was also said in a tone that told Solange it was immutable fact.

Solange's eyes widened in shock. "Surely not," she said, nearly choking on the sudden dryness in her throat. "Not because you tell him no."

"No." Kyra's braid swung over her shoulder as she shook her head. "Not because I tell him no. He'll kill me when I tell him I'm pregnant."

Solange gulped. This was the last thing she'd expected. "Pregnant. And how did that come about?"

Kyra managed a shaky laugh. "The usual way. You understand."

Unable to control the pink color that burned her cheeks, Solange stared at Kyra, the mixture of bravado and happiness on her face. "Yes, biologically I understand. But you—I thought you were concentrating on your schoolwork. Does Litsa know about this?"

"No. I haven't told her. She's going to be even more shocked than you are."

The understatement of the year. Solange tried one more time to inject sanity into the conversation. "Kyra, maybe you're mistaken. You've been under a lot of pressure."

Kyra laid her hand on her flat stomach, tenderly, as if to guard the life there. "No, I'm not mistaken. I'm having a baby."

Solange was beginning to wonder if she had fallen asleep and was dreaming all this. That this could happen to Kyra, a girl who had never been connected with any boys, who had never been the subject of the slightest gossip in a town where teenage girls were watched as if they were candidates for sainthood.

It wasn't possible. Yet everything about Kyra's demeanor reinforced the words she'd uttered. "Okay, you're having a baby. What about school? And what about the father of your baby?"

"My parents will kick me out when they find out—at least, my father will," Kyra said as matter-of-factly as if it were a comment on the weather. "I won't tell them until after the exams. Of course, I can't fail the exams. That would be fatal."

"A high percentage of students do fail," Solange reminded her.

"Even if I have to study day and night, I can't." She dragged in a deep breath. "Then after they kick me out, I'll go to university as I've planned. Tuition is free, and it won't cost much to live if I share with Litsa."

If Litsa's parents didn't object, something that was a possibility to consider. Unwed motherhood carried quite a stigma. "The father—where does he figure in this?"

"He'll marry me as soon as he completes his military service. He's promised."

A promise in the heat of lust? Or a real one? Realist that she was, Solange couldn't help wondering. "I take it he's not the man your father wants you to marry."

"Oh, no. Father would never approve of Niko. He's Sarakatsani. Father would say he's still got sheep muck on his boots."

"But the baby, won't that change things?"

"No. That just makes things worse. Father will know I slept with Niko. And the man he's picked won't want me."

Double standard, of course, Solange thought with a sinking heart. The one bright spot in the dilemma was that Kyra wouldn't be forced into the arranged marriage. Solange said as much.

"I know." The girl stared down at her clasped hands in her lap. "But I don't want you to think that's why I got pregnant. I love Niko and he loves me. But we knew how my father would react."

"How did you ever meet this Niko?"

"You know how I often go to baby-sit after school at my aunt's in Anhialos when she works afternoon shift? Well, Niko lives next door. We've known each other for about a year. When he was called up to report for his military service, we made love for the first time. I got pregnant."

"From once? Didn't Niko protect you?"

"It was more than once. And he did try, but one night—" she flushed beet-red "—we had an accident. You know—it broke."

"I see." Solange walked over to the window. Two children, barely old enough to know what they were doing, now about to be parents. What could she say? "I take it you want this baby."

She already knew the answer, but felt she had to ask, anyway. Not that she would be a part of the most drastic solution to Kyra's problem. Personally she would never do an abortion, but she didn't presume to judge doctors who did. Intellectually she knew there were situations where it was the only solution, a solution used surprisingly often here in Greece, in spite of being against both church and civil law.

"Yes," Kyra said fiercely. "I want this baby. I know, other girls at school have gotten pregnant and their parents sent them to Volos and discreetly took care of it. They could be back at school in a day or two. But I want my baby. We'll be able to manage."

"And where do I come in?"

"I would like you to be my doctor."

"If you go to Athens, that might be a problem."

"Just for the summer. In Athens I'll find somebody."

"Kyra, I don't know what to say. Your parents will have to be told. You can't hide this forever. How far along are you?"

"I've just missed a second period."

"Not far then. So you'll be able to keep it a secret until after the exams. Have you had any morning sickness? Your mother might notice something."

"She hasn't. They've been too busy with the new kiwi orchard to bother about me. I feel perfectly fine."

She looked well, too, Solange thought with a critical eye. A bit thin, but otherwise healthy with excellent skin tone. The family was well off, the owners of extensive almond orchards, as well as fruit trees. Kyra's three older sisters were married, her brother doing well in a military academy. Kyra's present dilemma would be exacerbated by her position as the youngest child, the child of her parents' middle age. No doubt she was her father's pet. She might very well be right that he would kill her. If not literally, then by disowning her as if she'd never been born.

Solange cleared her throat. "Kyra, I'd like you to come and see me in my office on Monday. Will that be a problem? You can drop in on your way home from school. I'll wait for you."

"Thank you, Dr. Solange. I'll be there. My last class is track and field, and I can find an excuse to get out of it, so I won't be late."

Cutting classes? Well, for once it wouldn't hurt. "Fine. I'll see you then. And for the moment, don't mention this to anyone. It may all turn out to be a false alarm."

"I won't, Doctor. If I did, it would be all over town in an hour." She turned with her hand on the doorknob. "But I'm sure it's real."

The door closed behind her. Solange let out a sigh and sank down on a chair, her shaking fingers gripping her skull and making a wild rat's nest of her hair. What a day this had been, and it wasn't over yet.

And what could she do about Kyra? At least the girl had courage and was being fairly realistic about her situation. But courage didn't buy baby food and diapers. And who would take care of the child while she attended classes? Obviously she hadn't thought of that.

Restlessly she got to her feet, wandering into the kitchen where half her groceries were still waiting on the table to be put away. Working mechanically, she stored the items in the cupboard and the fridge, folding the bags neatly and putting them in a drawer. The thought of eating lunch made her stomach churn.

And there was no one she could talk to, even if it didn't breach patient-doctor confidentiality.

Yes, there was someone. In this case confidentiality was less important than a second, unbiased opinion.

Taking her key and slipping some money into her pocket, she let herself quietly out. She would see Dion. He would at least inject some common sense into this.

CHAPTER NINE

DION MERELY LOOKED UP and cracked another egg into a bowl as Solange burst in. She was out of breath, as if she'd been running, and her chest heaved beguilingly under her loose shirt. A drop of sweat trickled slowly down her neck and disappeared under her collar. He watched its progress, unaware of the egg white sliding over his fingers. The longing to touch her again was an ache deep inside him. He wanted to put his mouth on her skin, lick away the drops of sweat, taste the salt and her sweetness, love her, love her...

He tore his eyes away, knowing his dream was doomed, destined to be annihilated by the nightmare that would become reality when he found Pavlou.

"Have you eaten lunch?" Tossing the shells into the garbage can, he rinsed his hands under the tap.

Solange shook her head. "No." She drew a last deep breath, but her heart still raced after the burning look he'd given her as she'd run in. He wanted her, no mistake. Had wanted her for days. Then why didn't he do something more about it than those few burning kisses they'd shared?

What did she want? Away from him, thinking of that unsettled, dark core in him, like the crater of a slumbering volcano, she was plagued with doubts. Near him, as now, she knew she could forget her uncertainties, especially if he pushed the issue. Sooner or later they would make love. In the meantime the suspense was nearly unbearable.

"You're beating those eggs to death," she said.

His hand jerked, as if he'd forgotten her presence. Not likely, she thought with a mixture of dismay and excitement. He'd been staring at her, those blue eyes hot and dark, hyperaware of her.

"Oh." He looked down at the bowl, his expression rueful. "Yeah, I guess I am."

Putting down the bowl, he scooped the onion and green pepper he'd chopped into the frying pan that was beginning to smoke on the burner. The vegetables sizzled, and a tantalizing aroma drifted up from the pan. Solange's mouth watered as she realized she was hungry, after all. Food. She would eat first, then deal with the erotic impulses that pooled with a painful pleasure in her belly.

"Shall I cut a salad?"

The smile he cast her was crooked and endearing. "Sure, since you seem to have invited yourself for lunch."

She moved the bowl of eggs aside, making a face as she did so. "Good thing I came by. There's enough cholesterol in here to overdose yourself for the next three days."

He shrugged, his tanned shoulders flexing under the sleeveless tank top he wore. "I'll work it off. What's on your mind, Solange? You didn't come by to criticize my diet."

"And you didn't seem surprised to see me."

"No. I figured that as soon as you'd closed your office you'd want to talk about Hatsis and Kissos. I could see curiosity written all over your face."

"Well, didn't you think it odd that both my family and yours had something to do with Kissos?" She sliced tomatoes, putting them into a bowl and adding chopped green pepper and onion.

"Not really. Many people from here went to Pelion and probably as many moved from there to here. And it's not my family that comes from Kissos. In fact, I doubt if my parents were ever there."

Baffled, Solange turned to look at him, the salt-shaker poised above the salad. "Then what makes you think this Hatsis can help you?"

"He's the only lead I have, now that Mavrakis is dead." His expression hardened, and he dumped the bowl from the eggs into the sink with a clatter. She saw his knuckles whiten, his tension out of proportion to the effort needed to stir the eggs in the frying pan.

"Then the man you're looking for isn't a relative." Some hidden meaning swam under the surface of their conversation, but for the life of her Solange couldn't figure it out. Dion had said he was looking for relatives, but his parents' death was somehow tangled into the search. The suspicion that he hadn't disclosed his real goal was growing stronger by the minute.

"No." He made a harsh sound that could have been a laugh. "No, I told you I'm looking for this man for information. Hatsis may be able to lead me to him."

"And then what?"

But Dion didn't answer, his face averted as he turned off the burner.

"Dion," Solange said with exaggerated patience, "when are you going to tell me what you're really looking for? I know it's not for long-lost relatives."

CASINO JUBILEE
"Match'n Scratch" Game

▼ DETACH AND MAIL CARD TODAY! ▼

BUSINESS REPLY MAIL
FIRST CLASS MAIL   PERMIT NO. 717   BUFFALO, NY

POSTAGE WILL BE PAID BY ADDRESSEE

HARLEQUIN READER SERVICE
3010 WALDEN AVE
PO BOX 1867
BUFFALO NY 14240-9952

NO POSTAGE
NECESSARY
IF MAILED
IN THE
UNITED STATES

If she hadn't been watching him closely, she would have missed the surprise that leaped into his eyes. It was gone at once, leaving his face a bleak, remote mask.

"Solange, I can't. Not yet." He dragged in a long, ragged breath. "The day may come when I'll have to, but not yet."

He dished up the omelet, setting the two plates on the table along with the bowl of tomatoes, which Solange had simply dressed with olive oil and a sprinkle of basil she'd snipped from the plant on the windowsill.

Silence sat awkwardly between them as they began to eat, a third guest at the table that neither knew how to evict. Dion broke it, forcing normality into his tone. "You took longer to get here than I expected. I thought you'd just stop by your office for a minute and then come over." He glanced at the clock ticking next to the pot of basil. "It's almost four."

The food might have been cardboard for all she tasted. Solange didn't like contention, especially when she wasn't sure what had caused it. But taking her cue from him, she pasted a smile on her face. "So it is. Does that mean we're eating lunch or supper?"

"In Canada it would be almost supper."

In Canada. Was she beginning to miss it? She hadn't thought about it much before Dion came. Now she was reminded every day, although his accent with its European cadence wasn't strictly Canadian.

"I've got a problem," she said as she helped herself to more salad. "Or rather one of the high school girls is in serious trouble."

"What kind of problem does this girl have? Or shall I guess?"

"Your first guess would probably be right. The thing is, she's a good girl, excellent student, not the sort you'd think would get pregnant. Actually I'm not positive, but the girl is.''

"The father? Is he from here?"

"From Anhialos."

"Then he's not a stranger."

"He might as well be, according to Kyra. She says her father will never allow their marriage because the boy is Sarakatsani. I knew there was some resentment at times, but I didn't know it could go this deep. It's possible, of course, that Kyra is exaggerating. Her father is going to be livid when he finds out about the pregnancy, never mind the name of her lover.''

Dion let out a low whistle. "Kyra? Oh-oh. You have got a problem with this Sarakatsani thing. In my interviews I've learned that there are others of the townspeople who resent the Sarakatsani ownership of great pieces of land. But Kyra's father has a personal grudge. He missed buying a tract of excellent land with a water well already drilled by not having the deposit in on time. A Sarakatsani shepherd beat him to it.''

"That's stupid, though," Solange declared. "Everyone had the same chance to buy the land. No one got any special favors.''

"But old Stavros won't see it that way. He lost his chance and he won't forget it. It's a Greek trait.''

Solange's mouth turned down. "You can say that again. It's the one thing I feel does most to cause dissension in this country. I could never understand this holding of grudges, these stupid feuds that go on for generations.''

"No, you wouldn't." Again depression washed over Dion. This was precisely why their relationship, if he could call it that, had no future. He possessed the very trait she despised, and was determined to exercise it.

It's not too late to back out, a little voice taunted him.

But I can't. I made the vow. It's not just revenge—it's honor and duty.

Slamming the door on his nagging conscience, he asked, "What are you going to do about Kyra?"

"First give her a pregnancy test on Monday. As I told her, maybe we're worrying for nothing. But Kyra has another problem, which compounds this one. Her father wants her to get married. Apparently he's arranging it. And not to Kyra's lover, whom he's not even aware of."

Dion whistled again. "Now, that's a problem. Simple pregnancy isn't the end of the world. A quick wedding and it's taken care of. Nobody pays much attention to when the first child arrives. But if the family doesn't approve..."

"Exactly. That's just how I read it."

"They could always elope," Dion suggested with a touch of mischief.

"Even that wouldn't be easy. Niko is in the army. He's taking his preliminary training someplace in the Pindos mountains. Kyra won't see him for at least three months and possibly longer."

Dion exhaled gustily. "So her father will have to be told. She can't marry anyone else while she's pregnant with this boy's child." He broke off, exasperated. "Boy, child. Do they even know what they're doing? They're only children and they're having a child of their own."

"Yes, it's sad, but with her family's support it wouldn't have to be a disaster."

"She's not going to get it."

"No." Solange crumbled bread between her fingers. "Not from them. She may have only Penny and me."

"Will it cause a problem for you when Stavros finds out you're her doctor?"

Solange shrugged. "I'll weather it."

Dion nodded, putting down his fork. "Maybe if I talked to Stavros. He used to think highly of my father, thinks it's great that I've come back to the family homestead, so to speak."

"Dion, not yet. Kyra wants to write her exams first. Then she'll decide what to do."

"Yes, the exams. Is she still planning to go to university?"

"She wants to. Her father doesn't approve, but he won't stop her from sitting for the exams."

"And she'll pass, won't she? Solange, did you ever have problems like this in Canada?"

"Sure, although more often the girl was already estranged from her family, or the family accepted the situation. The structure of Canadian society is more liberal. Here people worry more about what the neighbors think, but it's not so different when it comes down to emotions."

"Which is better, do you think?" Dion asked in a musing tone.

Tilting her head, Solange considered. "I don't know," she said slowly. "Neither, I guess, and both. They're just different. There are never easy solutions. People still have to work things out as best they can."

"Yeah," he agreed readily, knowing she was right, but also aware that he hadn't applied it to himself. Wasn't he acting on impulse, an impulse born of grief and anger years ago? It had never occurred to him that there might be a different solution than the one he was pursuing.

To distract himself from the unsettling thought, he asked, "Will you have dinner with me this evening?"

As soon as the words were out, he wished he could snatch them back, especially when he caught the startled look she gave him. What he wanted was to be alone, to reaffirm the rightness of his planned revenge. He didn't need more time with Solange.

Solange barely stopped herself from gaping at him. Although he'd been the sounding board she needed about Kyra, earlier he'd pulled back so far into himself that she thought he'd moved to another planet. She shook her head. She might as well give up trying to predict what he would do. "It's almost evening now."

Dion shrugged as he got up to carry their dishes to the sink. "Well, later then." Perversely now, he didn't withdraw the invitation. Live dangerously, he told himself, and enjoy the moment. It would be over all too soon, and Solange wouldn't be coming to him to discuss anything. "I'll take you to Volos for pizza, if you want. That place was good."

"How can I resist? Pizza by the sea." Out of the sight of their nosy neighbors.

"Sounds romantic," he said, falling in with the lightened mood.

"Definitely not us, is it?"

But he surprised her. "Why not? A man and a woman, the night, moonlight."

"I think the moon rises at about five in the morning."

"Stars, then. Is it so hard to imagine?"

It wasn't hard at all, Solange realized. But not practical. There were too many dark secrets in Dion, secrets she wasn't sure she wanted to know. That black river of emotion that ran through him—she would drown if she stepped off the safe, narrow path she'd laid out for herself.

She took their glasses to the sink and ran water in them, the cool liquid flowing over her hands. Next to her, Dion wiped up the counter with a sponge, his fresh, mossy scent drifting into her. He was close enough to touch, and she wanted to, though she hesitated to make the first move.

They turned at the same time, facing each other, so close they could feel each other breathing. Solange made up her mind. Who wanted to be practical all the time? ''Pizza sounds terrific,'' she said in a voice that sounded brittle to her own ears. ''I'll see you later.''

He bent his head, angling his mouth toward hers, but at the last second before their lips touched, Solange ducked away. Calling herself all kinds of a coward, she walked out, leaving him staring after her. She could feel his eyes boring into her back all the way to the door.

She went home and slept for two hours, waking groggy and disoriented. A cool shower woke her up, but the sensuous cascade of water over her body also woke up dormant feelings that were the twins of those she'd felt in herself that afternoon, and seen in Dion's eyes. The need to be with someone, to open herself to trust, possibly to love. Dion probably wasn't the right man, but she could become an old maid waiting.

This brought her up short. If Dion didn't have his obsession, the secrets he refused to share, would she see him differently?

Yes! Yes, she could love Dion, a man she didn't trust. That alone increased her disquietude. Her whole conception of love was turning upside down, forcing her to reexamine convictions she'd never questioned. Meeting Dion was changing her. And she was suddenly afraid to think of where it would end.

Drying herself briskly, she dressed in a practical cotton skirt and a loose camp shirt, twisting her hair into a knot at her nape. The severity of the hairstyle gave prominence to her strong features. Only her mouth spoiled the formal effect. Even without lipstick her lips were a soft pink. She remembered how she and Dion had kissed, the taste of him, and at the memory her lips grew tremulous.

She clenched her jaw, vowing to keep her runaway emotions under control.

But it wasn't so easy to be practical later when they sat on the Volos waterfront, listening to the slap of the waves against the seawall and the wail of a singer from the old-fashioned jukebox the restaurant owner had brought over from Toronto where he'd run a similar business.

The pizza was excellent, crisp crust and beautifully stringy cheese. With it they drank a sharp red wine, homemade from grapes grown in Anhialos.

The waterfront was busy, but not as busy as on Sunday evenings when half of Volos seemed to come out for the promenade. Although it was near midnight when they finally got up and paid the man, new customers were still arriving, mostly in their teens and early twenties, coming from seeing a late movie.

Her conversation with Dion had been pleasant. Dion's intensity was damped down, safely hidden behind his sense of humor. Relaxed and mellow, Solange didn't object when he took her hand and entwined his fingers through hers.

The night was dark, clouds coming up over the mountains and blotting out the stars. Blue-white heat lightning arrowed through the blackness, followed by a faint rumble of thunder.

"Angels bowling," Dion murmured whimsically. "There's no hurry to go back, is there?"

"Depends how early you want to start in the morning."

"Not too early. It's about a two-and-a-half-hour drive. If we leave at eight, we'll get there after church and before Sunday dinner."

Next to the park the wide seawall was deserted except for a couple of young boys fishing using a flashlight. They stared at Solange, recognizing a foreigner, probably because of her blond hair. In keeping with her image as a doctor, a highly respected profession here, she rarely wore it down. The thick golden waves were a flamboyant contrast to her appearance of reserved competence, and much too hot in summer. She'd often thought of cutting her hair, but it was her single vanity.

"Take your hair down," Dion said with that uncanny ability he had to read her mind. "It's so unusual."

"Too much so," Solange said ruefully, making no move to pull out the pins as they walked in the dark shadows under the ferny boughs of the silk trees.

Dion showed no hesitation as he gently brought her up against one of the smooth, curving trunks. The blossoms, just emerging, gave off a delicate but intoxicating scent.

Solange closed her eyes as Dion moved his hands around to her nape. He touched her skin, and she told herself it was the cool sea breeze that made her shiver. A light tug and the swath of her hair unrolled down her back. Dion stepped back, and she saw his teeth gleam in a smile as he tucked the pins into his shirt pocket. "There, now you can't do it up again."

"Dion—"

"No, don't talk." He placed his palms on her cheeks, framing her face and tilting it up to his. "Don't talk. Just feel."

A river of sensation ran through her as his mouth touched hers. Her mind told her to run for safety, but her body was frozen—no, not frozen—ice wasn't hot. She felt her skin burning, her heart pounding as if she'd slept in the sun and woken up with heatstroke. She was afraid. She couldn't do this. It had to stop.

But after a moment she forgot why she wanted it to. His mouth was sweet, gentle when she expected rough passion. In that tenderness she glimpsed the kind of lover he would be, wholehearted, giving as well as taking.

Shivering again, goose bumps coming up on her skin, she pressed closer, aligning her body to his. He shifted his weight, pulling her into the cradle of his thighs. She could feel his arousal against her belly, the summer clothes they wore a barrier that enhanced sensation rather than dulling it. Promises.

He rolled his hips slightly, testing her. "Solange, tell me you want me."

She was too honest to deny it, even when common sense told her she should. "I want you. But we can't."

"Why can't we?" In the heat of passion nothing mattered, not the past, not the future.

"You have unfinished business. After tomorrow, then we'll see."

He stiffened in her arms, then slowly backed away. In the darkness she couldn't be sure, but his expression looked stricken, deep lines drawn about his mouth. "After tomorrow," he said, so softly she could barely hear. "After tomorrow will be too late."

THE DRIVE HOME was accomplished in virtual silence. The tires hummed smoothly on the pavement, and at intervals the headlights picked up the glow of animal eyes from the side of the road. Korfalli lay peacefully asleep, the dark streets punctuated by pools of amber light from the streetlamps.

Dion dropped her at her door, not bothering to get out of the car. ''See you in the morning. Eight o'clock.''

''Good night. And thanks,'' she called softly after him, but the words were lost in the sound of the car engine accelerating.

Her bedroom was hot, despite the open window and the pungence of ozone and imminent rain in the air. Restless, feeling as if she itched in an unreachable place, Solange stripped and took another shower. The image of Dion's face, etched clearly in a flash of lightning when they'd gotten in the car, wouldn't leave her even when she closed her eyes against the water sluicing over her face.

Too late. After tomorrow will be too late.

What had he meant, and why had his face gone so pale and strained? Tortured. That was how he'd looked, however absurd that sounded. He looked like a man she'd had in the hospital once whose child had died due to the father's negligence in locking away a pesticide. Self-condemnation, the worst emotion to live with.

Didn't she know it, after the death she'd been blamed for in Montreal?

She stepped out of the shower and, without bothering to dry off, pulled on a loose sundress. Her wet feet slipped as she scuffed them into a pair of thongs. She picked up her keys, then paused. Unlocking a cupboard, she withdrew a couple of items before carefully locking up again.

Her mind resolutely blank, she let herself out into the night.

Clouds scudded across the sky, borne on a gusty wind that tugged at her skirt. She met no one as she covered the short distance to Dion's house. No lights showed, and for a moment she hesitated. But the drop of rain that fell on her cheek and ran coldly into the hollow of her throat decided her.

Somehow she was at a crossroad with Dion. How she'd gotten there and what it meant, she didn't understand. She knew only that she didn't want to be alone. Or perhaps she didn't want him to be alone with whatever memory tortured him.

Slowly mounting the step as more raindrops spattered into the dust on the path, she pushed open the door. It wasn't locked, but that didn't surprise her since Dion had never bothered to get the latch repaired.

As if in a dream, she walked through the house, past the dark kitchen and into the one usable bedroom. She'd never been there, but a flash of lightning showed her an old-fashioned brass bed, probably abandoned when his parents had moved out, and Dion lying sprawled under a sheet.

He was awake, his eyes moving over her as she came into the room and closed the door. "Solange?" He sat up.

She laughed shakily. "No, I'm a ghost." Nervous perspiration broke out on her skin. She'd never seduced a man before. Would he think her a wanton hussy?

She saw his smile, the quick gleam of his teeth. "Let me give us some light."

"No. Please." She put up her hand in protest, but he'd already struck a match and touched it to the wick of a candle on the nightstand. The illumination was faint, an amber glow barely chasing the shadows into the corners of the room.

He stood up on the far side of the bed, and she saw him limned in gold, broad chest with its mat of black curls, flat stomach, strong legs, also hair-sprinkled. He was aroused. Her knees turned weak as a sweet, languid need seeped into her bones.

"Come here," he whispered. "If you knew how much I've needed you..."

She knelt on the bed, then moved across it toward him. "You're the most beautiful man I've ever seen."

Dion laughed quietly. "I bet you say that to everyone you cast your spell on. Yes, I think that's what you've done, bewitched me, from the first moment we met."

His hands came to rest on her shoulders, and she could feel him fumbling with the straps of her dress. "You had a funny way of showing it, all those dark brooding moods." Her skin prickled as his calloused palms slid the straps down.

He closed his eyes, his hands gripping her upper arms. "Solange, I don't want you to be sorry."

She reached up and caressed his cheek, feeling the growing beard stubble, rough as velour. "Dion, I can't be sorry. No matter what happens, we'll have this."

His lashes fluttered down, and to her surprise a tear slid from under them, wetting her fingers. "No matter what happens," he said in a husky voice thick with emotion.

"Dion, can't you tell me?"

But he shook his head. "Not now."

A shudder racked his body. Solange drew back, but before she could move away he wrapped his arms around her and kissed her, a hot, searching, open-mouth exploration. It was as if he needed to absorb her texture, her taste, and store it away against future famine. As if this might be the only time they ever made love.

Sweat trickled down Solange's sides, rubbed away by Dion's hands as he pushed her dress to her waist. He touched her breast, gently, almost reverently, and the turmoil in her mind merged into one thought. She wanted him. She wanted to lie with him, explore him, love him. Even though he seemed to have no faith in a future for them.

For now there was only the present. And this moment could be forever.

She clutched at his shoulders as he put her down. Smiling a little at the sharp intake of his breath when he found her naked under the dress, she kicked it aside and welcomed him into her arms.

The heat in the room seemed to condense inside her as he gathered her close. Their skin was slick with sweat, the silky moisture heightening sensation. Outside the window the patter of raindrops in the fig tree formed a gentle counterpoint to their rapid breathing, and the rich smell of newly wet earth swam around them with an erotic perfume. Solange inhaled deeply, the green scent of wet grass blending with Dion's aroma, transporting her into a secret glade where there were only the two of them, safe from any intrusion.

He moved lower, suckling first one breast, then the other. Solange ran her hands over him, her fingers tangling in the delicious crispness of his chest hair. The muscles of his flat stomach quivered as she touched the raised scar, then moved sideways to explore the little dimple of his navel.

"A dent, not a bump, I see." Laughter bubbled from her throat as a crazy exhilaration seized her.

"Expert on belly buttons, are you?"

She could hear the smile in his voice and was fiercely glad she'd brought him this moment of happiness. "I should be, after all the babies I've delivered."

Sliding her hands down his body, she explored farther. He moaned when she caressed him with a gentle lover's touch, intimately searching out all the spots that gave him pleasure. He began to move against her, driven beyond thought, wanting only the ecstasy she promised.

"Dion, come to me now. I need you."

To her amazement he went still.

"Dion, what is it?"

"We can't do this." His voice was hoarse, tormented. His body trembled as if with fever, drops of sweat standing out like pearls on his skin as he hoisted himself on his elbows.

"Why not?" Solange struggled to surface from the haze of passion.

"The gossip."

"What are you talking about? No one knows I'm here. Why, you're blushing." Even in the candlelight she could see the flush that stained his cheeks.

"Solange, I'm not prepared. That's what I'm trying to tell you. If I went to the local pharmacy and bought a certain item, everyone would know. Solange, I didn't want to embarrass you." He sighed.

"Oh." For a moment she didn't know what to say. She touched his mouth, trailing her finger over his lower lip. "You're sweet, Dion, but you didn't have to worry." Reaching over the side of the bed, she retrieved her dress, withdrawing a little package from the pocket. "I'm a doctor, remember. I raided the dispensary."

With a soft laugh he took the packet. "Solange, you are truly incredible."

Whatever she would have replied was lost in the fierce heat of his kiss. Groaning with pleasure, she gave herself to his possession. He entered her slowly, with a tenderness that must have strained his control to the limit, as if he knew it had been a long time since she'd been with a man. She moved against him to ease his passage, elated as he voiced his own pleasure with incoherent whispers. She could feel the tension in his body, feel his urgent need as if it were her own. Raising her hips to meet his thrust, she gasped, "Once more. Yes, like that. Oh, yes. Oh, yes!"

The fire within her blazed higher, fiercely wind-whipped, and suddenly she was in the center of it, calm for a split second, then burning out of control as Dion followed her into the flames.

THEY LAY QUIETLY. Solange ran a languid hand over Dion's chest. He shivered. The air had turned cool in the wake of the rain. The candle had burned down, but a luminous starlight shone into the room. "You've killed me."

She cast an amused eye down his body. "I don't think so. In fact, I can detect distinct signs of life."

He muttered something that sounded vulgar and nuzzled his face against her neck, breathing in the fragrance of her body, his scent and hers mixed, the earthy essence of sex.

Love, he corrected himself. That cataclysmic meeting of souls couldn't be dismissed as merely sex. And he was too honest to try to.

Morning would be early enough for misgivings. Right now he wanted her again. "You don't happen to have any more of those things in your pocket, do you?"

She smiled smugly. "A doctor is always prepared."

CHAPTER TEN

KISSOS LAY in a verdant forest a little distance from the main highway, a village of steep streets and old stone houses. Beyond it a dirt track led to the hamlet where Angelo Hatsis was supposed to be living.

Leafy boughs formed a shady green tunnel through which the car bumped and lurched. They emerged after a mile or two into a little square bathed in bright sunlight. Dion braked next to a group of people coming out of the small church. Poking his head out of the open window, he called a greeting. *"Herete."*

A boy of about twelve came forward, though judging by the direction of his gaze he was more curious about the car's foreign plates than about its occupants.

"Where can we find Angelo Hatsis?" Dion asked politely.

"Hatsis?" An old man spit on the ground, but it might not have been personal.

The boy answered. "Up the path there. But you have to walk. A car won't go up the steps."

Dion parked the Renault at the edge of the square. He and Solange started up the path, uncomfortably conscious of the villagers' eyes following them.

"Is it my imagination, or aren't they very friendly?" Solange said as they turned a corner that took them out of sight of the square.

"Maybe just shy." Dion shrugged. "It's probably nothing."

The sun beat down on their heads. Solange squinted against the glare of it on the whitewashed walls, wishing she'd brought her sunglasses from the car. They stopped for a moment at the foot of the steps the boy had mentioned. Off to their right, under a willow tree, stood a travel trailer, an incongruous sight at the top of a steep gravel driveway.

"How did that get up here?" Solange gasped, wiping her forehead with a handkerchief.

"A hoist, maybe," Dion ventured. "German plates. Probably some returned villager who worked there."

They toiled on, climbing the steps made of flat stone slabs. At the top were two houses.

"Which one?" Both looked deserted, drowsing in the sun. A breeze that failed to relieve the heat sighed through the nearby trees, rustling the leaves. Far away, up the mountain, a cuckoo called, the sound tinny and mechanical.

The shriek of poorly oiled hinges brought Solange's head spinning around. The house on the left. An old woman clutched one of the upright bars of the gate with a gnarled, arthritic hand. A braid of a faded, indeterminate color escaped from the black scarf she wore on her head.

"Come here." She beckoned with her free hand. "You seek Hatsis?"

Hesitantly Solange edged closer, aware of the increased harshness of Dion's breathing at her back. "Yes. Is he here?"

Instead of answering, the woman asked another question. "You're Dr. Solange?"

Surprised, Solange glanced back at Dion, whose face was set and oddly pale. "Yes, I am."

The old woman pulled open the gate, stepping out of the shadows of the mulberry that grew next to it. Solange saw that her braid, though threaded with gray, had once been blond, not a common hair color in Greece. "I'm so happy you've come at last. I knew your mother."

"You knew my mother?" Solange asked in astonishment. "I've been to Kissos, but all my relatives are dead or gone away, and no one seemed to want to talk about them."

The woman made a derogatory sound. "Kissos. It's a nice enough place, but your mother was from here." She put out her hand, and Solange gently clasped it, mindful of the swollen, painful joints. "I'm Athena Galanou."

"Galanou?" Solange frowned. "I don't know that name. But then my mother almost never talked about Greece."

"After what happened, your mother marrying a foreigner and all, it's probably no wonder." Athena hugged her arms around her bony chest. "Her family didn't approve, especially since she had an understanding with a local boy."

Another arranged marriage, just like Kyra. Although it was probably irrational, Solange was glad her mother had escaped and married for love. And there had been love, despite the differences between them.

"She's dead, too, isn't she?" Athena asked.

"For some years," Solange said sadly. "She hoped they'd forgiven her."

"Her mother did. It was her father who couldn't. He was killed in an accident two years after she left. Your grandmother seemed to lose her spirit after that. She loved him deeply, you see, and since there were no other relatives to comfort her, it was as if the sun had gone out of her life. She died a year later, but her friends knew she really died along with your grandfather. Tell me, was Xanthe happy with that Frenchman?"

"Yes, she was happy."

"And you're her only child." Athena shook her head. "They've never been prolific, the women in your family."

"What about you?" Solange asked. "Are you related to my family?"

Athena jerked her head back in that peculiar upward tilt that indicated a negative in Greece. "Not as far as I know."

"What about Angelo Hatsis?" Dion asked.

Athena pursed her lips. "Angelo is a distant cousin of my mother's, much younger, of course. You've got business with him, have you? Strange, he doesn't receive many visitors." She pulled the gate wider. "Come in and have coffee. Angelo won't be fit for company until noon, and probably not even then. He stayed at the tavern until almost dawn. I know, because I heard him stumbling home when I got up to take a pill for my arthritis."

She made the coffee on a little gas burner in a tiny kitchen that was neat to a fault. A cat sunned itself on the doorstep, lolling bonelessly on a rag rug. A magnolia filled the still air with delicate perfume, its blossoms already dropping to lie like pale pink snow on the stone floor of the yard.

"You're a doctor, and you've been living in Korfalli," Athena said as she put the tray with the coffee things on the table. She had removed her head scarf, the long braids hanging down over the front of her faded dress.

"How did you know that?"

Athena laughed. "You should know by now that a foreigner living in this area would be talked about, especially if she's single, attractive and blond." Athena reached over and touched Solange's hair. "So soft and pretty. Rare."

"You're blond."

"Our family came from Epirus. There's a fair-haired strain up there."

"If you knew who I was, why didn't you contact me? Tell me you knew my mother."

Athena closed her eyes, her face sorrowful. "I thought of it many times. But I wasn't sure if you wanted to know about her. For all I knew, your mother might have made you hate her family. Heaven knows, she had enough reason, the way they kicked her out as if she'd never been part of them."

"She never said anything bad about her family." Nor anything good, either, Solange realized. She'd rarely talked about them at all. As a child, Solange had asked about them, and her mother had given her the bare facts. Later, as she grew up, Solange had stopped asking, sensing the distress it had caused her mother. "What was my mother like as a girl? How did they live? She never talked about life before she came to Canada, except in the most general way. Once she told me how much she loved the summer when the sun was hot and the apples ripening on the trees."

"Yes, she did." Athena's voice was soft, quiet with reminiscences. "She loved to be outdoors. She was like a wild colt or some woodland creature. She had to be free, but her parents were often restrictive. You can understand how they felt with an only child. But Xanthe was headstrong. In fact, no one in the village was very surprised when she ran off with that fellow. The man her father wanted her to marry was so different from her that it would never have worked. Didn't my mother warn her? But Xanthe loved her parents. She would have obeyed them. Xanthe, for blond—even her name suited her. You've got her hair, but then you know that.''

"Yes.'' Solange's voice caught in her throat. "She was almost gray when she died. The illness took the color and the life from her hair.''

"What was it?''

"A rare form of leukemia. She died the year I graduated from medical school. My father has since married again.''

"Do you see him? Family is important.''

Solange smiled slightly. "Not often. He lives in the Bahamas now. He's retired.''

Athena nodded, sipping her coffee. "I'm so glad we could meet—I was once your mother's friend and I wondered what her child would be like. But I knew you'd come sometime. Didn't I say to old Maria just the other day, Solange will come? I saw the pattern in the coffee cup.'' She looked at Dion, smiling at his patient silence. "In a moment I'll call Angelo for you.''

"Does he live with you?'' Dion asked.

"That *methesmenos?* I wouldn't have him here at all if he wasn't family. No, he lives in a little house at the back of the garden. He likes it that way. Drink your coffee. I'll read the grounds for you.'' She got up, rubbing a muscle in her back. "Excuse me. I have to stir my soup. Chicken soup for Sunday dinner.''

Solange and Dion looked at each other. "Do you believe that about the coffee grounds?'' he whispered.

"I don't know. A woman in Korfalli also professes to read the cups and what she sees sometimes—"

"Ah, you've finished your coffee." Athena came back to the table. Taking Solange's cup, she carefully up-ended it in the tiny saucer, then lifted it out and scruti-nized the pattern of the grounds. "Sadness first, but if you're patient and strong, you'll find much happi-ness."

Solange swallowed a laugh. Wasn't that what all for-tune-tellers said?

Athena took Dion's cup and repeated the procedure. This time she didn't speak at once as she stared into the cup. Dion found himself holding his breath, and a pe-culiar apprehension tickled the back of his neck. For a moment he wanted to snatch the cup from her hand and smash it on the floor. He even went so far as to stretch his hand across the table, but pulled back just in time.

The old lady's eyes were suddenly opaque, her ex-pression grim. Lines of strain—or perhaps it was pain—scored her face, deepening the network of wrinkles. "For you I see trouble. There is danger. You are look-ing for a man. No, not Angelo."

"Will I find him?" His throat was so tight that he could hardly force the words past his stiff lips.

"You will find him, but it's better if you give up this quest of yours now. Nothing good can come of it. I see death."

"Mine?" Dion asked with a resigned fatalism. He'd faced that eventuality long ago and dismissed it. If he died, it would be worth it, as long as he fulfilled his vow.

"No, not yours. Although if you go on, you may wish it was yours. A man has already died."

The bottom dropped out of his stomach, and he shiv-ered as if an icy breath had touched him. Mavrakis had died. Accident or murder. He didn't want to think about it, think that he might be responsible.

"Stop now." The old lady's voice rose. "Before it's too late."

"I can't stop," he heard himself say in a strangled voice. "I can't."

"You must. You must." The cup fell from her hand and crashed to the tile floor, shattering. Athena's thin body sagged back in the chair. After a long, tense moment, she opened her closed eyes. "I'm sorry. I'll call Angelo."

She ran from the room as if demons chased her.

Solange looked at Dion. He was slumped in his chair, his face white. "Dion," she said gently, "it's just superstition."

The smile he attempted looked more like a grimace. "I know. Just superstition."

"You can't take it seriously."

"I'm not." He forced a laugh. Getting up from the chair, he fetched the broom from the corner by the door. Methodically he began to sweep up the broken china, finishing by wiping the congealed coffee grounds with a wet cloth. The floor was clean. If only he could wipe out the future Athena predicted as easily. And the questions written all over Solange's face.

"Let's go outside," he muttered, taking her arm. "I need some air."

Solange sat down on an uncomfortable wooden bench under the magnolia while Dion paced restlessly around the yard. Down the hill a church bell harshly clanged the hour, and farther away, in Kissos, another tolled with a more mellow sound. At the house across the street a child played in the garden, her quiet singing an incongruous counterpoint to Dion's tension that was almost a suppressed violence.

Solange let out a long breath when Athena reappeared from behind a hedge with a stooped, aging man in tow. He was dressed in what appeared to be pyjama tops and a pair of black wool pants. His hair stuck out all over his head, and his jaw was dark with two days of beard stubble. As soon as he saw Dion, he left off his grumbling and stood up straighter, his stiffened muscles managing only a parody of military stance. "Yes? You wanted to talk to me?"

Get it over with so I can go back to bed. Dion heard the words beneath the conventional phrases. "Yes. Did you know a man named Costas Mavrakis?"

Hatsis's mouth twisted, and he spit into a flower bed. "Mavrakis? That coward. He could only follow orders, no matter who gave them. Lucky I only had to spend a year with him under my command."

A year? If the date of the photo was accurate, that year wasn't even significant. Disappointment tasted bitter in Dion's mouth. Still, he had to try. "Do you know where he went after he left your unit?"

"To another unit." The man spit again. "Athena, where's that coffee?"

"I only have two hands," Athena yelled from the kitchen. "It'll be ready in a minute."

"Make it half a minute." Hatsis turned back to Dion. "Why are you asking about Mavrakis? Who are you?"

"Dion Parris."

If he'd expected a reaction, Dion was disappointed. Hatsis fumbled in his pant pocket and drew out a crushed pack of cigarettes and a small box of matches. With shaking hands he took one out, straightened the bend in the middle of it and lit it. Acrid fumes fought with the scent of the magnolias.

"Parris, eh? What do you want with old Mavrakis?"

"I was hoping you could tell me. Mavrakis wrote me a letter, saying he had information for me. I was to meet him last Friday, but he was killed in an accident before we could talk."

A malicious light flickered through Hatsis's bleary eyes. "So he finally got it, did he? I can't say I'm sorry. It's a wonder somebody didn't bump him off years ago."

"Why?" Solange put in, unable to keep quiet any longer.

He seemed to notice her for the first time. He studied her briefly before turning back to Dion. "Pretty woman. Mavrakis was like one of those little dogs that want to play with the big dogs." He puffed on the cigarette and blew out smoke. "You know what I mean. Panting with their tongues hanging out. Can I play? Can I play? He was the one they always got to do the dirty work. One thing, he could be counted on to keep his mouth shut afterward. Probably scared of his own ass."

It came to Dion that whatever Mavrakis had planned to say to him might have more significance than he'd originally thought. Frustration made him clench his teeth, but outwardly he kept his face neutral. "Who's 'they'?"

Hatsis gestured with his cigarette, scattering ash. "The generals, higher officers. The Colonels. I got out as soon as I could. Didn't have the stomach for killing my own countrymen."

"You don't know anything about Nicholas and Zoe Parris."

Athena appeared with a tray of fresh coffee. Hatsis took one of the cups and drained it at a swallow, wiping his mouth with the back of his hand as he put it down. "Your parents, I suppose. Never heard of them. Like I said, I quit when things went crazy, about '68, '69."

He was telling the truth, Dion realized. Too early. Before he could frame his next question, Hatsis spoke again. "I got out and went to Germany. They wanted factory workers. Lived there for ten years." He laughed, a harsh sound that would have made a crow's caw sound musical. "Cold country. Gave me a taste for beer, though. When things got better here, I came back."

He glanced at the tray, the untouched cups obviously meant for Dion and Solange. "D'you want the coffee?"

Dion shook his head. "Take it if you want."

"Thanks." The man drained the two cups in quick succession, afterward lighting another cigarette. "Sorry I can't be of more help."

"There is one more thing," Dion said. "Did you ever hear of a Lambros Pavlou?"

The man's unhealthily pale face lost whatever color it had left. "Pavlou?" He choked and began to cough, a harsh, racking smoker's cough that made Solange wonder if she shouldn't have brought her bag. She stood up and started toward him, but he waved her back, wheezing into a soiled handkerchief. "I'm all right."

He stabbed out the cigarette and straightened in his chair, his eyes hard. "Pavlou is a psychopath. He enjoyed the killing. And the other little diversions that were officially against the law, but nobody paid that much attention. The news that leaked out kept the people from fighting back too hard. But Pavlou loved it, the power, the chance to— Never mind, it's not for women's ears. Or men's, for that matter. What do you want with Pavlou?"

"Is he alive?"

"He's alive. Someone like him doesn't die and rid the world of his worthless carcass."

"Where is he?"

Hatsis shrugged. "God may know. Or the devil. Unless Pavlou is the devil as we used to think he was. Last I heard he was living in some town in Thessaly, but that's years ago." He lit another cigarette. "That's all I know."

All? Dion wanted to yell, to shake the man until he remembered more, but instead he could only sit as if paralyzed. This was his last lead. What town in Thessaly? There were literally hundreds, perhaps thousands.

"I can't help you." Hatsis lurched to his feet. "Athena, when's the soup going to be ready?"

Athena came back out. "Won't you stay to eat? There's plenty."

Somehow Solange doubted that. She looked at Dion, her heart turning over at the sick look on his face. "No, I think we'd better be on our way." She offered her hand to Hatsis, who gave it a limp shake. "I want to thank you for your kindness to my friend Amelia in Korfalli when her son was killed. She appreciates the cards, your keeping in touch."

The strident laugh erupted once more. "That's Athena's doing. She felt sorry for the old lady, losing her son like that. Athena never had children of her own."

"Oh." For a moment she was nonplussed, staring at Athena, who said nothing. "Well, goodbye."

"*Adio,*" Athena said softly. She fixed her eyes on Dion, disconcerting him with the wise yet censorious expression in them. "Forget the past, young man. The future is what counts."

THE SQUARE in front of the church was empty except for Dion's little Renault. Still pale, he handed Solange the keys. "Would you drive, please?"

"Sure. Dion, are you all right?"

He didn't answer. They got into the car, and she started it and put it into gear. They bumped down the rocky track past the turnoff to Kissos and were soon on the main road back to Volos.

Dion was silent, his head resting against the window at his side. "Are you feeling ill?" Solange finally asked. His face was white, or as white as one could get with a tan. Little kernels of sweat beaded his upper lip and forehead. He looked as if he were coming down with flu. "Do you want to stop?"

His eyes popped open, and she gasped at the agony she saw in them. "Don't mother me, Solange." He clamped his mouth shut and turned even paler. "Stop the car."

She braked with a screech and pulled over to the side. He was out of the car in a single motion, and in a moment she could hear him being sick in the bushes.

Concerned, she set the hand brake and got out, stepping carefully through the stinging nettles that grew in the shallow ditch. "Dion—"

"Get away from me. You can't help."

She set her jaw. "You're sick—"

"Anyone would be sick."

Bewildered, she could only stare at him.

"I suddenly realized how it must have been for them in the prison."

"For whom?"

"For my parents, of course," he said as if she were a backward child. "God only knows what Pavlou did to them before he killed them."

Dion stumbled back across the ditch and opened the trunk of the car. He reached for the bottle of water he always kept there. The water was tepid, flat and unappetizing, but it moistened his dry mouth. Pouring some into his hand, he splashed his face, then drank deeply, rinsing the bitterness from his throat. If only he could erase the bitterness from his heart as easily.

"I'm going to kill that bastard Pavlou," he muttered without realizing he spoke aloud. "And enjoy doing it."

CHAPTER ELEVEN

"SO THAT'S IT." Everything suddenly fell into place in Solange's mind. "That's what you came to do, isn't it?" Her lips felt stiff, her face wooden. "Are you really doing a book on the Sarakatsani, or is that just a cover? And me, just a smoke screen?"

"I'm really doing a book. I didn't want to involve you, but it just happened." He capped the bottle and returned it to the trunk, closing the lid with a bang that echoed off the mountainside. "I think I can drive now."

She got in on the passenger side, fastening her seat belt. Her numbness was going, displaced by a simmering anger. "Dion, it was a tragedy, but you can't ruin your own life in this quest for revenge."

"He ruined their lives. He *ended* their lives. He has to pay." His voice was adamant.

Solange groped desperately for words to convince him that he was heading for his own destruction. "God will punish him."

"Where was God when they died? Why didn't he stop the killing?"

"I don't know," she cried, echoing the despair of every human who faces life and death and realizes the futility of attempting to control it. "I don't know why children die, either, but they do."

He heard the catch in her voice, and some of his own agony receded. "Is that why you left Montreal, because a child died?"

"Yes."

"Was it your fault?"

"Yes."

"I don't believe it," he said flatly. "You're too good a doctor."

She jerked her head toward him. "How would you know, Dion?"

"I know you. You don't see people as patients. You see them as human beings."

Solange sighed. "Yes. I've never been able to keep that distance and detachment they say doctors should cultivate. That's why I like working here. My patients are also my friends, shopping in the market for potatoes and onions the same days I do."

Dion reached across and squeezed her hand. "Tell me about it."

Her smile was brief and rueful. "Why do I feel you're distracting me from questioning you?"

"Later we'll talk about that. Now let's hear what happened to you."

"An intern we had fell asleep and didn't hear a monitor beeping. I was his supervisor and should have been watching him more closely. The child had stopped breathing, and by the time I realized it, I couldn't revive him. It was my fault."

"It wasn't," Dion retorted.

"The hospital board ruled that it was, and the intern didn't admit his part in it, and the administrator didn't even make him testify. I was in charge. I was blamed."

"Old boy network in action, I suppose." Dion's hands clenched on the steering wheel. "I would have choked it out of him."

Solange looked at him, torn between amusement and exasperation. "Yes, that's your way of handling it. It's not mine. What worked most against me was the hospital administrator's prejudice against female doctors. He considered women far too emotional to make rational decisions, and I confirmed his belief by yelling at him about the institutional, mechanical way he ran the hospital. So I lost my privileges, and he said I was lucky not to be sued for malpractice."

"But you told me you'd been reinstated."

"About a month after the inquiry the intern was caught sleeping on the job again, though this time nobody died. They reopened the case, changed their original verdict and gave back my privileges with an apology."

"I hope you told them what to do with it."

"As a matter of fact, I did," she said with remembered satisfaction. "I'd already made the arrangements to come to Greece with the earthquake relief group. And the final irony is that at the next board meeting the administrator was fired." She sobered. "But it doesn't change the fact that a baby died."

"Could you guarantee that it would have lived, anyway?"

Could she? She would have liked to say yes, but the child had been critically ill, hadn't been expected to last the week. "No," she admitted. "He probably would have died, anyway, but not that night."

"You can't save everyone, Solange." He felt her pain and tried to temper his cynicism but was only marginally successful.

"No," she said. "But we can help. If I didn't believe that, I wouldn't be able to go on living. Any death is a waste."

The tires squealed on the hot asphalt as he executed a sharp turn that would take them past the road to Zagora. The ski field, bare grassy patches on the mountainside, appeared on their left, the idle chair lift a spiderweb of cables threading upward on red-painted pylons.

"We Greeks take death more philosophically than Canadians."

"Do you?" Solange said with a bite to her voice. "Not from what I've seen. You want to personally avenge your parents, make someone pay for their deaths. That's hardly accepting the inevitable."

"That's different. That's—"

"As a people," she went on as if he hadn't interrupted, "you react differently, depending on the individual who dies. But philosophically? Not unless the person is very old. Then, and only then, there's the sense of completion, that death is an inevitable part of life. But when the person is young, there's only a sense of the injustice of it, the pain of loss."

"Then you can understand my pain when my parents died."

"Yes." She backtracked, realizing her quick answer was less than honest. She couldn't understand. Even though her mother had died, and she had experienced all the usual reactions—pain, anger, guilt—she couldn't understand how she would feel if the death had been violent, a senseless murder. "No, I don't understand. No one could understand that without going through it. But I also don't understand this burning need for revenge. It won't bring them back."

His mouth set stubbornly. "I know that. But the man has to be punished. He's already had almost twenty years more than he gave them. If he'd been locked up after the new government took over, I might have been satisfied. But he's been free all these years. My parents died for nothing."

"Not for nothing, Dion. They must have done something to have come to the regime's attention. That means their deaths would have made an impact, might have inspired others to carry on the fight."

"It inspired nothing," Dion stated flatly. "Didn't you hear Hatsis? He'd never even heard of them."

"How could he have when he wasn't even in the country? It's wrong, Dion, what you're planning. It's wrong and pointless. And it may end up with you in jail."

"Not if I handle it right."

"Going to the law and presenting your case is the only way to handle it right, Dion."

"They won't listen. I couldn't even get into the army records, remember? And look at Amelia's son's death. A highly convenient accident, if you ask me. And nobody's ever investigated it. They're sweeping that whole area under the rug. They don't want to hear about it."

For that she had no answer, and it was futile to argue with him when anything she said was only going to make him more stubbornly sure he was right.

In a way he was, she admitted deep inside her. A murderer should be punished. But not this way. She stared sightlessly at the passing scenery, the perfect summer day. It would be better if she spent her energy thinking of a way he could achieve his goal through the conventional channels. But convincing him wouldn't be easy.

They drove in silence for a time, reaching the twisting road through Portaria, just north of Volos, before Dion spoke again. "This kind of leukemia that your mother had—is it hereditary?"

As soon as the words left his mouth, he wondered why he'd asked them. The philosophy of life he'd adopted and stuck to had been to travel light, no emotional baggage, no attachments. Why should he care about her mother's illness when Solange had no part in his future?

"Why, are you thinking that I might get it, and you'll be rid of me?"

Her flippant question hid the deep hurt she felt. He knew it and wished he wasn't the cause of it. "No, Solange, I just wondered."

Solange let out her breath in a sigh. "No, it's not hereditary. I'm no more likely to get it than anyone else."

He kept his eyes on the road, edging the car close to the wall on the right in order to allow an approaching truck room to negotiate the tight curve. "I'm glad, Solange," he said quietly at last. "Believe me, I'm glad."

Volos lay below them, a city of modern buildings and not much obvious charm, sweltering under a heat haze. Dion didn't remember much of Volos from his childhood, but in the short time he'd been back, he'd grown to like it. It was a city that combined graciousness with a lively, forward-looking attitude, its economy strong, thanks to the burgeoning agriculture in the surrounding area and the growing shipping industry at its harbor.

The traffic was mercifully light, Sunday dinner in progress. In the evening the waterfront would be crowded.

"Do you want to stop for something to eat?" he asked.

"Where can you get anything on a Sunday noon? Everyone eats at home. Why don't we just continue to my house? I've got some pork chops that won't take long to cook."

Was that a good idea? Dion wondered. Although a truce seemed to be in force for now, all they had to do was get back on the subject of his past and his dubious future and they would be fighting again.

Stopped at the traffic light on the Larissa road, he glanced at Solange. She met his eyes with a challenge in hers. No, if he refused, she would think him a coward. He frowned, wanting to resist the pull she had on his emotions, but was unable to. Unwilling to.

"All right." He rammed the car into gear and sent it into a sweeping left turn, tires squealing.

"Such a gracious acceptance," Solange muttered.

He couldn't help the amusement that against all odds rose in him. "Thank you, Dr. Richards, for your kind invitation. There, is that better?"

"Much." She fidgeted with her hands in her lap for a moment. "Dion, I just want to say, uh, I'm sorry about what happened, with your parents, I mean. It was presumptuous of me to tell you what to do, or rather what not to. In your position I might feel the same way. I really can't predict something like that."

"Well, thank you," he muttered, wondering what had caused such a reversal.

"But I still think you should do it a different way," she rushed on. "What you're planning will only lead to a lot of trouble."

His jaw clenched. "My trouble, Solange. My trouble."

That was his final word. He dropped her off at her house and sent the little car roaring off down the street, barely giving her time to close the door. Solange looked after him as the dust slowly dissipated, her heart in turmoil.

KYRA CALLED the office on Monday morning, saying she was expected home right after school and couldn't make the appointment. "But you should find out," Solange protested.

"If I'm not, the test won't be necessary. If I am, a few days won't matter."

"If you are, you'll need to know certain things, like whether you need vitamins or iron—"

"Another time. I'll call you." The girl's voice was firm. "I have to go now. My father's coming down for breakfast."

"Damn." Solange muttered as she heard the click of the receiver being replaced.

The morning was a busy one, especially since Penny had the day off. The stream of patients, both with appointments and without, didn't let up until half past one. Solange had just settled into her desk chair with a sigh when Litsa came bouncing through the door on her way home from school. Oh, no, not another one, Solange groaned silently, irrationally.

"*Kali mera*, Dr. Solange," Litsa said cheerfully. "Have you heard about Kyra?"

Kyra? Solange's thoughts skittered wildly. Had Kyra confided in Litsa then? "What about Kyra?" she asked, forcing a smile.

"We just heard that she's made such a good mark in her English exam that she may be chosen for a trip to England. If she does as well on her final, she's sure to be."

Solange relaxed marginally. "How does her family feel about this?"

Litsa frowned. "I don't think they know yet. Her father..." Her voice trailed off. "Her mother would encourage her to go. She has relatives there, where Kyra could stay. But her father will probably give her trouble. He doesn't want her to go to university, either, and that's only in Athens."

So that was general knowledge. Knowing the active grapevine, Solange wasn't surprised. "How long would this trip last?" If Kyra went away, had the baby and gave it up for adoption, her parents might never find out. Solange and Penny would keep her secret. As for the ethics of such a course of action, the girl being a minor...well, Solange decided, she would worry about that when the time came. If it came.

"Probably a year," Litsa said.

Plenty of time. If the relatives in England went along with it, no one in Korfalli need ever know. Was that going to be the solution? It might well be the easy way out, though there was Kyra's young lover to be considered. Solange suddenly realized she'd never asked the girl if he knew about the baby.

And where did it leave Litsa? "Will that change your plans? Kyra was going to share an apartment with you, wasn't she?"

Litsa shrugged. "It wouldn't matter. I think this is a wonderful opportunity for her. I can always get someone else for a roommate. I wish I could go with her, though. But I'm a klutz at languages."

"And a math and science genius, from what I hear," Solange said with a smile.

Litsa blushed. "Thank you." She shifted her book bag to her other hand. "I'd better get going then and do my homework. *Adio.*"

"*Yassou,* Litsa," Solange said absently, pulling a stack of files closer. She stopped in midreach. "Oh, by the way, Litsa, how's your friend Helena?"

"She's fine. Her aunt introduced a boy from Mavrolofos to her family, and they're talking about an engagement as soon as school is over."

"Is Helena happy about it?"

Litsa shrugged. "She seems to be. He's just finishing his military service—the air force. She thinks he looks dashing in his uniform. It doesn't take much to make Helena happy."

Lucky Helena, Solange thought. "I guess we need some people like that," she said dryly. "Give my regards to your mother, Litsa. I probably won't see her until at least this evening. I've got a lot of work to finish here."

The girl left, but Solange found it hard to concentrate. She stared at the tan file covers without seeing anything. What was she going to do about Kyra?

And about Dion.

He was so determined, so set on his vendetta. And if he accomplished his mission, she knew it wouldn't make him feel better. Her own experience with the hospital administration had shown her that. She'd felt a brief moment of triumph when the intern had been found responsible and her own position reconfirmed, but she couldn't have gone back to work there even if she hadn't made her other plans. Despite the written apology, hard feelings remained. Revenge wasn't sweet; it was bitter and pointless.

SHE WAS MAKING a salad for her lunch an hour later when there was a quiet knock on her door. Kyra, perhaps? Below her, the household had settled down sometime ago for their afternoon rest. Heat, like a dense smothering blanket, lay heavily over the land, wilting blossoms and turning the wheat golden in the fields. Solange wiped sweat from her face with a paper towel as she headed toward the door. She'd never seen it this hot in late May.

Dion stood on the landing, his fist raised to knock again. His smile, when she opened the door, was faintly uncertain, as if he wasn't sure how he'd gotten there.

"Dion, what a surprise." After their parting yesterday, she hadn't expected to see him again. In fact, on her run that morning, she'd avoided passing his house, for her own protection as much as to save him embarrassment. She didn't think she could stand it if he snubbed her.

Yet here he was.

"Can I come in, Solange?"

She couldn't resist a little revenge of her own. "So humble. What a change."

He put up his hand. "Solange, please."

Stepping inside, he pushed the door shut. As he came into the brightness of the living room, she noticed for the first time how pale he looked. Mauve shadows lay under his eyes and lines of weariness etched his face.

"Solange, I'm sorry. You don't know the whole story, and I expected you to understand."

Her annoyance, petty, she admitted, faded. "Come into the kitchen. I was just having lunch. Have you eaten?"

"I had a sandwich. I'm all right." He sat down on a kitchen chair heavily, with none of his usual lithe grace.

"Then how about some iced tea?" Without waiting for his reply she went to the fridge and took out the pitcher and the ice, pouring him a tall glass.

"I had a letter today from some government agency, saying they'll deport me unless I give up the search for Pavlou."

Her eyes widened. "Can they do that?"

"No. I'm a Greek citizen. Greeks don't lose their citizenship even when they're naturalized in another country."

"But in the past undesirables have been exiled."

He smiled faintly. "Yes, but as it happens the letter came from the wrong agency."

"How do you know?"

He took a long drink from the glass she handed him. "I wasn't my parents' son for nothing. No, I think someone must have known about Mavrakis, that he wrote to me. This letter was dated a day after his, so it was before I went to see him."

"Does it mention him?"

"No, but that would be too revealing."

Solange picked up her fork. "I suppose. Well, if they can't deport you, there's no problem, is there? And the police are working on Mavrakis's death."

"Yeah. But I'm willing to bet they don't find much. Whoever is behind this is pretty clever. But that's not what I came to see you about, Solange."

"Oh? What is it then?" She began to eat, relishing the tart flavor of the mayonnaise that dressed the mixture of potatoes, beets and other vegetables, a dish inexplicably called Russian salad.

"Eat first, Solange. It's not urgent."

Taking his glass with him, he wandered into the living room. He adjusted the blind, although as far as Solange could see, it was perfect already. Going over to the bookcase, he pulled out a book on anatomy, examined the cover and put it back. He sank down on the sofa, only to jump up again at once and pace around the room.

"Why are you so jumpy?" Solange asked, putting her empty plate into the sink.

"Jumpy?" He gave a faint laugh. "Must be lack of sleep."

"Lack of sleep?" That explained the circles under his eyes.

"Yeah. I couldn't sleep last night." He hesitated, and Solange waited. "I thought about what you said...." His voice trailed off.

"Does that mean you've changed your mind?"

"I don't know." He sat down, rolling the glass between his palms. "I have cause, you know."

Solange took a seat in the chair opposite. "I don't doubt it, but it's not right to take the law into your own hands."

"What if the law can't touch the guilty person? For me this is a matter of honor and of justice."

The same argument he'd used yesterday. "Keep hammering until somebody listens. That's what I had to do."

"Your situation was different." He took a long drink from his glass, then raised his eyes to meet hers squarely. "I saw them die."

"You saw them die?" Heat washed through her, followed at once by an eerie chill and a sinking away of her stomach. "You were there?" She could hardly force her words past the hurting constriction in her throat. "Oh, Dion."

She would have run to him, but he stopped her with an imperious gesture of his hand. At the moment he couldn't bear her sympathy. If she touched him, he would shatter into a thousand pieces. "I was there. I saw the soldiers shoot them like ducks at a fair, dump their bodies into a ravine and start the rock slide that buried them forever."

Solange closed her eyes, his stark words creating a more vivid image than a film could have. "Dion, I'm so sorry. You were young, weren't you?"

"I was sixteen. I'll never forget it as long as I live." His tone made the words almost an accusation.

"Dion," Solange cried in pain, "I wouldn't expect you to forget it. Putting something behind you isn't the same as forgetting. It's just a letting go and moving forward."

He shook his head. "I can't move forward until this is resolved. Can't you see that?"

"There are other ways to go about it."

"None of them will work in this case. I have to find the man and—" he faltered "—punish him."

"By killing him."

Dion inclined his head, not bothering to deny it. "If necessary."

"As I said before, it won't bring your parents back. Have you asked yourself if they would want you to do this?"

"I didn't need to ask them. I made a vow."

"Dion, you were sixteen. After what you saw, it's no wonder you wanted revenge. But you weren't really responsible."

"I knew what I was doing. I knew what the soldiers were doing. It was Easter. Easter was late that year. The poppies were just coming into bloom on that mountain. Afterward I could hardly look at them without thinking they looked like drops of blood. Do you know what it's like, every Easter, to relive this?''

This time she didn't offer the easy platitudes. ''No, I don't. I can't even imagine. I guess I've had a sheltered life. It's easy to think of violence as something seen on TV that touches other people but not us.''

''It touches people. When it happens to you, or to someone you love, it rips out your guts and changes your whole life.'' He slammed his fist down on the arm of the sofa. ''Why did they have to die? Their only crime was to question and to make others question. No one has a right to absolute power over another.''

''How was it that both your parents came to the attention of the regime? What did they do?''

''They were writers. My father worked for one of the big Athens papers, and my mother was a novelist. She'd written a fictionalized version of student uprisings and the violence the military used to quell the demonstrations. The Colonels took exception to it, banned the book, although it was subsequently published in England and later translated into other languages.''

Solange's eyes lit up. ''Of course. Z. N. Parris. I didn't make the connection. We took that book in senior high literature. It's a wonderful book. You mean that happened?''

''Yes, it happened. I was, of course, too young to be involved or I might have died under a tank, too. As it was, my parents died. My father also wrote against the regime, even after they bombed our car as a warning. They only wanted to change things by peaceful means, by making people think. Look where it got them. Now do you see why I have to do this?''

''I understand, Dion, but—''

"There's always a but, isn't there? We Greeks don't give up."

"No, and that's why feuds go on for generations, even after everyone's forgotten what started them. I could never condone that. After a while it seems ridiculous to continue the animosity."

"This isn't ridiculous."

"No, it's not. It's just so sad."

He looked startled. "Sad? In what way?"

"That a man of your intelligence and your potential would risk his future on a vendetta that's futile." She dragged in a deep breath, discouraged by the hard set of his face. "Maybe you won't find this Pavlou. How long will you look?"

"Until I find him," Dion said stubbornly. "And I will. I spent the night going over every piece of paper in that packet from Mavrakis's flat. I found something that might be important—a record of several payments to a monastery northwest of here in the mountains."

"Payments to a monastery?" Solange frowned. "From what Hatsis said about Mavrakis, he didn't seem the kind of man who would support a monastery."

"That's what I thought. But I don't know if the payments were from him. The receipts didn't indicate who made them. But they were with his stuff. I tried to phone the place, but the lines are down. I'll try again tomorrow. I'm going to tackle the military records again, too, the regional ones. Pavlou must have served with Mavrakis at sometime, since Mavrakis wanted to speak to me. There must be a record. I'm going up to Larissa tomorrow to check at the base there."

"It'll be a hot trip. In Larissa the temperature has been running into the middle forties."

A brief smile touched his lips. "I can take it. Thanks, Solange." He got up and started for the door.

"Wait," Solange called, making up her mind. If she couldn't sway him from this path to self-destruction, perhaps she could defuse the cause. "I'll help you find this man. I make rounds to the villages between here and Farsala. I'll ask. If the man is in this part of Thessaly, I'll find him."

Dion gaped at her, then frowned as a questioning look crossed his face. "Why, Solange? Why the sudden turnaround?"

"Because I want to see this man for myself and get his side of the story."

Dion's shoulders sagged. "You don't believe me?"

"Oh, I believe you, but maybe you're after the wrong man. Even though Pavlou was an officer, someone had to give him orders."

"Don't you think I know that?" Dion cut in impatiently. "I have to find Pavlou, not only because he was directly involved, but also because of what he knows. There is another man, someone who has power, probably even to this day. Pavlou can give me his name. Then I'll have the right man."

CHAPTER TWELVE

THE WEEK LIMPED BY, a busy one that left Solange with little time to see Dion. He was on her mind constantly, especially when she drove to the isolated villages hidden in folds of the hills north, south and west of Korfalli. At home an outbreak of chicken pox kept both her and Penny busy advising calamine rubs and doses of aspirin substitute. To compound matters, several schoolchildren had turned up with head lice, a common affliction in warm weather.

By the end of the week Solange was ready for a Caribbean vacation. She laughed ruefully as she mentioned it to Penny and Aphrodite. "And this is the country where Europeans come to find the sun and the sea. Ironic, isn't it, that we have to work so hard?"

Tourist season had barely started, but the wheat harvest was in full swing, bringing with it the usual minor injuries. The town was inundated with strangers as lean and dark as Gypsies, who drove the huge green, yellow or red combines, working for wages or a share of the crop. The hot days and dry nights hummed with noise, as if the whole town lived in the middle of a factory.

Sunday afternoon, a week after her trip to Pelion with Dion, Solange sat on her shady back balcony dozing over a book when heavy footsteps pounded into the garden. She leaned over the rail to find Apostoli the plumber looking severely agitated. "Dr. Solange," he called in a stage whisper, mindful of Demetra's family having their siesta, "it's an emergency. A man has been hurt in the fields. He caught his arm in a baler."

Solange felt the blood drain from her face. She dreaded machinery accidents. A moment's inattention and a man lost a hand or an arm or a leg. "Just a minute. I'll get my bag and be right down."

She stopped to change her shorts for jeans, which would protect her legs in the prickly stubble fields, stuffed her bag with extra bandages and antibiotics, and ran out the door.

The baler stood in the middle of a small field of cut alfalfa, surrounded by the group of men, some of whom were crouched around a figure on the ground. In the wheat field adjacent two combines, abandoned by the drivers, waited like cumbersome, prehistoric monsters.

"Thank God it wasn't someone with a combine," Solange muttered as the pickup truck turned into the field, the cut grass scraping against its undercarriage. One year she'd seen a man drawn through the entire mechanism. Mercifully he had died almost at once.

"Baler's bad enough," Apostoli said laconically. He was a quiet man, strong and reliable, the best plumber in town.

Jumping down almost before the truck stopped, Solange ran across the stubble. To her surprise Dion knelt at the injured man's head, sponging his face with water from a canvas jug.

"Is it bad?" she asked, unsnapping her bag and taking out her stethoscope. Her fingers were already taking the man's pulse on the uninjured arm. She placed the flat circle against the man's chest, listening intently. His heartbeat was strong, precluding shock.

"There's little to see," Dion said calmly. "He was reaching to remove a stick jamming the packer section. The stick snapped and the packer closed on his arm. That's not supposed to happen—there's a safety catch—but something must have gone wrong."

Accidents were always the result of something going wrong, Solange thought grimly.

The injured man, whom she recognized as Spiros Dakkas, moaned faintly as she tucked the stethoscope back into her bag before turning her attention to his left arm. There was surprisingly little blood, but the arm was swollen to twice its normal size and was rapidly turning a livid purple from broken vessels under the skin.

"We'll have to take him to Volos. He needs X rays before we can determine how bad the injury is."

At the sound of her voice Spiros opened his eyes, focusing with difficulty. "Dr. Solange." His voice was thready with pain. "Please, don't let them cut off my arm. My children—"

Yes, he had five children and was the sole means of support for his family. "I'll do my best, Spiro. Don't worry." She filled a syringe, deftly expelling the air from the needle. "I'm just going to give you something for the pain." Rolling up the sleeve on his good arm, she injected the painkiller.

She fastened a sling around the injured arm, binding it close to the man's chest. While she worked she was aware of Dion quietly and efficiently dispersing the crowd and sending someone for a taxi. She applauded his sense; both her car and his were too small, and an ambulance, sent out from Volos, would take far too long. The sooner the injury was treated, the better the chance for recovery.

Solange sat back on her heels, repacking her bag. "Dion, I'll go with him in the taxi. I wonder if you could tell his wife and bring her to the hospital. She lives—"

"I know where she lives," he said promptly. "And I'll be glad to."

TWO HOURS LATER Solange sat in a noisy waiting room, her arm around Marina, Spiros's plump and pretty wife. Their youngest child, a toddler, clung to his mother's skirt, eyes round and apprehensive. When the child grew restless, Dion, seated at Solange's other side, picked him up and cuddled him close.

Patients came and went, the organized chaos typical of an emergency waiting room. "You didn't have to stay, Dion," Solange whispered.

"I do now," he said softly, ducking his head to indicate the child who had fallen asleep on his lap. "I don't want to wake him."

Another hour passed before the orthopedic surgeon came in. At the sight of him, fatigue-lined face above sweat-stained hospital greens, Marina gave an incoherent cry and sprang up from her chair.

The doctor took her shoulders in his hands, squeezing them reassuringly. "Be easy, Madam. Your husband's a strong man. He'll be fine."

"Oh, thank God. Thank God." Tears streamed down Marina's cheeks.

"His elbow may remain a little stiff, but since it's his left arm, that shouldn't cause too many problems." To Solange he added a brief, anatomical description of the injury. "It was mostly pressure damage to the muscle, although there was a bone chipped at the elbow joint. It will need some time to heal, but he should be able to manage light work in about six weeks."

"Thank you, Doctor. Thank you." Marina was in a delirium of relief. "When will I be able to see him?"

"You can see him for five minutes now. In a couple of hours he should be out of the anesthetic. Then you'll be able to talk to him. Do you have somewhere to go? It would be better if you had a rest."

"My cousin is coming. I'm going to her house for a while. Oh, there she is." A worried-looking woman came quickly across the room, enfolding Marina in an embrace.

"Dr. Solange," Marina said after a moment, wiping her eyes, "I want to thank you. I'll be all right now."

"Good. I'll let your children know." Her other children were being cared for by their grandmother, who lived in the house. They would be fine for a couple of days.

DION DROVE HER HOME. "Thanks, Dion, for your help. I really appreciated it."

He shrugged. "Anyone would have done the same."

"Not anyone. Plenty of people panic in an emergency, or they stand around wringing their hands." She pushed open the car door. "Why don't you come up for a moment? I think we could both use some coffee.

"You've started to care about these people, haven't you?" she added as they climbed the stairs and entered her flat.

He realized it was true. In less than a month, despite his resolutions to remain aloof and separate, the townspeople had insidiously woven him into their lives. He was allowed his independence but was already part of their joys, such as the wedding he'd been asked to attend, and their sorrows, such as this afternoon's incident, which fortunately had ended well.

"I thought I wouldn't," he admitted, staring out of her kitchen window as she filled the kettle and put it on the burner. "In fact, I was convinced I couldn't. But it's different here than in Athens. Here people still have time for each other. I like it."

"But not enough to forget this vendetta of yours."

His eyes clouded over, a muscle twitching at his jaw as he clenched his teeth. "Solange, you know the answer to that. It's justice. The guilty have to be punished."

"Have you thought about how it would be if the man you want turns out to be a friend or relative of one of these people who consider you their friend?" she persisted. "Have you thought about that?"

He had, though only since a complication named Solange had come into his life. When he was with her, the hatred he'd carried for so long didn't seem as consuming. He could feel it slipping, weakening, and sometimes it was hard to get it back. Was that what love did?

Love? He pushed the thought away. Once before he'd allowed himself to be deluded by a pseudo-love. He couldn't take the risk, not until it was over. "Solange, I can't forgive this. And I can't forget it."

Solange turned, opening the cupboard door to get out the cups. He reached up and took her hand in his, ignoring the shriek of the kettle as it came to a boil. "Please, Solange, let's not fight about it. I'm sorry you had to find out. I didn't want to hurt anyone."

His voice was rough with a plea that seemed foreign to him, and her heart softened. "The person you're hurting most is yourself, Dion. Can't you see that? Hating is self-destructive. It eats away inside you and ultimately destroys everything that is good. Dion, there's so much good in you. I know it. But this has to stop.

You've been hating for what? Nineteen years? Isn't it time you stopped?''

"I'll stop when Pavlou and whoever gave him his orders are punished."

She handed him his cup of coffee, and they went into the living room. "And if you don't find them?"

"I'll find them. I've given myself a year. Only a month has passed, and I've found all these leads. That's more progress than I made in three months the last time."

"Last time?" Solange's brows lifted. "You've never told me why you didn't pursue it further last time."

"A lot of things happened, but the end result was that I was told that all the leaders of the division involved in getting rid of dissenters were either in prison or dead."

"Executed?"

"Perhaps some, but I don't really think so. At any rate, there was nothing more in the army records, but since the government was going through a state of flux at the time, maybe some of the records were just misplaced temporarily. I met some people, former students who were willing to help me, but in the end their help was more of a liability than an asset. I went back to Canada, thinking there was nothing to be done. Then last winter, I talked with a new professor who's teaching political science at Simon Fraser University. He's quite an expert on Greek affairs and told me there was a cover-up. It was very likely that my man was still around. So I decided to move up the arrangement I'd made to take next year off to study the nomadic tribes of Greece and came here this year."

He related this in a calm, flat tone that told Solange nothing of his feelings. Yet she couldn't shake off the idea that there was more to the story than these bare bones. Perhaps it was his very lack of emotion or the way his eyes avoided meeting hers during parts of the narrative. Who were these former students who had helped him, and why didn't he seek their aid now? After all, they shared a common goal.

"Can't any of the people who worked with you then help you now? You haven't gotten in touch with them, have you? Otherwise you wouldn't have needed to talk to Mavrakis."

He got up and walked over to the window, his face closed and coldly remote. "No. They would be of no use to me, even if I could find any of them."

"You mean they've given up, and you're still carrying on with this exercise in futility? I'm glad somebody had some sense."

Stung by her tone, Dion snapped his head around. "It wasn't like that at all. Their leader died and they disbanded."

An odd inflection in his voice caught at her. "Did you have anything to do with that?"

"Their leader dying? If they were helping me, that's the last thing I would have wanted, isn't it?" He stopped, rubbing his hand across his eyes as if they hurt.

"But you said they were more of a liability."

"I did, didn't I? And they were when their activities came to the attention of the police. Don't forget, I was young, twenty-one, idealistic and politically naive, in spite of my parents. It was easy for the group to convince me that what they were doing would benefit the country. It was only at the end I found out their organization was well on the way toward becoming a terrorist cell and had grandiose plans you wouldn't want to hear about."

"Oh. What happened to their leader? He must have been very powerful to have resulted in their disbanding after his death."

"She was." At her startled gasp he smiled faintly. "Yes, the leader was a woman, Eleni Stamoutas. She held the power and she knew how to use it. Most of the other members were men. That was her specialty, manipulating men."

Bitterness laced his voice, and she knew he was one of the men Eleni had manipulated. "You looked up to her."

"More than that," he said bitterly. "We were close. Or so I thought. I really believed she was sincere until the night I refused to go along with them when they were going to throw a bomb into a popular nightclub frequented by American servicemen. I realized I wasn't cut out to be a terrorist. I only wanted to find the man who'd killed my parents and get on with my life."

"What happened?"

"As soon as they left, I called the police. When I wouldn't give my name, they said they could do nothing, that they received prank calls all the time. So I went to warn the nightclub myself. I arrived just as Eleni and her friends pulled up in a stolen car."

He remembered the night as if the intervening fourteen years had been fourteen seconds.

The Plaka, the old section of Athens, had still been open to car traffic then. Many of the nightclubs had been brashly modernized, the entertainment and decor at odds with the age of the buildings that contained them. Lurid neon lights, since banned, flashed off and on, often in time to the beat of heavy rock music.

He had found the nightclub easily enough. Nodding to the young man who stood outside to advertise the club's amenities, he climbed the steps. At the sound of tires screeching he whirled around. Eleni leaned out the open window of a Mercedes. The neon lights painted her red hair with startling purple highlights, and under it her face was a mask of hatred. In her hand she held a blazing bottle. "Pigs," she screamed, and threw the bottle.

Without pausing to consider his own safety, Dion leaped up and caught the makeshift bomb in his hand before it could fly through the club's open door. He jerked the rag wick from the bottle as the flames licked ravenously over his skin. Clenching his teeth against the pain, he dropped the burning rag and stamped on it. The bottle slipped from his other hand, smashing on the cobbled street, the spilled gasoline igniting into flames that died harmlessly as they consumed the fuel.

Staggering, clutching his scorched hand, Dion collapsed against the side of the building. He was dimly aware of people crowding around him, their concerned voices, someone suggesting they call the police and an ambulance.

"No." He pushed himself away from the wall, shaking his head to clear it. A wave of dizziness threatened to overwhelm him, but he managed to keep his feet. Turning, he ran down an alley, his feet scrabbling on the rough ground as he lurched to keep his balance. Behind him someone shouted and a police whistle shrilled, but by ducking down another narrow lane, crossing a low hedge around a garden and passing through a rubble-covered vacant lot, he soon left his pursuers behind.

Reaching a tiny churchyard that was disturbed only by the singing of crickets, he stopped at the pump, his breath heaving in and out of his lungs. His throat hurt and his eyes stung from the acrid smoke of the burning gasoline.

He looked at his hand, which had mercifully gone numb. Black soot hid most of the damage from his eyes, but on his palm rising blisters already oozed a clear fluid. Grasping the pump handle with his left hand, he awkwardly worked it up and down. Water gushed out and, gritting his teeth against the agony, he thrust his burned hand into the cold liquid.

He thought he could hear his skin sizzle, but that had to be his overwrought imagination. Stuffing his wadded handkerchief into the drain in the little stone sink, he kept his hand under the water, sagging into a sitting position on the ground as his knees gave way. The adrenaline firing his blood receded, leaving a bone-deep weariness that made him want to lean his head on the cold stone and sleep forever, shutting out the horror of people who warred against their own countrymen. He'd stopped them tonight, but what about tomorrow night, and the next, and the next?

"I'm getting out," Dion told them the next day, his words ringing with a hollow echo through the room. He glared defiantly at the raised faces, seeing the various expressions, contempt, derision, a reluctant admiration on one at the back, that of the newest recruit.

Eleni snapped out an obscenity, the livid red of anger washing up her face and into her cheeks. Her eyes glittered with hate. Dion almost reeled under the malevolence she directed at him. "Coward. You haven't the stomach for killing, have you? How would you feel if you knew the man you're seeking is helping to finance this organization, although he's been careful not to let anyone see him? He lives in the house where we've met a few times."

The room spun. The blood pounded at his temples, and he trembled with outrage. Betrayal. All the time they were pretending to help him, they had been hiding the man. He'd been so close. His stomach heaved, and for a moment he thought he would be sick, putting an ignominious finale to the whole episode.

With an effort he'd summoned his control, wrapping it around his emotions with icy precision. In that moment he'd vowed he would never make himself vulnerable again, never give anyone complete trust again.

He came back to the present with a jolt, Solange's overly warm living room spelling security rather than discomfort. Across the street a caged canary sang an ecstatic aria, the liquid beauty of the notes raising goose bumps on his skin.

"And what happened after that?" Solange asked quietly, her expression concerned and curious, registering none of the shock he might have expected.

"I walked out. I was surprised that they let me go. But that wasn't the end of it. I went to the house and found no one there. I planned to try again. And I thought after a reasonable time I might even go to the police with their names, not that I expected to be believed, since I had no proof and the group was constantly changing headquarters. But the very next night, as I walked home, Eleni and a couple of her most besotted goons jumped me. Luckily a drunk stumbled down the alley before they could finish the job. And equally luckily I happened to be near a doctor's house. I made it to his door, and he removed the knife from my belly and sewed up the wound."

"So that's how you got that scar."

"Yeah, a little souvenir."

She sat up straighter, setting down the mug she gripped between her hands. "What happened to the group? You said they disbanded."

"Yes. The following week, while I was recuperating at the doctor's surgery—he'd been a friend of my family and agreed to let me hide there until I could get out of the country—a bomb blast killed Eleni and three core members of the group. I guess they got careless with explosives. I knew I was safe. And what was even more interesting was the fact that they were in the basement of the house that Eleni had mentioned. The owner also died in the fire. According to Eleni, he had to be the man I was looking for, so that's when I gave up the search."

"Did Eleni know the man you were looking for had six fingers?"

Dion nodded. "But I never met this man, and I'm not sure Eleni ever did."

He raked his fingers through his hair, gripping his temples for an instant. His palms were wet, and he dried them on the thighs of his shorts. "I assumed Pavlou died in the fire and only found out different when Stefan told me he was alive later. The death certificate confirms that the man who died in the fire wasn't the Pavlou I want. There's no mention of the extra finger."

"Is it possible that he faked his own death and substituted someone else's body?"

He shifted restlessly, getting up to walk around the room. "I've thought about it over and over, but what seems most likely is that someone else died in the fire and Pavlou took advantage of it and disappeared. On the other hand, Eleni might have been lying when she told me the man financing the group was the one I wanted. She wanted to hurt me, and since she'd lied to me all along, what would one more matter?"

Solange heard the bitterness in his voice and had to ask the question regardless of how much she might dislike the answer. "Were you in love with her?"

His muscles flexed under his tank top as he shrugged. She noticed for the first time that he had a dark smudge on his shoulder that was turning into a bruise, probably from wrestling with the baler to free Spiros's arm. "I thought I was. I'd had no time for women, working and going to school on my own. I was flattered by her attention—what young man wouldn't have been? When we became lovers, I thought it was exclusive and forever, naive that I was. She was probably laughing behind my back at my clumsy efforts and extravagant promises."

"It was a rite of passage." Solange hid the brief, irrational jealousy that grabbed her heart and just as quickly let it go. No man of thirty-five hadn't had lovers. It was just more comfortable not to know about them.

"Yeah," Dion said, his thoughts turning inward. "Stupidity. But I didn't make that mistake again, and I won't."

"But you've told me. You must trust me a little."

He jumped as if the thought startled him. "I did, didn't I? I wonder why... why you're different."

Trust. Meeting Solange had changed him. He had let his guard down with her. And had told her about his past, without considering whether she would use it against him. For all he knew there might be a warrant out for his arrest on charges arising from the bombing incident. Not that that was likely, since he had gone through passport control with no trouble.

You're different. His words hung in the hot room. Solange felt them burrow into her heart with almost the same force as a declaration of love. Perhaps from Dion this was a declaration of love. "How am I different?" she asked softly.

He turned from the window, his eyes seeking hers, their gaze clear and direct, lit from within with blue fire. "Because you don't make judgments. Solange, you care about people. You care about me."

CHAPTER THIRTEEN

CARE? Such a trite term for what she felt. Despite her inability to fully understand his vendetta, much less to condone it, Solange knew she loved him. She was glad, finally, to acknowledge the depth of her feelings, if only to herself.

Perhaps it wasn't wise to love him. She hadn't known him long, yet on some psychic level she felt she'd known him forever.

She loved him.

As for the future—well, that would have to take care of itself. At the moment she couldn't visualize anything beyond the present. Love implied a future, but between her and Dion, the obstacles remained. Only he could remove them. Until then she could only pray that some of what she'd said would make a difference.

He admitted he trusted her. He had told her his story, declared his determination to carry out his vow. Yet she had detected shades of defensiveness in his manner. He was beginning to have doubts, to lose some of the strength of his convictions. She didn't see him as innately vindictive or violent. He was too sensitive in his relations to others for that. No, the wall of hate was beginning to crack. There was hope.

"Yes, I do care, Dion," she said in a quiet voice that hid the deep emotion filling her heart. "And what you've just told me doesn't change that. In fact, it only reinforces my position. What you're planning is wrong. You got into trouble last time but escaped. This time you might not be so lucky."

He sighed heavily. "I know that. Do you think I haven't thought about it, especially since I've known you, with your tolerance and goodness? Solange, can we leave it until I find this man? I promise I won't go off the deep end just like that."

That was more than he would have promised even last week. Solange let out a long breath of relief. "Okay, Dion."

She gathered together their coffee cups and carried them to the kitchen, glancing at the clock. "Why don't we go for a swim? At this hour on a Sunday there won't be a soul at the beach."

He grinned. "Give me a couple of minutes to change, and I'll be back to pick you up."

The fields shimmered in the hot sun, the combines silent in the late afternoon. Behind the car dust plumed up in a banner, dissipating lazily on the breeze and adding another layer to the white mantle coating the roadside shrubbery. The sea was calm, deeply blue, the small, pebbled beach deserted, and their privacy assured.

It was still early in the summer for swimming. Solange was still surprised how rigidly people used the calendar to define the swimming season rather than the weather. After the hot spell they'd been having, the sea had warmed up. Still, tradition died hard. Only crazy people sea-bathed much before the second week of June.

They parked the car and by mutual consent walked along the hard-packed sand at the water's edge. A hundred yards down the beach a small freshwater stream lined by flourishing bamboo ran from a marsh into the sea. Solange lifted the hem of her skirt as she waded across, gasping as the cold water bit into her bare feet. Sharp little indentations in the ground indicated that sheep had been there recently to drink, but the water had already resumed its normal clarity.

"Come on, Dion. Just a little farther. We can leave our towels on the grass."

They came to a small seaside meadow, closely grazed grass surrounded by thickets of reed and bamboo. Tough weeds grew in clumps here and there. What Solange had at first taken for pale stones tangled in their leaves turned out to be snails that clung to the stems.

Dion crouched down and detached one. "We used to use these as bait for fishing when I was a boy. Of course, it was easier then when the sea wasn't so heavily fished. All you had to do was cast a line from the shore. Now the fish seem to stay farther out."

As if to dispute his words, a fish rose in an arc out of the water fifty feet offshore and vanished again with a splash. Solange laughed. "He's making fun of you."

"Probably. They used to do that, too, when I fished— jump out of the sea but never take the hook. All I ever caught was little guys. Ten of them would hardly make a meal."

She shuddered at the idea of unhooking a fish, knowing it was silly to be squeamish when she'd treated the victims of car accidents and sewn up their lacerations without a qualm. "I think I'll stick to the fish market, thank you very much. Someone else can catch and kill the poor things."

Dion smiled and ran his fingertip gently down her cheek and over her jaw, tilting her face up as he dropped a light kiss on her mouth. "You know, you really are a very nice lady."

The demons he'd awakened by relating the story of Eleni had gone back into hiding much quicker than they usually did. Before, when something reminded him of her treachery, he'd always felt depressed for hours. But this time it had seemed less personal. Perhaps the humiliation was fading, becoming part of his past rather than a force in the present.

Solange's doing. When he was with her the hatred he'd nurtured for so long didn't seem as powerful. At first it had alarmed him when he felt it slipping. Sometimes he had to search to get it back.

The idea disturbed him, yet he couldn't seem to stop dwelling on it. He was changing, and so were the philosophies he'd formed for his life and followed all these years. That alone was a revolutionary concept. Was his desire for revenge, his need for it, weakening? He'd deliberately led a solitary life to prevent such a circumstance, but suddenly he was questioning his choices.

He'd never noticed his loneliness until Solange.

He glanced at her. She had dropped the sandals she'd carried next to her towel. Raising her arms, she stripped her loose T-shirt over her head. Her breasts, small but prettily rounded, strained against her blue bikini bra. He remembered how they had felt in the dim candlelight when they'd made love, and wondered if it would be different in daylight under the hot, brilliant sky.

His body stirred at the thought and his lips formed her name. "Solange."

She looked around, tilting her head up from her concentration on her skirt button. "Yes?" Her eyes were the same deep brown as he'd seen in the shadows of the stream, a color that was natural and earthy, warm as the heart they revealed.

Confused by the depth of emotion that made a lump come into his throat, he looked away, pulling off his shirt and unzipping his khaki shorts. He tossed his clothes beside hers and ran for the water, plunging in and stroking out with long movements of his arms. A moment later, as he came up for air, he heard the splash Solange made as she dived in.

She resurfaced next to him, standing in chest-deep water. Lifting her hands, she swept back her long hair, fastening it at her nape with a rubber band she'd carried fastened to her bikini strap. Meeting his eyes, she must have seen the intensity in them. "The water's really too warm, isn't it?" Her voice shook a little, and she bit her lip. "Not refreshing at all."

"It feels like a bath." As soon as the words were out, he realized they only increased the tension between them, the promise of intimacy that he wasn't sure he should act upon. His mission still stood between them. They had made love once, but that was before. Now she knew. Would she still want him, knowing he couldn't renounce his need for vengeance?

Her lips parted, and she staggered a little as the wake from some boat, unseen beyond the horizon, washed against them. "If this is a bath, we're overdressed."

She still wanted him, the desire he couldn't damp down traveling unerringly across the small distance that separated them. His heart sang as he grinned. "Yes, aren't we? I dare you to take some of it off."

Her face lit up with the anticipatory smile of a woman who knew her lover was watching her and wanting her. She unclipped the front clasp of her bikini bra and let the two halves float free. "Anything else?"

"Well..."

"Your turn next."

"Okay," he said. "But let's get a little closer to shore. I don't want to lose our suits."

They waded to hip-deep water, the sun lowering on the horizon behind Solange, creating a golden nimbus around her head.

Dion pulled off his swimsuit, and she did the same, handing both pieces to him to toss onto the shore. They moved together, their bodies sleek in the warm sea. Instant, intense arousal.

He ran his hand over her hips and around to the inside of her thigh, and she trembled, her breath coming out in a gasp. "Dion, please—"

"Please what?"

"Touch me. No, don't. I'm about to explode."

"How do you think I feel?" He took her hand and wrapped it around him, closing his eyes to savor the exquisite sensation.

"Dion," she breathed. "Love me."

He could have lifted her, joined their bodies as they stood in the water, but then it would be over too quickly. Instead, he scooped her up in his arms and waded to the beach. There were pleasures he wanted to give her first.

He put her down on their towels, arranging the bundle of their clothes under her head. The sun's rays slanted over them, heat that no longer burned, touching Solange's skin with gold.

On his knees beside her, Dion gazed at her beauty, the high flush on her cheeks, her mouth slightly parted, rosy, inviting. He accepted the invitation, exploring her with his tongue and lips, tasting her, wanting more.

She kissed him back ardently, her love blazing from her eyes, from the tense yet willing languor of her body as it molded against his. "Let me, sweet. Let me," he murmured when she lifted herself as he moved his mouth slowly down her throat to her breasts. "I want to give you this. It'll be your turn another time."

She tasted of the sea and of flowers weeping their perfume under a spring rain. He could smell the residue of her jasmine scent on the fragile skin beneath her breasts and at her navel. The wet of seawater was being replaced by the slick sheen of sweat, the musky scent of it arousing him unbearably.

He paused, dragging in a deep breath, willing his body under control. He'd never felt a hunger this urgent, never dreamed that sharing this profound act of intimacy with a woman he loved could be so much more than simple sex.

He closed his eyes, the intensity of his hunger to be one with her, body and soul, almost a pain. This was real. This was what he'd never thought to experience. It was frightening. In his heart he knew the agony he'd felt at his parents' death was as nothing compared to what he would feel when Solange turned from him.

As she would when he killed Pavlou. And destroyed his own soul.

She must have sensed his stillness. Questioningly she whispered his name.

"Solange, I'm here." Heedless of danger, he submerged himself in the elemental sweetness that was hers.

Yes, he loved her. Tears stung his eyes, escaping and mingling with the sweat running down his face. She would never know.

He loved her. With a corner of his mind he wished it could be forever. But permanence was not for him. He could find the man tomorrow, could be in prison the next day. He could promise her nothing.

Except this. With a moan that revealed only a portion of his agony he caressed her velvet skin, his hands and his open mouth moving softly over her.

"Yes," he breathed, inhaling the hot scent of her, feeling the quivering of her thighs as he put his mouth against her. She was wet, slick with arousal, and he needed so badly to kiss the soft, secret places that she had offered only to him. He loved the delicious femaleness of her and wondered how he had ever thought he could walk away from her. He wanted her, he wanted all of her, his, forever.

When his tongue touched her, she gasped in surprise. "Dion! Please, Dion! Oh..."

Sparkling lights were spinning through his head. He could feel her trembling, and he nipped gently at her with his lips, then opened his mouth and kissed her with ravishing passion, sweeping his tongue over her, pleasure flaring in him as he felt the convulsions begin inside her.

"Dion," she cried, and he could have wept at the wonder in her voice as she exploded in a million fragments of ecstasy.

Before the last quiver died he moved up, burying himself deep within her, catching the final aftershocks that were strong enough to send him over the edge. With a cry of triumph he let go of his control and gave the utmost of his love.

"OH, MY," Solange said after an interval that might have lasted moments or might have been hours. "Oh, wow."

Dion laughed, a rumble that seeped into her ear as she lay with her head cushioned on his chest. "Yeah, wow."

Around them the sky had taken on a lucent deep blue color as the sun slipped below the horizon. The sea lapped serenely, a rhythmic shushing that emphasized their isolation. Far away Solange could hear the musical tinkle of sheep bells, and an errant breeze stirred the bamboo fronds near their heads, clattering the leaves so that they sounded like distant voices.

Peace. It settled into her, entering all her cells as if it meant to stay. Not only a sense of well-being from Dion's loving pervaded her body and soul, but a sense of rightness, a conviction that she belonged. Not just here, but anywhere with him.

If only he wasn't so set on destroying what they had and himself along with it. Ruthlessly she pushed the thought aside, slamming the door to the back room of her mind and locking it.

Not fast enough, for she shivered a little. Dion, mistaking the faint tremor, propped himself on his elbow, his palm resting comfortably at her waist. "Cold? We can take another swim. The water's so warm."

She shook her head. "No, I'm not cold. Just thinking."

He flopped back, pulling her in close to his body. She snuggled up, savoring the warmth of his skin, the faint stickiness of drying sweat that made the contact even more intimate. Their bodies had joined, their sweat had mingled, their scents mixed until they were identical. A oneness such as theirs should last an eternity.

"We ought to get back. Demetra knows we came back from Volos. She'll wonder where we are if we're not at the square for the evening promenade." Solange smiled. "She'll be thinking all kinds of things."

Against her cheek she felt the corner of his mouth turn up. "Does it bother you?"

g every spare moment studying for those infer-
ns.''

and Litsa were deep in conversation, their heads
r as they walked, their hands entwined in the
ss that Solange had found so foreign when she'd
rived in Europe but now accepted as common-

hey came abreast, the girls smiled and said hello.
, how is your work going?'' Demetra asked.
're welcome to come and study with Litsa, you
''
.
know,'' Kyra said with a shy smile. ''But my fa-
ikes me to come straight home from school.''

e girls moved on, and Demetra shook her head. ''I
t understand the man. Kyra is a good girl, but he
s her as if—well, I don't like to say. But it's so un-
She's such a good student and she may not even
e the chance to go to university.'' She threw up her
ds. ''And I thought only grandparents kept up these
fashioned ideas that going to university would ruin
l for marriage and family.''

olange murmured some reply, her mind on Kyra's
sical health. The girl looked pale, and her wrist bones
collarbone were far too prominent. She'd lost weight
e the day she'd visited Solange's flat. And she'd
er come in for the pregnancy test. If she was indeed
ecting a baby, she had to have some prenatal care,
fast, by the look of things.

hey made the turn at the end of the plaza and started
k. The crowd was thinning slightly, keeping a lan-
d pace that suited the early summer night.

hen Solange felt her senses prickle to alertness as
eone cried out ahead of them. Demetra paused in

''No. That's what everyone had in mind when you
first arrived—to get us together.''

''It worked.''

Frowning, she lifted herself on one elbow. ''As long
as you didn't feel pressured.''

Dion lazily traced the tan lines along the slope of her
breasts. ''No, I didn't feel pressured. Not by your
friends. I felt pressured by my own reaction to you. Solange, you made me question. You're still making me
question.''

Hope surged in her. If he questioned, he might give up
his senseless vendetta. But she was careful not to pursue
the matter. They could argue another time. Right now
she wanted to savor the pleasure of being with him.

Dion's mind was following another track. ''Did you
ever think, when you were young, that you would be lying on a beach in Greece someday with a man like me?
Did you ever dream about the future?''

''Sure I thought about the future.'' She lifted one arm,
draping it around his neck to give him freer access to her
breast. ''I thought I would be a respected doctor, one
with a practice in some large Canadian city. I would have
time for research into prenatal care.'' She sighed as his
touch began to arouse her again. ''Dion...''

''Hmm?''

''Yes, keep doing that.''

''If you'll keep talking. There are so many things I
want to know.'' And perhaps little time left to hear them.
''Didn't you ever see a man in your future, even one you
would have a grand affair with, something to write in
your memoirs?''

''Only in my memoirs?'' Her breath shortened.
''I...think...if I met a man for a grand affair, I'd fight
to keep him.''

His caressing hand slowed, stopped when it reached her chin. He tipped her head up. "Solange, look at me."

She forced her heavy eyelids up, meeting the intense dark blue of his eyes, the identical shade the sky had taken on now that twilight was fading into night. "Solange, would you fight for me?"

She didn't hesitate. "Yes, Dion," she said fiercely. "I'd fight for you. Isn't that what I've been doing?"

"And you want to win." A brief sadness passed over his face and was gone as he lowered his head toward her. "Solange, just think of now, this moment, the love..."

The words drifted away as she gave herself up to the tenderness of his renewed caresses.

THE TOWN SQUARE was crowded by the time they returned to Korfalli. They went to their own houses to shower and dress, meeting at the main street to walk together past the lighted shop windows to join the Sunday promenade.

Demetra, accompanied by her son Taki, who was dressed and scrubbed and combed to an inch of his life, spotted them and hurried over. "I'd almost given you two up for lost. Solange, Marina phoned earlier. Spiros has come out of the anesthetic. He's complaining to the doctors already, says he wants to go home. Marina has threatened to tie him to the bed."

"Good. I'll be going to see him in the morning. Penny's taking the office."

"She's here somewhere if you want to talk to her," Demetra said. Her voice dropped conspiratorially. "She's with a man, a man who drove here in a Mercedes."

"Oh, probably Vangeli's cousin," Solange said with pretended nonchalance. Penny had been unusually si-

---

lent after her dinner with the man e[...] lange, eaten up with curiosity, had [...] the nerve to ask her directly. But now [...] Penny that was unprecedented. "He'[...] in Thessalonika," she explained whe[...] her brows.

"Well, maybe there's hope for her.[...] knowing look from Solange to Dion [...] "How about you two? Off together hal[...] coming back wet and bedraggled. Cou[...] thing." She arched a brow at Dion. "Do[...] you'll be staying in Greece?"

A shadow passed over his face, along [...] grin. "It's too early to tell. I'm working o[...]

Demetra laughed, enjoying his discomf[...] none of my business, right?"

"It seems to be everyone's business here [...] forgotten that."

"Gossip," Demetra admitted while Ta[...] "It's the lifeblood of small towns." She gla[...] at the boy, ruffling his smooth dark hair. "G[...] with your friends if you want." Taki left, [...] dately for ten steps before breaking into a [...] spotted a group of children his own age perc[...] low wall around the fountain.

"Where's Vasili?" Solange asked as the thr[...] began to walk slowly down the square.

"He had to check something in the orchar[...] body's been driving a motorcycle through [...] fields. Probably kids, but he wants to know w[...] he can get their parents to lean on them. They [...] one of the irrigation lines last night, causing [...] flood a corner of the field. Wait, isn't that [...] Litsa? I haven't seen that girl in days. Of cours[...]

midstep, her hand clutching Solange's arm. "Was that Litsa?"

"Oh, no." This time the cry carried clearly to them as the crowd slowed and converged on a spot near the fountain.

"Yes, it is Litsa." Demetra began to run, her skirt flaring around her knees. "I wonder what's happened."

Solange ran after her, a dreadful premonition setting her heart pounding in her throat. Kyra. Something had happened to Kyra.

She was right. Litsa sat on the edge of the fountain, her arm tightly around Kyra's shoulders as the other girl sobbed into her palms. Kyra's white skirt had a dark stain along the hem, and blood seeped onto the flagstone floor to gleam wetly in the lamplight.

CHAPTER FOURTEEN

THE SOFT SUMMER NIGHT took on the proportions of a nightmare. "Please stand back," Solange begged as she pushed through the crowd. She spotted Taki, round-eyed with curiosity. "Taki, will you get my bag? You know where it is, in the hall closet. Here are the keys. Hurry."

Solange crouched beside the two girls, the crowd regrouping and hemming them in. The crush of bodies, the chattering of worried voices pulsed around her, making her head pound with an almost claustrophobic anxiety. If she was uncomfortable, what must Kyra be feeling? "Dion, can you make some room for us? And find a blanket?"

Calling on her training, Solange dragged in a long breath and gently lowered the girl to the flagstones. Kyra's arms fell limply to her sides, and her face was so pale that even her lips were colorless. Litsa sank down and cradled Kyra's head in her lap. Tears ran down her cheeks as she tried with shaking hands to arrange Kyra's dress so that the bloodstains were hidden.

"It's all right, Litsa," Solange murmured with a calm she hardly felt. "Don't cry."

She realized she couldn't do a proper examination here, and even if it were a simple miscarriage, it would be better if a gynecologist checked the girl out. Looking up, she was relieved to notice that Dion had convinced the crowd they had business elsewhere. "Demetra, could you find Kyra's parents and phone Dr. Andropoulos. He should be at home.''

"Of course, Dr. Solange.'' Shaking her head but offering no comment, Demetra set off toward the nearest kiosk, her expression sober.

Dion touched Solange's shoulder, and she gratefully accepted the blanket he handed her and wrapped it around the girl. Lifting her skirt slightly under its cover, she noted that the bleeding had eased somewhat. As sparing as possible of the girl's modesty, she wadded up the towel Dion also gave her and pressed it between Kyra's legs.

"You haven't seen Penny, have you?''

Dion shook his head. "I think she left with her friend. The Mercedes is gone. Do you need her?''

"No, I can manage.''

Litsa, her face as pale as Kyra's, spoke quietly to her friend. "Don't worry, Kyra. By tomorrow you'll be fine. You'll see.'' As she uttered the soothing but largely meaningless words, she stroked Kyra's forehead, brushing back the dark hair that was damp with sweat.

Kyra's lips moved. "Don't tell my father. He'll kill me.''

Solange's grip tightened on the girl's hand, feeling its iciness. Kyra's life could well be in danger, and she was worried about her father's reaction. It might be funny if it weren't so tragic. She set her jaw. Maybe it was time somebody had a serious talk with old Stavros and set him straight on a few things concerning his daughter.

The thought had barely coalesced when Taki trotted up with her medical bag. She threw him a grateful smile. Pulling out the stethoscope, she inserted the earpieces and listened to Kyra's heartbeat. Strong and even, no suggestion of shock. Apparently no uncontrolled internal hemorrhage. She wondered if Kyra had been mistaken, after all, and this was only her period delayed by the pressure of school.

She was relieved to see Demetra bustling across from the kiosk, her worried look replaced by a smile. "Dr. Andropoulos will be here directly. Kyra's parents are visiting relatives in Nea Anhialos, but there's no answer on the phone there. They're probably out to dinner. I'll try again later."

Dr. Andropoulos, an elderly man with a shock of white hair above a patrician face, loped up in his usual harried manner. His glasses teetered precariously on the end of his formidable nose. "What have we here? Kyra, if you were having problems, why didn't you come to see me?"

"I wasn't," she said with a wan smile. Then her face crumpled, and she stifled a sob as tears slid from the corners of her eyes toward her ears. "Uncle Andreas, I'm so sorry. I should have come to you."

Solange suddenly understood why Kyra had confided in her that day, and also why the girl hadn't kept the appointment at her office. She must have thought she'd be slighting her uncle to be seen visiting another doctor when he had his practice right here, as well, especially if later her pregnancy became obvious. If indeed there had been a pregnancy.

"It's all right, child," Andropoulos assured her. "Now, let me listen to your heart." He glanced up at Solange, his smile kind. "I know you have already, Doctor, but I have to hear for myself."

After a moment, he squatted back on his heels. "Are you having any pain?"

"Only a few light cramps. When it started I had a strange sinking sensation but no severe pain."

Dr. Andropoulos nodded. "That's the way it is sometimes. Kyra, I have to ask you..."

Kyra shook her head. "Please, Uncle Andreas, not now." Her eyes swiveled to Solange's. "Dr. Solange, please don't tell my father."

Beside her, Litsa gasped. Solange knew she'd realized the truth for the first time. Solange let go of Kyra's hand to give Litsa's a reassuring squeeze. "I won't, dear. But he may guess."

Kyra closed her eyes, but not before Solange saw the fear in them. "He can't. He can't."

"He will," Litsa muttered darkly. "Everyone knows now."

"Here's the stretcher," Dion said. He turned to Dr. Andropoulos. "Shall we get her on it and move her down to Solange's office? It's the closest."

Dion and Dr. Andropoulos unrolled the canvas stretcher and moved Kyra quickly onto it, then tucked the blanket close around her. Each lifting an end, they raised it and started off down the square, ignoring the curiosity of the few remaining bystanders. Solange picked up Andropoulos's bag as well as her own, overtaking the men in order to unlock her office door. She let Litsa come in with them, asking Demetra to stay outside and tell anyone who asked that Kyra had a female problem brought on by stress and that she would be all right. She hoped it was true, and there was no use feeding the avid gossip mill with any possibility of a pregnancy rumor.

Once inside, the two men placed the girl on the examining table. Dion stepped discreetly into the waiting room. Dr. Andropoulos busied himself laying out his instruments as Litsa and Solange stripped off the girl's clothes and replaced them with a hospital gown.

Litsa's hands shook, and she looked as if she might be in need of medical attention momentarily, too. "Do you want to stay with Dion until we know what's going on?" Solange suggested, noting the sick look on Litsa's face as she wadded up the bloody clothes and stuffed them into a laundry hamper.

Litsa shook her head, gripping Kyra's hand again. "No. Kyra needs me. I'll stay."

Dr. Andropoulos completed his examination with quick but thorough efficiency, thanking Solange as she handed him the instruments he asked for. "I believe she's had a miscarriage. I want to admit her to the hospital in Volos overnight. I may have to do a minor cleansing procedure in the morning."

"The exams start Friday," Kyra said, her voice cracking. "Will I be able to write them?"

Dr. Andropoulos patted her hand. "My dear, by Friday you'll be fine."

"If her father doesn't figure it out," Litsa muttered grimly. "We'll have to be careful."

"I can't lie to him," Dr. Andropoulos said with a frown. "I won't volunteer anything, but if he asks, I'll have to tell him the truth."

After half an hour Kyra's color began to return. Dr. Andropoulos decided it was safe enough to move her. "I'll drive her to Volos and check her again in the morning. There may be nothing else needed, and she'll be home again by noon."

He settled the two girls in the back seat of his car, covering Kyra with a blanket against the cool night air. Solange followed in her own car.

Once Kyra was admitted there was little for Solange to do. Litsa, her eyes heavy with worry, needed to rest. She wanted to stay, but the head nurse on the ward assured her that Kyra, under mild sedation, would sleep all night.

"Come, Litsa," Solange said, placing her arm around the girl's shoulders. "Time we got home."

Litsa looked back at Kyra's motionless figure under the white hospital sheet, dark brown hair tangled on the pillow. "I should have brought a brush."

"The nurse will fix her hair in the morning. And by that time somebody will have tracked down her mother." A second call to the relatives in Anhialos had produced only a sleepy comment from their teenage son that his parents and Kyra's had gone to a nightclub in Volos and would return late. Solange had left a message that Kyra had been taken ill and for the parents to contact Dr. Andropoulos, since Kyra was now technically his patient.

Feet dragging, Litsa allowed Solange to walk her to the car parked in the hospital lot. "Let's hope her mother comes to see her and not her father."

A hope that Solange shared. She started the car and turned it toward the street, swerving around a rotating sprinkler that managed to keep the hospital lawn green even through high summer.

"You didn't know, did you?" Solange said quietly as they left the outskirts of the city with its drab industrial areas behind.

"About Kyra, that she might be pregnant?" Litsa's mouth turned down. "No, I didn't. It's the first time she ever kept a secret from me. Dr. Solange, I didn't even know she was seeing anyone. Do you have any idea who it is?"

Even to Litsa, Solange couldn't betray Kyra's confidence. "Kyra told me, but she wants to keep it a secret. It may come to nothing, anyway."

"Especially now." Litsa sighed gloomily. "If her father finds out who it is, he'll kill him and Kyra both. Poor Kyra."

Yes, poor Kyra. So young and soon to face some very adult choices that might be forced on her. "Thanks for standing by her, Litsa," Solange said, reaching over and touching the girl's hand. "You must have been a little hurt that Kyra gave you no clue what was going on with her."

Litsa was silent for a long moment. "Not hurt exactly," she said contemplatively. "I just didn't expect it to happen this soon. But we're almost adults. We can't expect to share everything. Do you think Kyra will marry this boy...man—" she floundered awkwardly "—the father of the child she's lost?"

Not if her father had anything to say about it. "I don't know. She's very young and still under her parents' roof."

"Well, at least her father can't make her marry Alecko Venetis."

A hell of a way to accomplish that end, Solange thought.

Demetra and Penny were waiting for them in the front garden when Solange pulled up outside the house. "How is she?" Demetra asked at once. She reached out a hand to Litsa and pulled her into a tight hug.

"Kyra will be fine. She should be home tomorrow." Solange forced a smile. "She was sleeping."

Penny put her hand on Solange's arm, her body tense. "Is it true what they're saying, that she had a miscarriage?"

Solange's shoulders slumped as she bent to lock the car. "I was hoping that rumor wouldn't circulate."

"Well, no one's confirmed it."

"And no one will," Solange said hardily. "If I have anything to say about it."

"What did her father say?" Penny's hand clenched into fists at her sides.

"So far, nothing. Her parents don't know yet. Dr. Andropoulos stayed to wait for them. In any case, they probably won't be able to talk to Kyra until tomorrow."

Demetra rolled her eyes toward the star-studded sky. "Thank God for some mercy."

"Until tomorrow," Penny said. "Well, if they kick her out, I'll take her in." She looked at her watch. "I'd better get home. Good night."

"Good night, Penny."

Demetra frowned as Penny walked off down the street. "I hope she doesn't make things worse. I can just see her storming over and telling off old Stavros."

"She hasn't up to now," Solange said mildly. "I think we can trust her discretion."

"I hope so." Demetra's frown remained as she dropped a kiss on Litsa's drooping head and turned toward the house. "Come, Litsa, it's time you were in bed. School tomorrow. And Dr. Solange probably wants to get some rest, as well." Pausing at the door, she winked.

The sly innuendo was explained when Solange entered her flat. Dion sat in the chair by the window in the dark. He jumped at the click of the lock, startled out of either sleep or a deep reverie. Pushing himself out of the chair, he came toward her, clasping his hands at the back of her neck and massaging the muscles there. "You're tense." He dropped a light kiss on her mouth, promising more if she wanted it.

"Who wouldn't be?"

"It'll be worse when Kyra's parents find out."

She closed her eyes, giving in to the soothing stroke of his fingers. "You heard."

"The window's open."

"Mmm." She leaned against him, savoring his strength and the woodsy scent that emanated from his skin. "Stay, Dion. For tonight. I need you."

He chuckled low in his throat. "That's quite an admission. I'm not sure how to take it."

"At face value. This is tonight. Tomorrow everything may be different again."

Temporary. Why did he feel the sharp stab of disappointment? Hadn't he been the one who'd emphasized they could have no future? So what was his problem? Or was it just that he wanted the upper hand in their relationship? The man called the shots. Who'd made that law? A stupid one, but sometimes he realized he was just as conditioned as the next guy.

Solange's hands were working their way inside his shirt. Distracted by the gentle exploration, he gave in to the pleasure, consigning philosophical questions to oblivion. Picking her up in his arms, he carried her off to bed.

HE WAS GONE by the time Solange got up for her morning run. Sparing the sensibilities of the household, no doubt. Or her own.

She followed her usual route, but he wasn't on his porch. Probably sleeping off the effects of the night before. Pleasant aches in assorted parts of her body reminded her of the passion they'd shared. By rights she should have slept in, too, but her internal clock was too insistent.

She had half a mind to pop in and douse Dion with cold water but restrained the impulse. Let him sleep. She might need his support later in the day, and a happy, well-rested man would be more help than someone who was tired and out of sorts.

Like old Barba Stavros, Kyra's father.

THE CONFRONTATION came sooner than she'd expected. With Penny opening the office, Solange went to the greengrocer's to have first choice of the morning's fresh produce. Her string bag bulging with leeks, tomatoes and some slender eggplants, she was crossing the town square when Stavros jumped up from his chair in front of the coffee shop and strode toward her.

"Oh-oh," she muttered, bracing herself for the onslaught promised by his thunderous expression.

"What did you do to my baby?" He hurled the words from twenty feet away as if they were stones from a catapult. All the morning shoppers, and there were plenty of them, turned to watch the altercation.

"Kyra will be fine."

"Fine." He spit on the ground. "Depends on what you call fine. She's ruined. No decent man will have her now."

"What happened to Kyra will have no lasting effect," Solange reiterated with determined calm.

"No lasting effect?" he bellowed. "She's no longer a virgin. When I find the man, he'll curse the day he was born. Before he dies."

So he knew the truth. There was no use prevaricating. "Kyra loves him."

Stavros bristled. "Oh, she told you that, did she? As if that excuses anything. Women seem to think that anything is all right if she loves him. What does a girl of Kyra's age know of love?"

More than you, most likely. The rash words leaped to Solange's lips, but she bit them back. "Kyra will overcome this if you and her mother help her."

"Kyra will never overcome this. She's marked."

Solange had difficulty restraining her temper. "Marked? Isn't that a bit harsh? Kyra's a lovely girl. In a few months people will have forgotten, especially since they don't know."

"They don't know?" He made a rude noise. "Madam, they know. They aren't stupid."

"Barba Stavros, her best friend didn't know. Unless you make a fuss and start more talk and speculation, no one will ever know."

"Except her future husband."

"Whom she hasn't met yet. Aren't you getting ahead of yourself?"

"Well, Alecko has already been to see me this morning. He's worried about her child-bearing ability."

Solange's temper flared. "Which shows you that he's not the right man for her," she said hotly. "He wants a brood mare, not a wife. Besides, I think it's Kyra's right to choose her own husband."

The old man's face turned an alarming crimson as rage blazed in his eyes. "Kyra must obey her father. It's your fault, coming here with your foreign ideas. Before you came she was a quiet girl. She didn't talk about going to university."

Not to her father, perhaps. But Solange knew that Kyra had confided in Litsa her ambition of becoming a kindergarten teacher from the time they were in grade school. "Barba Stavros," she said, reining in her anger, "I have never talked to Kyra about anything that I didn't talk to Litsa or her mother or anyone else about. You can ask anyone in town."

"Didn't you advise Helena Vrakas to use birth control?"

She had, but even then she hadn't supplied the means, only made the suggestion. Stavros saw the brief uncertainty and jumped in. "See, you have corrupted our children."

The injustice of the accusation and the vitriolic force with which he issued it made her take a step back. "I didn't," she said firmly. "I told Helena she was too young for sex."

"You had no right to tell her anything. You should have gone straight to her parents. They would have taken care of it."

"How? By locking Helena up and throwing away the key? Or by arranging a quick marriage to some man she doesn't even know, as you tried to do with Kyra?"

The man's eyes narrowed. "Maybe you've influenced Kyra into this even more than I thought. Maybe you put the whole idea into her head as a way for Kyra to avoid marrying the man I chose."

He knew Kyra objected? And was plowing ahead regardless? Solange wanted to swing her load of vegetables against his head and knock some sense into him. "If you knew she didn't want to marry the man, why were you trying to force her?"

"I'm her father." The flat statement said it all. "You made her change."

Solange clenched her fist until the handle of her bag bit into her skin. The small pain allowed her to maintain control. "I had nothing to do with it," she said tightly.

"You had everything to do with it. It's your fault that Kyra isn't the good girl her mother and I raised. Look at her sisters, all married with children. No fancy school for them. And her brother, isn't he in officer's training and engaged to a major's daughter? They're amounting to something while Kyra will be reduced to living on the streets.''

Solange's mouth dropped open, and she couldn't utter a word. Living on the streets? Was Penny right then? Were they really going to throw the poor girl out? "I'll take her in," she declared recklessly.

"Will you? Then educate her well, *putana*."

She gasped at the epithet, virtually the worst insult a man could hurl at a woman. The lump in her throat prevented the angry words crowding there from escaping. Before she could swallow it down, Stavros stalked away, his worry beads swinging in an agitated manner from his fingers.

A gentle hand touched Solange's arm. Grandma Amelia looked at her with sympathy in her faded blue eyes. "He's wrong, child. And he knows it. No one blames you for Kyra's trouble, and neither will Stavros once he has a chance to think about it."

"He's going to kick her out," Solange whispered, the tears finally streaming down her face. She made no protest as Amelia led her over to a bench under a lime tree. "He's not going to let her come home."

"He'll change his mind." Amelia pulled out a lavender-scented handkerchief and held it up for Solange to blow her nose, as if she were a child. "In the meantime Kyra's mother has made arrangements for her to stay with friends in the next village, at least until the end of school."

"But what about university?"

"Her mother will sell one of her dowry fields if necessary. She'll go."

How would Kyra feel, exiled from her family? Solange, drying her eyes and beginning to feel embarrassed at breaking down in public, determined that she would go and see her at the first opportunity.

By noon the story of Barba Stavros's confrontation with Solange was all over town, every shouted sentence repeated and no doubt embellished. The townspeople's support lay mainly with Solange, though a few whispered against her and against Kyra.

Solange, having sent Penny and Aphrodite home at one, was locking up at half past when Dion came striding across the square, a shovel and a rake over his shoulder. His clothes were streaked with red mud, dried to a rust color, and his hair was plastered to his head with sweat. He smelled salty and hot, and Solange had a sudden urge to bury her face against him in primitive possession.

"What's all this I hear about you and Barba Stavros? I had three people come and offer me bottles of water just to regale me with every detail. I hope you gave him hell. He has it coming, kicking out his daughter just when she needs him."

Tears burned again as she heard his simple declaration of faith in her judgment. "Dion, he's not thinking straight right now."

"No, probably not, but it's generous of you to see his side."

"But I didn't. I yelled right back at him. Where have you been all morning? I didn't see you when I went for my run."

"After I left your place, I got my tools and went to water those young olives the man who's renting my fields planted last year. He's busy with the wheat harvest and asked me to look after them for a few weeks. Why, did you miss me?''

She grinned, her dark mood lifting. ''Not a chance. I was busy fighting World War III.''

Dion chuckled. ''You'll see the funny side of this someday. I wish I'd been here.'' His face changed. ''By the way, I may have another lead to follow. Someone mentioned this morning that our old parish priest from Athens is still alive and living in Rigion. I'm going to go see him. He may know what happened to Pavlou.''

Solange bit her lip, hiding her disappointment. She'd really believed that Dion might give up his vendetta. ''What about the monastery? Have you heard from them?''

''The telephone lines are still down. Apparently they have a lot of trouble with them. I wrote a letter, but so far I haven't had a reply.''

''When are you going to see this priest?''

''As soon as possible.''

She squared her shoulders, tossing back her head as if to defy his objections before he could list them. ''Then I'm going with you.''

CHAPTER FIFTEEN

THEY WALKED TOGETHER as far as Solange's place. Her mind in a turmoil, Solange barely heard Dion's brief goodbye as she opened the garden gate.

She had stripped off her clothes and was about to step into the shower when she heard a ferocious pounding on the door. Who on earth? Flinging on a robe and tightening the belt, she ran to the door as the pounding threatened to break it down. "I'm coming. Keep your shirt on."

She flipped up the latch and Dion stormed in, slamming the door back against the wall. His fist was clenched on the collar of Barba Stavros's shirt. The man looked terrified, his mouth working as he tried to speak.

"Dion, you're choking him."

Dion shook the man as if he weighed no more than a bundle of rags. "Choking's too good for him. Why didn't you tell me what he called you?"

"What he called me?" She backed away, his fury like a red cloud between them. "I thought you knew. You said—"

"I said I heard the story, but no one told me what he called you until just now. I'll smash his face, but first he's going to apologize." He pushed Stavros ahead of him. "Talk, you pitiful excuse of a man."

"Dion, stop it." Lunging forward, Solange grabbed his arm, but she might as well have tried to move an oak rafter. "Dion, please. You're hurting him. He's a distraught father. He didn't know what he was saying."

"He knew all right. And he's going to say so." With a look of disgust, Dion hauled Stavros to a chair and dropped him onto it.

Stavros sat in it, the picture of misery, his shoulders hunched. "I was on my way here, Dr. Solange. My wife wouldn't let me come to the table until I apologized. Forty years and she never missed a meal, and now she's refusing to feed me."

Solange's mouth twitched, and she controlled her smile with difficulty. "Then maybe you'd better get it over with so you can go home to eat."

Stavros looked fearfully at Dion. "If the Kyrios here will let me."

"He'll let you." She tightened her grip on Dion's arm. "Won't you, Dion?"

"Maybe." His voice was a low growl. "Depends."

"I'm sorry, Dr. Solange," Stavros said, his gnarled fingers twisting the chain that held his worry beads. "I didn't mean it, and everyone knows that. It's my temper. And I was so upset over my little girl. When I find the animal who attacked her—"

"Barba Stavros," Solange interrupted gently. "She loves the boy. He didn't attack her."

"Then tell me who he is."

"I can't do that. Kyra will have to tell you herself."

"She refuses." Stavros threw up his hands, raking his fingers through his grizzled salt-and-pepper hair. "It's a fine thing when a man can't even control the women of his household. First my wife refusing to serve my dinner, and then Kyra."

Dion stepped forward. "I think that's enough. You can go now, Stavros. And from now on you'll be polite to Dr. Solange."

"Oh, I will," the man promised, clearly relieved to have gotten off so lightly. He stood up and scuttled toward the door.

"Wait." Solange moved to block his path, a frown creasing her face. "Is Kyra at home?"

The man looked shamefacedly at the floor. "No, she's at her aunt's. I'll let her come home when she tells me the boy's name."

Solange knew Kyra would never do that. Her heart ached. Kyra would go off to university, make new friends and a new life, either with or without Niko. Her father would grow old and bitter, setting his grievance in cement until it would never be resolved.

"Barba Stavros, do you remember when Kyra was born, how happy you were? Your other children were already in school and you had Kyra at home, a sweet little girl who adored you."

Stavros blinked his pale blue eyes. "Yes, she was my baby. But he's stolen her away. She'll never be my baby again."

"But she'll always be your daughter, won't she?"

Wiping at a tear that rolled down his weather-beaten cheek, Stavros swallowed a sob. "I kicked her out."

"You can take her back."

"People will say I'm weak, that I can't control her."

"This isn't about control, Barba Stavros. Do you love Kyra?"

Another tear escaped. "More than my life."

"Then let her have hers. You want her to be happy, don't you? Then give her a chance. Kyra is still a good girl, but she needs to be her own woman. And she is a woman now. You have to accept that. Please, Barba Stavros, let her come home."

But he set his jaw stubbornly. "She has to learn her lesson. When she has, I'll let her come home. Good day, Dr. Solange. I'm sorry I upset you."

He passed through the open doorway, and they could hear his boots clumping down the stairs and the outer door closing. In the downstairs hall another door also closed, more softly. Solange shut her apartment door, leaning back against it with a sigh. She hoped not too much of their conversation had been audible, not that anything was ever secret for long in this town.

"Well, I hope your honor and mine are appeased," she said to Dion without opening her eyes.

He stepped in front of her, bracing his hands on the door panel on either side of her head. "You handled that admirably, Solange. Saved face all around."

Solange opened her eyes and found herself looking deep into his. She wished she could read him as easily as he read her. "Would you have beaten him?"

Dion shrugged. "I wanted to. He had no right to call you a whore. But I don't know. He's an old man. He was upset."

"Does that mean revenge isn't always a solution, Dion? I understand feuds have started over lesser insults than the one he paid me."

"In the past, maybe. We're a little more sophisticated than that now."

"Are we, under the skin? Are we really?"

SINCE PENNY was scheduled to look after the office during the evening, they decided to drive up to Rigion after the siesta hour. Dion, more familiar now with the often incomprehensibly winding hill roads, drove them in his car.

Rigion sprawled on a hillside in the midst of a rolling landscape marked in patches, some of them naked under stubble, others clothed with tall green corn. Only an occasional clump of trees dotted the fields that had been claimed from unproductive scrub.

Below the village the rail line connecting Volos with Karditsa, Trikalla and Kalambaka snaked across the countryside. A passing train looked like a toy, its whistle a lonely echo that rebounded against the hills.

Once this had been wild country, inhabited by Sarakatsani and Vlachs in winter and by Gypsies in summer. Now it was prime farmland, the breadbasket of Greece. Solange wondered what the old people thought of the changes.

"It must look different from when you were a child," she said to Dion.

"We didn't have a car—hardly anybody had one in those days. The only times I've been here was passing on the bus or the train on the way to Saloniki. Everything was different then, but without a frame of reference it didn't mean anything to me. I was a kid. The world was how it was."

"Until it changed when you were sixteen."

His mouth tightened, lines of tension etching from his nose to his jaw. "Yeah, it changed." He relaxed his grip on the wheel slightly. "Actually it changed a number of times, like when we moved to Athens, but I changed when my parents died."

She felt his pain, and the rage he must have felt then and which still smoldered in him. "You can change again, Dion," she said, wanting to smother that destructive fire inside him with her love, to put it out once and for all.

"I'm seeing this through." He slowed as he turned into a narrow street, the car's engine echoing loudly between the close-set houses. "Yes, here it is."

The garden enclosed by a neat iron fence was well tended, filled with red geraniums and pink roses whose fragrance vied with that of a bed of mint next to an outdoor sink. A bougainvillea, not easy to grow away from the coast at this latitude, tumbled its magenta blossoms over the porch roof. Toward the back of the house rows of tomatoes, beans and peppers thrived in a vegetable garden.

Dion knocked on the door, an old-fashioned one with glass set in a wrought-iron frame, and with lace curtains shielding the interior of the house from view. They waited a moment, but no one came. Dion turned away. "Must be out."

The words had no sooner left his mouth than they heard footsteps in the back garden. "Pesky kids." The voice grew louder. "I'll get you this time. Oh!"

A short, portly man popped his head around the corner of the house. His round cheeks above a sparse white beard were red and glossy, his square hands dark with garden soil. A Montreal Expos baseball cap sat on his head, an incongruous counterpoint to the white hair drawn back in the traditional priest's bun at the nape. "*Herete.* Forgive me, I thought it was those kids knocking on the door and then running away." He walked toward them, the black skirt of his robe swinging jauntily as he moved to the sink set against the front of the house. "Excuse me while I wash off some of this dirt. Calliope," he yelled. "Bring some chairs. We have visitors."

"Oh, don't bother," Dion said. "We don't want to keep you from your work."

"Work. There's always work." The priest dried his hands with the towel hanging on a nail above the sink. "Now, visitors—that's more rare these days. When you get to be my age, your friends keep dying. No stamina, not like the old days when we worked in the fields all day and danced all night."

He put out his hand, his grip firm and calloused. Solange liked his handshake. It was honest and straightforward, a barometer of his character. "I'm Yanni Melas. And who might you be?"

"Solange Richards."

"Ah, the new doctor in Korfalli. All the way from America. No, Canada, isn't it? We used to think of them as the same country, but that's not correct, is it? I've heard good things about you." He turned to Dion, pausing only to yell once more, "Calliope!"

He shook Dion's hand with the same brisk familiarity, his eyebrows lifting when he heard his visitor's name. "Nicholas and Zoe's son, all grown up. Well, well." He turned and bounded up the steps, throwing open the door. "Calliope!"

"I'm here." The tall, lanky woman who came out of the house with a chair in either hand had to stoop under the lintel. Her wiry hair was drawn back into an untidy bun, wisps framing a face that had the benign serenity of a good-natured sheep. "You can stop shouting, you old fool. I'm not deaf."

Solange stifled a laugh, her face reddening as she caught the look Dion cast her, the amusement in his eyes. Pulling a tissue from her pocket, she pretended to cough and blew her nose with unwonted vigor. "What's wrong, Solange?'' Dion murmured. ''Hay fever bothering you?''

Solange felt a fresh burst of giggles bubble up but managed to control them by stepping forward and taking one of the chairs.

''Thank you.'' The smile with which Calliope favored Solange transformed her face to near beauty, then disappeared when she turned to her husband. Her Roman nose twitched as she glared balefully at him. ''Nice to see some people still have manners.''

Papa Yanni took the other chair, reaching up and playfully pinching his wife's wrinkled cheek. ''We can't all be perfect, dear one.''

''We can try,'' she said with mock severity while a twinkle lighted her eyes.

''Fetch our visitors a drink,'' Papa Yanni said. ''I could use a little something myself.'' He wiped his sleeve across his perspiring brow, pulling off the baseball cap, then resetting it. He grinned broadly. ''A gift from my son. Do you know Montreal, Kyria?''

Solange was used to these kinds of questions. The village people in Greece had no concept of the size of Canada, gaping in disbelief when she explained that it was farther from the west coast to the east coast of the country than from Canada to the shores of Europe. ''Actually, I know Montreal well. I grew up there.''

''Your Greek is very good.'' He leaned back in his chair, slapping his thighs with his palms and raising a small cloud of dust. ''Ah, Calliope, you've brought the drinks.''

Jumping up again, he dragged a small wooden table up so that it sat between their chairs. He took the tray and set it down, pouring a dark red wine from a crystal decanter into thin-stemmed glasses. With a flourish he handed the first one to Solange. "This is my own wine, made from a secret recipe."

She drank, tilting the wineglass with the delicacy it deserved and rolling her tongue around the wine before she swallowed. It was delicious, fruity and exotic on the tongue, smooth going down the throat, and settling into her stomach with the warmth of a kiss. "It's lovely." She lifted her glass. "A long life and happiness."

Lifting his own glass, Dion echoed the toast. "Happiness."

Papa Yanni gave a snorting laugh. He dug a finger into Calliope's skinny ribs. "With this woman I wouldn't dare be anything else."

Calliope rolled her large expressive eyes. "See what I put up with. No wonder no one comes to visit anymore."

Papa Yanni turned to Dion. "It's been years, hasn't it, since those days in Athens? You went away to school, then to Canada. I suppose you're rich."

Dion laughed. "Not really. I teach sociology at the University of British Columbia."

"What, no restaurant? I thought all Greeks went to Canada to open restaurants."

"Not quite. Papa Yanni, you remember my parents, don't you?"

"How could I forget them? They tried so hard to fight, and what did they get for it? An ignominious death. Dion, the story was that they betrayed our cause, but I never believed it."

Dion turned white. "Betrayed the cause? No, they didn't. They refused to. That's why they were killed."

"The regime must have anticipated a fuss, for in the days after your parents' disappearance they circulated documents that made it look as if they were Communist sympathizers. We soon put a stop to that. In those days I was part of a secret organization recruiting new political leaders who would overthrow the regime. We recovered their bodies and gave them a decent Christian burial.''

Excitement rippled along Dion's nerve endings. He leaned forward, an intense emotion blazing from his eyes. ''They're buried somewhere, not on that mountainside? I thought they were lost forever under the housing development that's gone up in the place they died.''

''No, they're buried in a cemetery just outside of Athens, near the house they hid in before they were imprisoned.''

''The house? You mean it's still there?''

''Of course it is,'' Papa Yanni said complacently. ''We used it even after their deaths as a secret meeting place. And we published the last articles they'd written, putting to rest the rumor the regime spread.''

''Then why haven't I seen any of this?''

''It was published in underground newspapers. But they were distributed all over the country. It helped. They didn't die for nothing.''

''Do you have copies?''

''Of course, my boy. Calliope has them put away. They're yours. I'll give them to you before you go.''

''Thank you.'' Dion didn't quite know how to convey his gratitude. His eyes burned and a lump closed his throat.

''There was a key,'' Papa Yanni said reflectively. ''Hidden in the cellar. It must still be there, in a wine bottle. It's to their safe-deposit box.''

''So there might be other personal things.'' Dion swallowed convulsively. He couldn't get his parents back, but claiming whatever inheritance they'd left him would be like having part of them again, and might allow him to say his final goodbyes.

"Quite possibly. Your father's last words to me were: 'See that Dion gets the key.' But after the political situation stabilized several years later, your aunt in Vancouver had died and I didn't know how to contact you."

"Yes," said Dion. "After she died, I was living in a university residence and didn't have a telephone listing."

Papa Yanni frowned. "Your parents were working on an important story at the time they were taken. They kept it very discreet, fearing reprisals if it came out prematurely. It had something to do with a rising light in politics. Unfortunately we never learned his name, and afterward no one knew where they'd hidden the work. I've often wondered if something had leaked out. Their arrest was very sudden." He passed his hand over his eyes. "And their death even more so. After all this time who is there left to ask?"

Pavlou. Dion glanced at Solange, sitting quietly listening. Her fingers gripped her wineglass, the white knuckles the only sign that betrayed her tension. He could feel what she was trying to tell him, but there was no way he could stop now.

"Papa Yanni, do you know where I can find Lambros Pavlou?"

"Dion, no." He heard Solange's whisper, the distress that drew a white line around her mouth, but he ignored it, and the clamor of his conscience.

"He's the man who carried out my parents' execution."

Papa Yanni shook his head. "Yes, but—"

"I saw him myself," Dion said vehemently. "He was there, a man with six fingers on his left hand."

"Raptis." Papa Yanni spit out the word as if it were an obscenity.

"What?"

The priest drew in a deep breath, his hand trembling as he wiped it over his beard. "That was the name he used later. Raptis."

"Raptis?" Dion slowly let out his breath. "No wonder I couldn't track him down. He must have changed it after the fire."

"Dion, please." Solange pleaded. "You know where your parents are buried now. You know they didn't die for nothing. Can't you let it go?"

Papa Yanni reached over and took Solange's hand in his. "Dear lady, a promise made over a death is sacred. You can't stop him." His eyes held an infinite sorrow, a grief such as she'd seen in the eyes of saints on the oldest icons.

"No, you can't, Solange." Dion's voice was flat, yet she could hear the echo of hidden emotion, the uncertainties that she'd suspected were growing stronger. But it was as if he couldn't draw back from the path he'd taken, as if a chain held him and didn't allow him to turn back. She could only hope that an alternate route would miraculously present itself.

Papa Yanni looked from one to the other. Beside him Calliope was silent, waiting with a thick manila envelope in her hands. At last the old man sighed. "I will pray for you, Dion. Raptis is in the Monastery of the Transfiguration, fifteen kilometers from here."

THE MONASTERY sprawled over a hillside, almost lost in a pine grove. The half-timbered main building was old, probably a thousand years, Solange estimated. Later additions formed wings on either side, the architecture blending or clashing, depending on the time period it had been built. Ivy and grapevines softened the walls, changing disharmony into a homogenous form. Beside the stone path the delicate petals of scarlet poppies fluttered in the breeze.

Low in the sky the sun gilded the edges of the slates that covered the multilevel roof. Solange squinted against the glare as she got out of the car, breathing in the astringence of resin and sweet clover. A low, rushing sound, like distant surf, surrounded them—the wind in the pines.

"This is the place you tried to call, isn't it?" she asked Dion. He stood next to the car, staring up at the building, as if he were afraid, now that he'd come this far. "This is where Mavrakis was sending money."

"Yes."

"Why would he send money to a monastery?"

Dion shrugged. "Penance. Guilt. Maybe we'll never know. Odd thing about our people when they get old. Often they begin to realize their mortality and try to make amends for past sins."

"And if that's what Pavlou is doing here?"

For this he had no answer, only a closed look that warned her to leave it alone.

The wooden gate in the stone wall surrounding a cloistered courtyard stood open. From a cage attached to the overhanging roof a canary warbled an ecstatic trill of notes, breaking off abruptly as a hooded monk came out of the building. The massive door banged closed behind him, a hollow echo in the open space.

"Come." With one crooked finger he gestured to them, turning so quickly they didn't have a chance to see his face.

Dion tensed, his mouth thinning to a grim line. Her heart pounding in tune with the frantic rhythm of her thoughts, Solange followed. She couldn't stop him. He was going to kill a man, and she couldn't stop him. In a monastery, no less.

Her lips moved in a wordless prayer. It couldn't happen, could it? Desperately she tried to grasp the unraveling tendrils of faith, hanging on to the belief that Dion was a good man, gentle. He wasn't a killer. She clung to the thought, willing it to be the truth.

The monk led them to a door, turning the handle only to unlatch it before he walked away, his sandals slapping softly on the flagstone floor.

"How did he know?" Solange whispered, her eyes wide. She felt cold all over.

"My letter, probably." Dion seemed to accept the fact without question.

"But then he must know why you're here." The realization dried her mouth, making it hard for her to speak. "Why didn't he stay?"

"Does it matter?"

The emotionless tone of his voice chilled her further. She hugged her arms around her chest, willing away her pain, her fear as Dion pushed open the door.

He sucked in his breath, and she let hers out. The man who lay on the narrow bed in the infirmary was no threat to Dion or anyone else. And Dion knew it.

Nevertheless, he moved closer, skirting the three beds that stood between him and his objective. They were empty, made up neatly with white sheets, ready for the next patient who might need them.

Lambros Pavlou Raptis lay without moving, unaware of their presence, unaware of the shaft of sunlight that illuminated the cross over the bed for an instant before the sun slid below the horizon. His hands were crossed on his chest, as if he already rested in his coffin, the left one with its extra deformed finger, lying on the right. The man himself was little more than a skeleton, the skin covering his flesh as smooth and yellow as parchment. The only indication that he lived was the soft, labored whistling of his breath in his throat.

The physician in Solange came momentarily to the fore. "Some kind of cancer, I'd say," she murmured, barely aware of speaking aloud. Her voice was low, but the man on the bed wouldn't have heard if she'd shouted. "He's a dead man."

Dion stood by the bed and stared at the man, his face an expressionless mask, as if he'd shut down every emotional reaction he'd ever had. What would he do?

Minutes passed, five, perhaps ten, measured by the ticking of a clock in the hall. Solange couldn't stand it any longer. Spinning around, she went out the door, almost running by the time she reached the open courtyard. She stopped, gasping for breath, her face turned up to the sky where the first stars winked into being.

Dion. Her heart screamed his name.

A monk, perhaps the same one as before, came out. "Miss," he said awkwardly in broken English. "Sit down."

He led her to a bench under a sweetly blooming honeysuckle. She felt too tired to protest as he held a glass to her mouth and made her drink the cold water in it. She smiled her thanks, and he pulled the hood more closely around his head, but not before she saw his face, young and quite handsome, with a winsome smile that came and went.

Sitting down next to her, he began to talk quietly in a mixture of Greek and English that made him hard to understand. Solange let the words flow over her. As long as he talked, she didn't have to think, to worry about what Dion was doing in there.

"Your friend, he knows Raptis?"

"No, not personally. But he's been looking for him."

Raptis. A little jolt went through Solange at the name, and she frowned. Where had she heard it before? It was somehow familiar, but in their headlong drive from the priest's house, she hadn't had a chance to think.

"It's too late," the monk said gently. "Raptis has been ill for two years."

She jerked back to attention. "Like that?"

"Yes, although he had good days at first, but now he never speaks." The monk shrugged fatalistically, quickly crossing himself. "He will die. Tonight, tomorrow, next week."

"Do you know who he is?" Solange asked, curiosity breaking through her numbness.

"Yes. He has paid. For three years he lived in silence, in poverty, in prayer." The monk crossed himself again. "Whether it is enough, who can say? It's up to God. We cannot judge."

An admirable philosophy, Solange thought. Too bad Dion hadn't learned it. Or had he? At that moment he emerged from the building, almost invisible in the dusk. Without a word he walked past her, going to the car.

Solange jumped up, hating herself as she ran into the infirmary. A light glowed above the door, making her own shadow flee before her into the corner. The man lay in the bed, a corpse that breathed, just as he had before. Nothing in the room was disturbed.

Going out, she paused long enough to thank the monk. He said nothing, merely inclining his head. As she passed the offering box in the inside of the door, she dropped a thousand-drachma note into it, a meager atonement that did little to assuage the irrational guilt inside her.

CHAPTER SIXTEEN

"WAS THAT THE MAN you wanted to kill?" They had
gone past Rigion and joined the national highway for the
last stretch home before she spoke. The words burst out
like water from a breached dam, once started quickly
becoming an unrelenting flood. "Was that the man, that
dried-up husk who hasn't known whether he's dead or
alive for two years? Why didn't you do it? Why didn't
you put him out of his misery? He might have thanked
you."

Dion closed his eyes, but not before she saw the agony in them. "Solange, don't. Please don't. I couldn't
bear it if you hate me."

"And I don't know if I can bear to love you."

"I warned you, Solange," Dion said raggedly. "I
warned you."

Some of her anger faded. Yes, he had warned her. It
was her own fault for falling in love with him.

Pressing her foot down on the accelerator, she sent the
car up the curving hill above Velestinou. Solange had
insisted on driving. The inaction of being a passenger
after what Dion had put her through would have caused
her to explode. As it was, she felt reckless, angry and
invincible.

The headlights of oncoming vehicles flashed by, and
a sprinkler briefly spit water onto the windshield. The
speedometer was nearing a hundred miles per hour, and

the engine had reached a screaming pitch before she slowed down. She took the exit turn as decorously as a lady on her way to church, just as well since the traffic police had a radar trap set up just beyond it. Giving them a wave and a quick toot of her horn, she cruised by, just below the limit.

"Dion, it's over now, isn't it?" she asked as they entered the outskirts of Korfalli. She held her breath, waiting for his answer, hoping, but with half her mind braced for a negative reply. There were loose ends. Would he let them lie? Or would he insist on following up every unraveled thread?

"No, it's not over."

Solange's heart sank. "But Raptis is already as good as dead, and he can't talk. You've reached the end."

"No, I haven't," he said stubbornly. "This is a setback, but it just means I'll have to get the name of Raptis's superior from another source." His voice was firm, his jaw set.

"And kill him?" Solange braked in front of her house. "Dion, when will it be enough?"

"When justice is done. When honor is satisfied." He frowned. "The lost military records, the warnings from people like Captain Demos, Mavrakis's 'accident'—there's someone behind them, and I'm betting it's the man who gave the orders. Someone with a lot of power, maybe even that general who lives in the house on Penteli. I have to find my parents' last work. The answers will be there. Tomorrow I'm going to Marathon."

Solange didn't hesitate. "I'm going with you."

His head swung around. "Why?"

"Because I'm still sane even if you aren't. You're carrying this obsession too far."

"You can't stop me."

"Maybe not, but I can try to keep you out of trouble."

His shoulders slumped as if he were suddenly weary. "Okay. Can you be ready at six?"

BUT THE DAY wasn't over. As soon as Solange entered the house, Demetra stepped out into the hall, followed by a young man she had never seen before. He wore the tan summer uniform of the army and an anxious expression. "Solange, this is Niko. He wants to see Kyra's father. I managed to persuade him to wait until you could go with him. After what Stavros has been saying around town, I don't know what he would do if Niko shows up at his door."

Good advice, Solange thought as she offered her hand. His clasp was strong, unhesitant. Solange looked into his face, liking the resolute lines, the earnest gaze of his dark brown eyes. Her spirits rose. At least for Kyra things would work out. This boy wasn't the type who would use her and discard her. The first words he spoke confirmed her assessment.

"Dr. Richards, I love Kyra. When I heard—" He blinked rapidly as tears of pain filled his eyes. "She had to go through that without me."

"Kyra is young. No—" she put up her hand as he was about to protest "—it has to be said. Kyra needs to finish school. Are you willing to support her in that, even if her family is against you?"

He drew back his shoulders. "Yes. I have some money, and my army pay. We can't get married now, but as soon as I'm through, we will. Eighteen months. I'll take care of her, Dr. Richards."

"And she won't get pregnant again, I trust." Solange hated to be so hard on the boy, but she knew he had to face reality. If he couldn't accept this, there was no use risking the confrontation with Stavros.

Embarrassment painted Niko's cheeks red. "No, I promise." His eyes turned bleak. "We'll hardly be able to see each other, anyway. I'm to be stationed in Kalamata for the next year."

"How did you get out now?" Solange knew that leaves for new recruits were few and far between.

He looked faintly guilty. "I told them my grandmother was dying. My commanding officer is a kind man. He gave me forty-eight hours."

"And if anyone asks when you go back?"

His mouth quirked in a wry smile that washed his face with endearing humor. "She made a miraculous recovery."

"Okay, we'll go see Stavros."

"Would you like me to go, too?" Demetra asked.

Solange considered, chewing her lower lip. "No, I don't think so. But if I'm not back in an hour—" she glanced at her watch "—say, by midnight, send someone to rescue us."

While the introduction wasn't easy, it went better than Solange had dared to hope. She found that Kyra was back home, her mother Thea's doing no doubt, and an uneasy truce seemed to have been established between the girl and her father.

Thea, obviously curious but silent except for a murmured greeting, admitted Solange and Niko to the house, leading them to the kitchen where Stavros sat watching a drama on television. Solange noted with relief that the in-laws were nowhere in evidence. Just as well—they didn't need their interference. Maybe this could be handled in a civilized manner, if only Stavros would be reasonable. Solange crossed her fingers.

Kyra was the one who almost blew it apart, inadvertently pouring fuel on the fires of contention.

As soon as Niko walked in the door, she threw herself sobbing into his arms. Her father couldn't help but see the way they clung to each other, body to body, leaving none of their young passion to the imagination. Solange watched Stavros's face turn red, then purple, and alarming thoughts of possible stroke raced through her, making her wish she hadn't left her medical bag at home.

Stavros lurched to his feet, his bulk formidable in the low-ceilinged room. "So you're the bastard who took advantage of my baby. I ought to kill you."

Gently handing Kyra into her mother's arms, Niko faced Stavros squarely and without a sign of fear. Or deference, for that matter. Solange's heart swelled with admiration for him.

"I love Kyra. I would never hurt her. And I want to marry her. I intend to do so with or without your consent."

"She's a minor!" Stavros roared.

"In a year she won't be. And I can't marry until I complete my military service. You won't be able to stop us."

"I could. I can send her away where you'll never find her. Or marry her to another."

Niko's mouth turned up in a grim smile. "It won't be easy here. Everyone knows she was mine first. And if they don't, I can make sure they will."

Solange held her breath in horror. That was a challenge of the most provocative kind. Niko was literally risking his life to make it. Reputation was everything, more than money, property or connections. Reputation was a good name, the essence of what a person was.

Stavros couldn't ignore a threat to Kyra's reputation, for it reflected back on his whole family. He had to respond, either to throw Niko out on his ear, accomplishing nothing, or to give in gracefully.

A dozen emotions flitted across Stavros's weather-beaten face. Finally he inclined his head. "I love her, too, young man. But there is one condition. You can't see her for a year. She will go to school."

Go to school. Solange could barely contain her elation. Stavros had been threatening to stop her schooling only a few days ago. This was true capitulation. From the corner of her eye she saw Kyra and Thea exchange triumphant grins. And Thea, catching Solange's glance, winked broadly at her. Obviously Stavros only thought himself master of his household. He had been gently manipulated by his wife.

"She will do well," Stavros went on. "And when you finish the service, if you both still feel the same way, I will provide Kyra with an apartment or house as dowry and you will marry. And name the first child after me."

"Done." Niko extended his hand, and the old man took it. Each winced at the strength of the other's grip.

With tears in their eyes Kyra and her mother joined the two men. Solange, leaving them hugging one another, slipped away into the night.

She found Demetra waiting for her in the hall, pacing anxiously. She gave her a brief victory sign as she came in. "It's all right. I never thought it of Stavros, but he's mellowed."

"Enough people took him to task after the way he spoke to you. And I think after he thought about it, he realized he would have to come down or lose Kyra entirely." Demetra took Solange's arm and led her into her own immaculate kitchen. "But that's not why I waited up."

She waited until Solange was seated at the table, then poured them both a glass of orange soda before she continued. "It's about Grandma Amelia. She came to see me today. She was so worried that Dion would find this Pavlou and bring shame on her. You see, her husband was distantly related to Pavlou."

"And you knew this? Is that why at first you wouldn't talk about the six-fingered man and why you warned Dion?"

"Yes. But it didn't stop him, did it? Men. They're always doing these crazy things. He had to have revenge, even if it wouldn't bring his parents back, even though he must have known how they despised violence."

"He probably forgot. But I'm betting he's finding it out now. We saw his old priest. And we saw Pavlou, or Raptis, as he seems to be calling himself lately. That's Amelia's last name, isn't it? I knew it was familiar, but I couldn't place it."

"Yes," Demetra said with marked bitterness. "Pavlou was kicked out of the family years ago, even before the recruiting business. He dropped the name Raptis and used his mother's maiden name."

"In order to spare his relatives? I find it hard to believe, if what Dion and Hatsis say is true."

"No, not to spare them. He was involved in some shady business during the civil war, although he was young at the time. When the wrong side won, he found it prudent to change his name. But we all knew him, since he came from here. And by the time of the Colonels, we thought he'd changed. Apparently his politics had, but that probably was only expediency."

"Then why didn't someone tell us this as soon as Dion asked about a man with six fingers? Many people must have known who he was talking about."

"Of course they did. But with the connection Lambros had with the Colonels and the mysterious aspects of Dion's parents' deaths, it didn't take much imagination to figure out what Dion was up to. We wanted to protect him." She passed her hand over her eyes, but not before Solange saw the tears in them. "And to protect ourselves. It was our shame that such a man was allowed to live and prosper."

Solange shook her head in bewilderment. Even after five years in the country she still couldn't understand the soul of the Greeks, their irrepressible devotion to honor and their ferocious independence, both individual and collective. Four hundred years of Turkish rule hadn't decimated their Greekness. Neither had the vicious civil war that had pitted brother against brother and father against son after the Nazi retreat. Compared to those monumental events, the seven years of the Colonels were only a blip.

Except for someone like Dion, who had seen his family brutally destroyed.

Demetra touched her arm, bringing her out of her introspection. "Solange, you're tired. Go up to bed. I'm sorry I kept you so long."

Solange got up, her movements stiff and jerky, like an automaton. The woolly pressure in her head and the heaviness of her limbs reminded her of her intern days when sixteen-hour shifts had been the norm. "It's all right, Demetra. By the way, I'll be in Athens for a couple of days. Dion has something to clear up and I'm going with him."

Instead of looking happy that the matchmaking scheme seemed to be working, Demetra frowned. "Again? I thought he'd give it up now that he found Lambros."

"So did I," Solange said soberly. "But he has to carry it out to the end and visit his parents' graves."

Demetra's expression lightened marginally, but the concern in her eyes remained. "Take care of him, Solange. Please."

On impulse Solange threw her arms around Demetra and hugged her tightly. "I will, Demetra. You can bet on it."

Solange had reached the door when a thought struck her. She turned. "Demetra, Grandma Amelia's son was killed in a jeep accident in the army. She told us her husband died not long before. How did he die?"

Demetra's face turned bleak, and for a long moment Solange thought she wasn't going to answer. At last she said heavily, "He was shot. It was a political killing."

"GRANDMA AMELIA'S husband was murdered," Solange told Dion the next morning.

He sighed. "Yes, I know. He was active in politics at the time. There's an editorial about his death in one of the old newspapers Papa Yanni gave me."

"You didn't go to see Grandma Amelia last night, did you? To tell her about Raptis?"

Dion, his face lined with fatigue, glanced at her before turning his attention back to the nearly empty highway. Poplars stood like sentinels along the road, flashing long shadows over the speeding car. In the fields wild poppies danced, blood-red in the amber light of the early-morning sun. They were near Lamia, a third of the way to Athens.

"No. I didn't see any point in upsetting her. But eventually she'll have to be told. Even though she didn't say so the day she showed us the photo, she must have questions about both her husband's and her son's deaths. I didn't have time to read everything Papa Yanni gave me, but I found enough to show that my parents knew there was something strange going on. It was just too convenient, both of them dying so close together, and her husband's death clearly an execution."

"But it happened before the military takeover."

"There were schemes afoot for years. The government was very unstable with plots and infighting going on all the time. Why, the politicians sometimes even came to blows in the house of parliament. No one had enough authority to run the country, and there was trouble between the promonarchists and the antimonarchists, not to mention a few Communist former resistance fighters just to liven things up. All of it contributed to a situation ripe for a revolution."

"And you think Amelia's husband knew about it?"

Dion nodded. "I know he did. My father wrote that he and his distant cousin Lambros had already been at bitter odds during the civil war. Lambros changed his politics afterward, but Amelia's husband never trusted him. Lambros being the man he was, a psychopath who was inclined to be paranoid, probably had him removed."

"And possibly his son after that. Dion, do you think Amelia knew?"

"I'm certain she knew but was afraid to talk about it, or she put it so far out of her mind that it was like a form of amnesia."

"Then at least Hatsis showed some conscience. Not that it seems to have made him a happy man."

Dion shrugged. "We all react differently. Some of us give in, and some of us fight back."

And Dion was a fighter.

"As long as you remember when to stop," she muttered.

His mouth tightened. "When it's finished."

THEY FOUND THE VILLAGE without any trouble, a small huddle of houses on a vast plain just south of Marathon. Scattered flocks of sheep grazed the sparse vegetation, their bells a mellow chiming on the morning breeze.

Dion drove first to the cemetery, easily located by its characteristic row of cypresses. The grass inside the fenced plot was uncut, already turning a soft tan in the summer heat.

Solange waited in the car, and Dion was grateful for her sensitivity. He had to do this alone.

Mixed emotions assaulted him as he crunched through dying weeds to the far side of the fenced plot. Grief, a profound sorrow at the waste of productive lives. Gratitude that someone had cared enough to risk recovering his parents' bodies from the rock slide. The fragile beginnings of hope. He found suddenly that he could pray again, deeply, something he had only been able to do superficially for years.

The graves were marked by twin granite stones, the names and the dates engraved without embellishment. His mouth twisted in irony. Poppies, the flower he'd seen as a symbol of betrayal, grew bravely against the stones, gossamer petals the color of blood and as fragile as life itself. But the sight of them could no longer hurt him.

Contrary to common custom, the graves were undisturbed, the bodies left in place rather than dug up after three years and the bones interred in the charnel house. He had a lot to thank Papa Yanni for and vowed that when this was over he would do so.

He closed his eyes and whispered a prayer, a wordless plea for understanding, forgiveness, peace. Yet underneath he knew his anger simmered still. A surprisingly strong anger that frightened and horrified him. Anger at the killers, the mindless obedience to orders given by men without conscience?

No.

He realized all at once the anger was directed at Nicholas and Zoe, and he'd never come to terms with it because of the circumstances and his vow to avenge their deaths.

They had left him. They had lived in a way that was guaranteed to put them in danger. They had continued in the face of threats. Though they'd protected him, they had done nothing to protect themselves. And they had deserted him.

Guilt clawed at him, but it couldn't kill the anger, the rage that made him want to hit out at somebody, anybody.

SOLANGE SAW the rigidity of his body as he left the cemetery, and a worried frown creased her brow. Dion picked up a rock and began to pound it against the drystone wall at the edge of the dirt road. "Damn! Damn! Damn!" Over and over.

Solange watched, saying nothing as pieces of stone chipped off and flew through the air. Let him get it out of his system, she thought. He was finally admitting rage, facing up to the reality everyone who has had a loved one die must come to terms with. And it was just as difficult for him as it had been for her when her mother had died. The sense of desertion, betrayal.

When the rock was reduced to fist-size, he threw it aside and walked toward the car.

"You're angry, aren't you?" she said calmly as he got in behind the wheel. "And it's not what you expected. Dion, this should have happened years ago, but because of your youth and the big upheaval in your life that you had to deal with, you suppressed it."

His lashes were stuck together in clumps from tears she knew he wasn't aware of shedding. "How can I be angry when I loved them so much?" he said thickly.

"And they loved you, Dion. You have to believe that."

"Then they should have gotten out when things heated up. They shouldn't have gotten killed."

"In their place would you have run away? Would you?"

He thought of his search for Pavlou-Raptis, his own determination. "No, I wouldn't have been able to."

"They couldn't, either."

"They had me. They should have thought of what it would do to me."

"You were only one, their son to be sure, but they had to work to ensure a future for the others who fought with them. Ultimately it was your freedom that had to be preserved. What kind of a country would it have been if their work had failed and it went from dictatorship to anarchy and possibly another civil war that would have left nothing but destruction for your generation to inherit? That was what they fought for, and they won."

She let out her breath, feeling slightly foolish after her long, impassioned speech. "I'm sorry, Dion. This doesn't help you."

To her surprise he was looking at her with unmistak-able admiration in his red-rimmed eyes. "Yes, it does, Solange. I didn't think you understood before."

"I'm not sure I understand now." She smiled tenu-ously. "Shall we go and find the house?"

He pulled out a handkerchief and blew his nose. "Yes, let's find the house."

CHAPTER SEVENTEEN

BIRDSONG in a gnarled apple tree gave an air of normality to the cottage at the edge of the village. It was separated from its nearest neighbors by rows of flourishing grapevines and surrounded by a steel picket fence. The gate was unlocked, but the house remained secure, nestled against a hillside.

A large padlock hung on the door, and the windows were hidden behind sturdy roller shutters. Closed in this way, a house was inviolate. Solange knew of people in Korfalli who spent years out of the country, coming back and opening their houses and moving back in with nothing more than sweeping and dusting.

"How do we get in?" she asked, eyeing the padlock. The flower beds along the fence were filled with weeds, dry after a month without rain, their brittle leaves rustling in the faint breeze. A cricket chirred, then leaped explosively out of the grass onto the dusty road.

"We'll break it." Going back to the car, he returned with the tire iron.

Wedging the iron bar between the lock and the steel door frame, he had little difficulty twisting it off. The lock clattered to the pitted concrete step.

"Hey!" The shout spun them around guiltily.

A man stood on the road, a hoe and a shovel over his shoulder. "What are you doing? You've no business disturbing that house."

Dion walked over to the fence, his gait confident, even arrogant. "Isn't this the house where Nicholas and Zoe Parris lived?"

The man lifted his battered cap and scratched his head, replacing it without regard for the disarray of his grizzled hair. "So they say. I wouldn't know. I've only lived here ten years." He crossed himself. "Some say it's haunted."

"Well, I'm Dion Parris, their son. I'd like to look inside."

"Dion Parris? Can you prove that?"

For answer Dion pulled out his wallet and extracted a business card. The man squinted at it. "I don't read English. I suppose this is English. Just a minute."

Moving around to the corner of the fence, he yelled at someone in the field. An old man came slowly through the grapevines. "Eh, Mitso," the first man said. "Can you read this?"

The old man took his time putting his glasses on his nose and closely examining first the card, then looking Dion up and down. Solange, he dismissed with a perfunctory glance.

"You have the look of your father, Dion Parris," he said in passable English. He handed back the car. "Be careful that you don't share his fate. It might not be healthy for you here."

Before Dion could say anything, both men tramped out into the field, vanishing into the tall corn that bordered the grapevines.

Shrugging, Dion returned to the house. The door had a second lock, but to Solange's astonishment Dion inserted a key from his own key chain and opened it.

"You were carrying a key to this house and you never came here?"

The long-disused hinges creaked mournfully as he pushed the door open. "I kept the key. I don't know why. For good luck, a connection with the past—whatever. But I didn't know the house would still be here as they left it. I thought they'd sold it to help pay my school fees. I always stayed with them in the Athens apartment the last few years whenever I wasn't away at school."

"But you didn't even come to check it out."

"No reason to," he said with seeming carelessness.

"No reason to? Dion, you had plenty of reason to. But you were afraid."

They were still standing on the doorstep, Dion blocking Solange's way. Was he afraid now, too, afraid of the memories?

His eyes were hard as he locked them with hers. "Yes, I was afraid. We had good times here. I didn't want to remember until I'd completed what I set out to do."

Another obstacle to the mourning process. He'd denied the obvious and gone after the unattainable. Why? To punish himself for being alive while they were dead? Solange touched his arm, feeling the sweat that matted the soft hairs, sweat that was the product of nerves rather than the day's heat. "Shall we go in?"

Chaos met their eyes. Chairs and tables were overturned, and a television set lay smashed on the floor. Books were scattered out of the bookshelves, their spines broken, pages torn.

Solange gasped in horror. "An earthquake?"

"No, not an earthquake," Dion said grimly. "Look at the calendar."

She followed his pointing finger. A poster-size depiction of the Delphi Charioteer hung askew on the wall, as if someone had looked behind it, perhaps for a wall safe. The month shown was March, nineteen years ago.

"They were arrested in March, killed at Easter, nearly two months later. Someone searched this house, probably after their arrest."

"Then who locked it?"

"I'm guessing Papa Yanni's group, when they buried them. No one's been in here since."

"But it's been searched. Anything of value would be gone." Solange's shoulders sagged in disappointment.

"Not necessarily. Depends how far they searched." He led the way into the kitchen, which was less of a mess than the living room. The cupboards stood open, but were bare except for plates and cups stacked in one of them. A musty smell of damp wood filled the room. "Neither of my parents cared much about cooking. When I wasn't here, there was little food in the house."

"Good thing," Solange said, wrinkling her nose. "Otherwise we'd be battling a million bugs."

"Not after all these years, although we may find an odd one in the cellar."

Pushing aside a dusty rag rug, he uncovered a trapdoor set in the concrete-slab floor. Long-unused hinges creaked as he took hold of the ring and raised the steel panel, then pushed it aside.

Solange shuddered as the dank, chill odor rushed up into the room.

"We'll need a light," Dion said.

But Solange wasn't sure she wanted to know what was in the cellar. The dampness and the cold raised goosebumps on her skin. An irrational apprehension gripped her, and for a moment she found she could believe in the existence of ghosts.

She wanted to run from the house, leave it to its memories of violence and death. Besides, the condition of the rooms indicated a thorough search; it wasn't likely that the cellar had been overlooked.

Dion, apparently less sensitive to the oppressive atmosphere, was already rummaging in a kitchen drawer. "Here it is. A candle and some matches." The matches were damp and limp with age, useless, but in the little alcove that held the gas hot plate he found a lighter. Miraculously it still worked.

The candle's flame flickered as he carefully climbed down the steep, rickety stairs. Keeping her eyes on the light, Solange followed reluctantly, not wanting to let Dion face the past alone. The edge of the lighter bit into her palm as she held on to it. She was taking no chances of being stranded in the dark.

The cellar was just that, an unfinished excavation that extended into the hillside behind the house, earth walls that smelled moldy and old. At one side of the roughly square room were bins that had once held vegetables, flanking empty shelves for canned goods. The wood looked in surprisingly good condition except where it had been broken, probably by a crowbar during the search of the house.

"Good," Dion muttered. "They didn't find it."

"Didn't find what?"

"The secret room."

"The secret room?" Solange echoed in disbelief.

"Yes. Don't you know that secret organizations have to have secret rooms?" The note of humor in his voice seemed macabre under the circumstances, but Solange realized it was his way of fighting off the demons. "I thought it was a wonderful feature to have in a house when I was about fourteen, especially since I was strictly forbidden to talk about it."

His wistful tone showed that he had regressed to some happy childhood memory when tragedy didn't seem possible. Solange wasn't sure what to think about his dispassionate attitude. Ever since they'd come to the house he'd appeared astonishingly cool, as if he were only visiting a museum rather than a place that must be filled with recollections of both joys and pain. If he was repressing strong emotion, she wondered how she would handle it when it came bursting out.

Reaching into a large bin where a couple of round mummified objects that might once have been potatoes lay in the bottom, he manipulated a bolt that was invisible to anyone who didn't know where to look. With a faint click a whole section at the back of the bin slid away, disappearing into another dark passage.

Dion took Solange's hand. "It's a bit of a squeeze here, but in a minute you'll be able to stand up."

After a moment she found herself in a square, concrete-lined room. In the center stood a table surrounded by chairs and covered with dust. Along the wall were a couple of cots, and several more stood folded in the corner. Shelves held canned food, books and files, and even bottles of wine.

"This is where they hid political dissidents on occasion," Dion said, his voice only slightly above a whisper. He lit the lantern that stood on the table, pumping the air supply so that the light brightened and extended to the far corners. The pungent smell of kerosene filled the small room.

"Well, it looks as if nobody found it." Solange browsed through the books and papers, mostly notes on university courses. A box of photographs included shots of a student riot with army tanks converging on the advancing crowd. She remembered the event, the students killed and the outcry over it that had filled the world's news reports. On the back of one of the larger photos was a poem, a long epic, which, as nearly as she could figure out, was a graphic retelling of the killings and an expression of rage against the perpetrators. She shivered at the despair and helpless anger evident in the writing and wondered if the author had lived to see his world change.

Dion poked among the wine bottles, taking out first one and then another and holding it up to the light. "Ah, this looks like the one." He shook it and a small object on the bottom rattled against the thick green glass.

"Champagne? Now?"

"Not champagne," he said, heading for the sink in the corner. He ripped off the foil and gently pulled out the cork without the aid of a corkscrew. "It's light vegetable oil," he explained, pouring the contents of the bottle down the drain. "Superficially it looks like any bottle of white wine." The bottle empty, he shook it over his open palm. A small flat key dropped out. "This is it, the key to the safe-deposit box."

"Isn't it strange that your parents didn't tell you about the key?"

"They never had a chance to. I was only allowed to speak to them once after their arrest. There was a guard watching the whole time. I only saw my father. It was a week before the execution. They said my mother was too ill to leave her cell."

His voice broke, but after dragging in a long breath, he went on. "Father told me to see a certain man who had been a colleague of theirs—the name he used was a code, but I knew who to see. This man gave me the air ticket to Canada and a passport I'm not sure was completely legal. But it got me out. As far as I knew, my parents hadn't had this house for two years, and all their work had been confiscated. It was a critical time. Nobody was safe.''

"I wonder why Papa Yanni didn't open the box,'' Solange said thoughtfully. "It might have contained something useful to the organization.''

Dion shook his head. "Even if he'd felt within his rights, he couldn't have. Bank regulations. I'm the only one who can get in it, the heir to the estate.''

"Will the bank still honor that after all these years?''

He touched her shoulder, squeezing it for an instant. "We'll see. If we hurry, we'll just have time to make it before they close for the day.''

Luckily the bank was in Kifissia, not far away. To their disappointment, the box, readily opened by the bank manager who had been sympathetic to Dion's parents and who had gotten to know Dion during his efforts to free them by bribery, contained nothing but another key. But it was a key Dion recognized.

"It's a duplicate of the one we had in the apartment to the storage area. Is it possible the government agents didn't clean that out? But then again, if they never found a key they might not have known there was a storage area.''

The storage compartments weren't contained in the same building as the apartment, Solange soon found out. The center of Athens was relatively quiet as siesta hour descended, the streets carrying only taxis and buses due to traffic restrictions. In defiance of the law and knowing foreign licenses had certain privileges, Dion drove through the tangle of streets to a building on the outskirts of the Plaka.

The manager remembered Dion and enfolded him in a hug. "Of course, my boy, I'll take you to the warehouse. And don't worry, no one's been in your parents' things. I always knew you'd be back someday."

"It's been a very roundabout journey."

The man led them through a narrow hallway and out the back of the building. From there they followed a tortuous route of back alleys in which skinny cats drowsed in the sun or rummaged in garbage pails put out for collection. Once a dog, disturbed from its siesta, ran ahead of them, its gait loose-limbed and as floppy as an inadequately stuffed toy.

"Not much farther now," their guide said, puffing with exertion. He paused beside a formidably barred door, at least four yards high, set in a stone wall. Above the door the wall was smooth, set with a couple of tiny windows protected by heavy wire mesh. "This is where they kept their valuable papers, where they worked to put out their underground newspaper."

Lighting a cigarette, he blew out smoke that rose on the still, close air. Three foreshortened shadows flowed before them as the sun shone straight overhead. The quiet of the street was so profound that Solange couldn't shake off a sense of unreality, as if she were walking in a dream and would soon wake up to find herself in her own bed in Korfalli.

The door opened smoothly, no betraying creak to wake the neighborhood. Inside, an old-fashioned printing press sat in the middle of an open space, lit by the single bulb that hung from the ceiling. By its light, Solange could see other cords and sockets, but the bulbs had long been removed from them.

The man led them to the far side of the room where he opened another locked door. "There. It's the second locker on the right."

Hands trembling so that he could hardly hold the key, Dion inserted it into the lock and turned it. The mechanism clicked and the heavy steel door swung outward.

Inside were only two cardboard boxes, each about twice the size of shoe boxes.

"That's it?" Solange's voice was flat with disappointment.

"Remember what Papa Yanni said. Most of their work was published. This has to be the last story they were working on, the one they were keeping secret. And probably their background research notes are also in the boxes. Let's get them out to the car."

The man who had accompanied them helped to transport the light load back to the apartment building. "Can I rent out the space? Or will you be coming back?"

"I don't think I'll be back," Dion said. "I suppose you rented out my parents' apartment long ago?"

The man inclined his head. "Years ago. I'm sorry." He gave an apologetic shrug. "You understand. They'd signed a release, instructions to be followed in case they were arrested, and I sold the furniture for the last month's rent."

"What about their personal effects?"

Nervously puffing on a cigarette, the man shook his head. "The police took all of it when they were arrested. I couldn't say much or they would have taken me, as well."

"You were part of the underground movement."

"I was. But I didn't advertise it. Not like your parents. Their feelings were obvious to everyone who read their work. We carried on after they died, but it wasn't the same. It was as if the blood had drained out.''

Dion grasped the man's shoulder. "I'm sure you did the best you could."

"Not good enough. The same situation may happen again. The present government is in deep trouble. Too many scandals. It's ripening again." Crossing himself, he lowered his voice. "There's a rumor. One man. No, I can't say more." He turned back toward his apartment door, pausing only to say goodbye. "Good luck, Dion Parris. God go with you."

"SHALL WE GO back to the house, or would you rather stay in a hotel?" Dion asked when they were in the car threading through the city traffic.

This morning she'd wanted to flee the house, but oddly since she'd seen the cellar, seen there was nothing sinister hidden there, she didn't have any qualms about going back. But did Dion? "Will it bother you to go back to the house?"

"No. Why should it?"

"Remembering."

"I've come to terms with it. I can handle the memories. Most of them were good ones. You were right. It is kind of a good feeling to go back to where we lived, to remember the early days when we were together and happy."

He went on to tell her how he'd gone to the village school for a while and played soccer on Sunday afternoons in a dusty field that the village kids had dubbed the stadium.

"When I started high school, we moved to the apartment, but we always came back to the house for the summer. Until the last two years. I missed it. I missed them, too, when I was away at school.''

They had been close, the three of them, Solange realized. A picture emerged of Dion as a self-sufficient child, mature beyond his years. Only children were relatively rare in Greece, especially at that time, but Dion had apparently not been spoiled or unnecessarily indulged. Perhaps because his parents had both been busy with their careers.

In Amaroussi Dion abruptly turned off and drove toward the police station. ''I'd like to talk to Captain Demos for a moment.''

''Captain Demos?''

''Yes,'' he said almost impatiently. ''Remember when I was arrested for hit and run and you came to my rescue. He warned me about looking for Pavlou. So I've been wondering if he knew something he wasn't telling me. Now's the time to pin him down. Do you want to wait in the car?''

''Yes, but you'll have to park in the shade.''

Fortunately Demos was on duty, going through paperwork in his office. A ceiling fan whirred overhead, but with little effect on the heat. He looked up when Dion was announced, mopping his sweating face with a handkerchief. ''You're still here, are you?''

''Yes, I'm still here.'' Dion sat down on the wooden chair, which was as hard as he remembered it. ''Have you got anything new on Mavrakis's death?''

''Not much. We found the car that hit him a couple of days later. It had been stolen. We checked out the estate where you lost the man who posed as a policeman.''

Dion's heart sped up. ''Did you talk to anyone there?''

''Not likely. Do you know who lives there?''

''A retired general, Adoni Gallos.''

Demos looked surprised. "You're well-informed. However, the general has been in poor health for some time and he's gone with his daughter to a spa in Switzerland for a cure, they say. The daughter and her husband live with him. And I wouldn't like to be the one who disturbed them."

"Why?"

"Because I'd soon be walking a beat in Soufli."

"Soufli? Isn't that up near the Turkish border?"

"Exactly," Demos said, putting a wealth of meaning into the single word.

Dion smiled faintly as comprehension dawned. Every policeman's ambition was to be stationed in Athens. Soufli was used as a euphemism for profound disgrace, one step above suspension.

"The general's son-in-law is a politician, isn't he?"

Demos nodded. "A powerful politician who will bring the country to its knees if he's elected. And all the signs point to the probability that he will be. I wouldn't like to be the one to mess with him."

"I'M SORRY." Solange's voice shook and tears stung her eyes. "I just can't seem to turn off my head."

They lay in bed in the house where Dion had spent his childhood. Next to her Dion stirred, gathering her close, his eyes heavy with the lassitude of satisfied love that she had been unable to share.

"It's okay." He stroked his hand up and down her back, her skin soft and sleek under his palm. Would they ever lie together like this again? To ward off the unthinkable, he said with a determined optimism he was far from feeling, "It's not as if it's the last time we'll ever make love."

But the question hung between them, weighty and dark: what if it was?

The room was hot, the mattress still faintly musty, even though they'd aired it. The sheets smelled like the potpourri with which they'd been stored in a cedar blanket chest. Solange lay in Dion's arms, her arm cramped under his shoulder, but she didn't care. Her skin was sticky with perspiration. She needed a shower, but the need to hold him was stronger. If she could only keep him here, he would be safe; she would make him forget.

Ever since he'd talked with Captain Demos, Dion had been preoccupied. He'd refused her help in going through the papers in the two boxes. "But I have to do something," she said.

"You can make something to eat."

Feeling rejected, she'd turned to him, words of resentment trembling on her lips. But the odd, pleading look in his eyes had stopped her. "Please, Solange. I have to do this alone. I just have this feeling that it's going to get complicated."

And she'd complied. Since there was nothing to eat in the house, she'd taken the car and gone into Marathon where she'd been lucky to find a restaurant that sold her a roasted chicken. From a stand beside the road she'd purchased fruit, but any other shopping would have to wait until the stores opened.

She shifted, and his arms tightened around her. "Don't go," he murmured, his breath stirring the fine hairs at her temple.

"I wasn't going. Dion, what did you find?"

He laid his fingers across her lips. "Sshh. Tomorrow. We'll talk tomorrow."

Tomorrow it would be over. Tomorrow he would confront the man who was really behind his parents' deaths. After that it was in the hands of God. He might be in jail. Or facing the firing squad for treason.

Captain Demos had been right to warn him. Trifon Drakos, the general's son-in-law, was a powerful man. But Dion had the means to stop him. In the boxes he had found a thick file of information that Nicholas had accumulated—information that would cause a scandal that would make the present ones look like nothing at all. All Dion had to do was confront Drakos and show him what he knew. Drakos would have no choice but to resign from his party and from public office. That might cause a stir, but not nearly the cataclysm that would explode if his secret activities were made public.

Or he could kill him. And he would. Drakos was the man who'd ordered his parents' death.

"I have to stop him," he said aloud. "Or there will be a bloodbath like no one's seen."

Solange's heart lurched in her chest. "You found something in your father's papers, didn't you?" she asked in a resigned tone. "Who is it?"

She didn't hold out much hope of an answer, but he surprised her. "The man who lives at the estate on Penteli. Trifon Drakos."

"Drakos? The politician."

"Yes. And he has to pay."

The bleak tone of his voice pierced her heart. The miracle she was praying for wasn't going to happen. "Dion—"

He touched her lips with a gentle finger. "Solange, don't. Please don't. I have to do it, see it through. It's been part of me for so long." His eyes fell closed. "And I don't know how to stop it anymore."

He laid his cheek against hers, regret twisting in him. He needed this night—to love her, to absorb everything she was, her sweetness, her essential goodness, to lock the memory of her love deep within him. "Solange, don't think anymore. I need you."

Moonlight turned her body to silver. With an exquisite tenderness he began to touch her, caressing her with his hands and with his mouth, arousing her, driving out every thought except the reality of his love. No matter what happened she would remember him, and he wanted her to remember him with joy, not sadness. As he would remember her.

He couldn't take away the pain she would feel tomorrow, but he could give her this night.

Dion, I love you, don't go. The words echoed in Solange's mind. But as he kissed her, at first gently, and then with a feverish desperation, the echo grew fainter until it faded altogether. Her blood quickened in response to his touch, and the barriers that had earlier held her back came tumbling down.

Moving against him, she pressed her hand to the base of his spine, trembling in anticipation when she felt the moan that reverberated through him. He lifted himself, framing her face with his two hands as he made their bodies one. "Solange, remember. Remember that...that I... Remember me."

He surged into her once, twice, pausing as the first ripples of fulfillment chased over her skin. "Yes, go with me. Yes, all the way."

He led, and she followed, into a world where there was no past, and all futures were possible, to a world where dreams became reality, and two souls fused into one.

I love you. She heard the words as clearly as if he'd said them out loud, and she struggled to answer. But then he touched her, his fingers gentle, and coherent thought fled. She stilled for a second, then arched wildly against him, the shock wave of her completion taking him with her. A feverish heat engulfed them, forging a bond that only death could break.

Solange lay next to him afterward, too wrung out to move. *Please, God,* she thought, *let Dion abandon this quest.* If he did, their love would endure, and she'd have a chance with him. A future—in Canada or Greece or wherever. She didn't care as long as she could have him.

"Remember, Solange," he murmured so softly that she might have dreamed it. "No matter what happens, I'll get word to you."

And with that she knew there was nothing she could do.

After a time Solange fell into a troubled sleep. When she awoke, in the deep darkness before dawn, Dion was gone.

CHAPTER EIGHTEEN

TO DION'S SURPRISE the gates at the Drakos estate stood open. No one challenged him as he drove straight up the paved driveway to the house set in a cluster of pine trees. He stepped out of the car, the moonlight casting pale shadows around as dawn approached. In the distance he thought he could hear waves breaking on a rocky shore.

The massive front door of the house swung inward at his touch, but he no longer felt surprise. Instead, apprehension prickled over his skin, lifting the hairs at the back of his neck.

A small hunting knife strapped to his ankle gave him little reassurance. He didn't even know if he would be able to use it. How did a knife feel sliding into a body? Despite the cool night, sweat ran down his sides, dampening his shirt.

He was a fool, bent on self-destruction, and the only ammunition he had was a sheaf of papers.

At least he'd taken what precautions he could. When Solange's even breathing had told him she was asleep, he'd crept out of the bed and dressed. He'd found a print shop in Kifissia where he'd been able to bribe the janitor to let him photocopy the critical information. Then he'd put everything into a plain envelope and mailed it to Stefan in Vancouver, to be opened in case he didn't contact him within a reasonable time.

Change by peaceful means. He hesitated in midstride as he walked silently down the marble-tiled hall toward a lighted doorway, his father's words slipping through his mind as if printed on a ghostly banner. A message? In the tiny chapel where he'd stopped to pray on his way here, the monks had just started their predawn mass. "Peace be with you," they'd chanted. He shook his head. He couldn't have second thoughts now.

He reached the door, pushed it farther open.

The man who sat behind the desk stood up as soon as Dion crossed the threshold. Even dressed in pyjamas and a robe he was imposing, tall with broad shoulders and the substantial look politicians seemed to cultivate. His black hair was combed back from a widow's peak that accented the angular lines of his face. Smiling, he looked benign. Now, with a guarded, watchful look in his pale gray eyes, he looked dangerous.

"I've been expecting you, Dion Parris." His voice was low, resonant, touched with irony that brought a faint smile to his lips but left his eyes cold as a frozen sea. "I knew the moment you arrived in that village and visited your parents' graves."

Nothing could surprise Dion anymore. "You know why I've come, then." He glanced around the luxurious room, noting the leather-bound books that filled the shelves, the original art displayed on the walls and in a curio cabinet. "I suppose the bodyguards are hiding out back?"

Drakos shook his head. "No bodyguards. This is between you and me." Sitting down, he gestured for Dion to do the same.

"I'd rather stand, thank you."

"As you wish." Setting his elbows on the desk, he steepled his fingers before his face. "I sent the bodyguards away. I didn't want any witnesses."

Again fear laid icy tracks up Dion's spine. This was a ruthless man. Killing Dion would be akin to stepping on an ant for this man, whose history was documented in the papers Dion held in his hand.

He pushed away the fear, pushed away the image of Solange's face soft with sleep as he'd left her, shut out the agony she would feel if he didn't return, an agony that even now gnawed at his own heart. He had to do this, regardless of the consequences.

"Considerate of you." He was amazed that his voice sounded cool, detached and steady. "I, too, don't need witnesses."

He tapped the thick manila envelope he carried. "It's all here, dates and places, substantiated by statements from witnesses."

Drakos glanced over the papers Dion spread on his desk. His expression didn't alter, his eyes remained hooded and faintly contemptuous as they met Dion's. "This is all in the past. Everyone knows I've changed my politics since then."

"You know that's a lie. You want to take over the country, turn it back into a dictatorship. You see this name?" He stabbed at the top document with his finger. "As late as last year you still called this man your friend, although now you're on record as saying he betrayed you. But these papers prove that you knew the man twenty years ago and helped him to gain the directorship of a bank that soon made astonishing progress and was until last year one of the five largest banks in Greece. A bank that's now almost in bankruptcy because you helped this man siphon off funds into Swiss accounts. What are you going to do, Kyrios Drakos, when you become dictator, bleed the country dry and then leave it to blow away? Well, I'm not going to let that happen."

Drakos leaned back in his chair, the paleness of his cheeks the only sign he was affected by Dion's vehement words. "And how will you stop me? By killing me?" He paused, then added contemplatively, "You'll have to, you know. I have connections in high places who'd be only too glad to expedite the departure of an unwelcome tourist. No, perhaps that would be too easy. I hear your jails in Canada are quite luxurious. Perhaps you'd like to experience a real prison."

Dion laughed humorlessly. "Do you think I'm stupid? I've mailed the originals of these documents to someone in Canada who will see that they're published if I don't tell him otherwise."

Unperturbed, Drakos slid his chair closer to the desk. "As you've pointed out, I have money. I could pay off your friend. Anyone can be bought."

"Not anyone," Dion said, his throat tight. "This man's mother and sister were tortured, raped and killed in 1973 by people connected with you. He isn't going to be bought off."

"Then I'm going to have to kill you," Drakos said softly. He brought his hand up, and Dion found himself looking into the innocently small black hole at the end of the barrel of a sleek gray pistol.

SOLANGE PAID OFF the taxi driver outside the gates, doubling the fare accumulated on the meter. The man had driven her in record time, speeding through the gray dawn down the deserted roads and suburban streets without regard for safety or laws.

He grinned broadly as he tucked the money into his pocket, restarting the taxi and sending it into a wild spin as he turned on the road. The pungent fumes of burnt rubber stung her nostrils as she walked slowly up the driveway.

At the sight of Dion's car she paused, her heart clenching painfully in her chest. She touched its hood in passing. Cold. He'd been here well before her. If only she hadn't fallen asleep, she might have been able to stop him.

The front door stood ajar and she walked in, following the sound of voices.

Dion's voice, taunting and harsh. "Go ahead. Pull the trigger. Your career is over whether you do or don't. You might as well be indicted for murder as for fraud."

Through the half-open door of the study, Solange could see a man holding a gun. Trifon Drakos. She recognized him from newspaper photos, although at the moment he presented an image far removed from that of the affable politician, the friend of the common people as he called himself.

She pushed the door farther, trying to see Dion. Drakos must have noticed the subtle movement, for he suddenly swung the gun over and fired. A splinter flew off the edge of the door frame, the report momentarily deafening her as she dropped to the floor.

The marble tiles were cold under her cheek and hands. For a stunned moment she wondered if she'd been shot. She moved experimentally, flexing her arms and legs. No pain, only a buzzing in her head. Percussion, she realized.

Through the ringing in her ears she heard the sounds of a scuffle. Forcing herself to her knees, she peered around the door, tensely ready to duck.

The game had changed. Dion held the gun, and Drakos sat in the desk chair, blood dripping from his nose. Eyes glittering in futile rage, he pulled out a handkerchief and wiped his face.

Slowly, her limbs lethargic with dissipated adrenaline, Solange stood up, pushing the door wider. Dion moved around the desk and pressed the muzzle of the gun to Drakos's temple. Turning his head slightly, he looked at Solange. "Go and wait outside." His voice was cold, his face that of a stranger, starkly white and stripped of all emotion.

She gripped the door frame, her nails biting into the wood. "Dion—"

"Go!" he snapped.

The word sliced through her, as cutting as shards of glass. She turned away, her heart a dead lump in her breast. He was going to do it. She couldn't stop him.

DION STARED DOWN at the man cringing in the chair. On Drakos's temple he could see a little red circle where the gun barrel had bruised the skin. Dion laid paper and pen before him. "Write. First a letter of resignation from your political party, citing health problems. Second, a complete confession regarding your activities during the military regime when you pretended to help the resistance but were really a spy for the government. People here have long memories, as you well know. When this is made public, people will spit when they hear your name. Third, write a suicide note. Say you've been consumed with guilt at last."

Trembling, the man wrote. When he was finished, Dion, perched on the edge of the desk, glanced over the sheets. "Good. Now sign them."

Drakos signed. Dion folded the papers and tucked them into the envelope with his other documents. He smiled almost gently as he lifted the gun and pointed it at Drakos's head. His finger tensed on the trigger.

"Wait." Drakos lifted his hand. "I have money in Switzerland. My wife and father-in-law are there now. One phone call and I can transfer any amount to any bank in the world."

Dion's jaw clenched. "Do you think you can pay for what my parents suffered with money? Nothing can, but this."

SOLANGE HUDDLED on the steps outside the front door, shivering in the amber light of morning. A mist rose from Drakos's lush garden, the dampness penetrating the thin shirt she wore. She should have phoned the police; Captain Demos would have been discreet. But up until that moment in Drakos's study she had believed that she could stop Dion, with no need to involve anyone else.

Now it was too late.

When she heard the gunshot, she jerked as if the bullet had buried itself in her body. Agony tore through her, a shaft of white-hot steel. *No, Dion. No!*

Wrapping her arms around her chest, she walked to Dion's car, a small square shadow under a sky turning gray with dawn. The keys were in the ignition. She could leave, turn her back on him forever.

A sound from the house spun her around, her heart jumping into her mouth. Dion stood on the steps, his face familiar once more, looking strangely at peace.

She saw the gun in his hand, heard his words, and the hope died.

"It's over."

Bitter sickness rose in her throat. She swayed on her feet, the pain of disillusion clawing in her stomach. Turning from him, she clutched the roof of the car, her breath rasping in harsh, gulping sobs.

Up to this moment she had still believed he wouldn't do it. The gentleness she'd seen in him, the sensitivity he'd shown with her and with the people of Korfalli weren't the marks of a man who could kill another, no matter what the provocation.

And provocation he had. She knew it now. She'd known it for some time, even before she'd seen the article he'd left behind. She'd read it as she waited for the taxi earlier, her horror and anger growing with each word. Drakos was a psychopath, devoid of human feelings. He would trample anything and anyone in his path in his quest for power. If he'd become prime minister—and there was every chance he could have—there would have been a holocaust such as Greece had never seen. Future generations would thank Dion for having assassinated such a man, not condemn him.

So how could she?

Because no matter how she tried to rationalize it, she couldn't condone cold-blooded murder. Not even the murder of a man as evil as Drakos. And if Dion could murder, then she couldn't love him. Now he could only have her sympathy.

She spread her hands on the mist-dewed metal of the car, forcing away her numbness. Dion would need a good attorney. He should be able to get a light sentence on the basis of moral justification, perhaps even calling it a crime of passion. She considered the people she knew. The lawyer who'd helped settle some of the earthquake claims might be available. . . .

"Solange." She shuddered when he put his hand on her shoulder and pulled her close to him. "Solange." He shook her a little. Her eyes were glazed with horror, but he took heart from the fact that she didn't push him away. "Solange, I didn't do it."

Tilting back her head, she stared at him. Her eyes were blank, black pools in the pearly light, her skin fragile and transparent with lack of sleep. A tear trembled on her lashes. He wiped it away with his thumb. "Solange, I didn't kill him."

"You didn't kill him?" She sagged against him, and he tightened his arms around her waist. "Why? You had the gun. I heard a shot."

"Yes, I fired, but not at Drakos." He smiled faintly, ironically. "I'm not sure I know why I didn't kill him. I was pointing the gun at him, and I knew what he'd done, not only to my parents but to others, but something stopped me."

His throat thick, he swallowed, choosing his words with difficulty. "I realized that by killing Drakos I would gain nothing. I already had him checkmated. Already had my parents' article and the confession I forced him to sign. I still *wanted* to kill him but..." Dion shook his head.

As he'd stood over Drakos, he'd had the strangest sensation that someone else had entered the room. Then he heard the words that had been chanted in the candle-lit chapel that morning: "Peace be with you."

"I remembered what my father used to say. 'Change by peaceful means.' It was almost as if he were there. I suddenly knew that finding the man and stopping him was enough. I didn't need to kill him."

Dion sighed heavily. "At the last moment when my finger tensed on the trigger, I swung the gun aside and fired into the wall. But Drakos has been stopped, and he'll be punished. There was no need for me to be his executioner."

And what a relief that was. It was past time for him to put the past where it belonged, not buried but on record as a warning. And now he had to move forward into the future, making sure it was a future that would nurture his children—his and Solange's.

"So many years I lived with this," he said with a catch in his voice. "But you made me doubt, Solange. I began to see the futility of always trying to even the score. You made me feel again, made me care about people. I found I couldn't do it. I couldn't risk losing you."

She pulled free of his arms and walked a little distance away. "I was so scared," he heard her whisper.

"Well, it's over now. I've called Captain Demos. The police should be here shortly."

Solange turned. Her face was as pale as the morning glories that twined around the base of the chestnut tree behind her. "Will he be convicted?" she asked in a low voice.

"With the evidence I have and his written confession, yes. Drakos is a criminal, just as if he'd robbed the bank himself instead of only siphoning off the profits. He won't be doing it again."

He lifted his hand, staring at the gun in it as if it were something foul. Pulling back his arm, he flung it as far as he could, satisfaction filling him as it clattered down the rocky cliff at the edge of the garden.

Solange followed its path with her eyes, then turned back to him. "It's really finished then?"

"Yes, it's finished. And I can say it now. Solange, I love you. I love you more than life."

Solange stood for a moment as if frozen, and despair clawed at him. Then she moved into his arms. "Dion, you were right. You had to do this, had to track this man down. Not to kill him. Not for revenge. But for justice. And I'm proud of you for doing it."

He held her against him, relief making him dizzy. Happiness surged up in him, so much that he couldn't talk. He could only stare at her, her beautiful face flushed with color, the sick pallor gone, her cheeks wet with tears.

"I'm not perfect," she said. "I doubted you, but I never stopped loving you. But if you ever put me through a night like this again, I'll kill you." Stretching up, she pressed her open mouth against his. "I'll never—" she kissed him again "—never let you go."

He laughed shakily, though he felt closer to tears. "Never is a long time."

"Yes, forever."

HARLEQUIN®
OFFICIAL SWEEPSTAKES
RULES

NO PURCHASE NECESSARY

1. To enter, complete an Official Entry Form or 3"× 5" index card by hand-printing, in plain block letters, your complete name, address, phone number and age, and mailing it to: Harlequin Fashion A Whole New You Sweepstakes, P.O. Box 9056, Buffalo, NY 14269-9056.

   No responsibility is assumed for lost, late or misdirected mail. Entries must be sent separately with first class postage affixed, and be received no later than December 31, 1991 for eligibility.

2. Winners will be selected by D.L. Blair, Inc., an independent judging organization whose decisions are final, in random drawings to be held on January 30, 1992 in Blair, NE at 10:00 a.m. from among all eligible entries received.

3. The prizes to be awarded and their approximate retail values are as follows: Grand Prize — A brand-new Mercury Sable LS plus a trip for two (2) to Paris, including round-trip air transportation, six (6) nights hotel accommodation, a $1,400 meal/spending money stipend and $2,000 cash toward a new fashion wardrobe (approximate value: $28,000) or $15,000 cash; two (2) Second Prizes — A trip to Paris, including round-trip air transportation, six (6) nights hotel accommodation, a $1,400 meal/spending money stipend and $2,000 cash toward a new fashion wardrobe (approximate value: $11,000) or $5,000 cash; three (3) Third Prizes — $2,000 cash toward a new fashion wardrobe. All prizes are valued in U.S. currency. Travel award air transportation is from the commercial airport nearest winner's home. Travel is subject to space and accommodation availability, and must be completed by June 30, 1993. Sweepstakes offer is open to residents of the U.S. and Canada who are 21 years of age or older as of December 31, 1991, except residents of Puerto Rico, employees and immediate family members of Torstar Corp., its affiliates, subsidiaries, and all agencies, entities and persons connected with the use, marketing, or conduct of this sweepstakes. All federal, state, provincial, municipal and local laws apply. Offer void wherever prohibited by law. Taxes and/or duties, applicable registration and licensing fees, are the sole responsibility of the winners. Any litigation within the province of Quebec respecting the conduct and awarding of a prize may be submitted to the Régie des loteries et courses du Québec. All prizes will be awarded; winners will be notified by mail. No substitution of prizes is permitted.

4. Potential winners must sign and return any required Affidavit of Eligibility/Release of Liability within 30 days of notification. In the event of noncompliance within this time period, the prize may be awarded to an alternate winner. Any prize or prize notification returned as undeliverable may result in the awarding of that prize to an alternate winner. By acceptance of their prize, winners consent to use of their names, photographs and/or their likenesses for purposes of advertising, trade and promotion on behalf of Torstar Corp. without further compensation. Canadian winners must correctly answer a time-limited arithmetical question in order to be awarded a prize.

5. For a list of winners (available after 3/31/92), send a separate stamped, self-addressed envelope to: Harlequin Fashion A Whole New You Sweepstakes, P.O. Box 4694, Blair, NE 68009.

PREMIUM OFFER TERMS

To receive your gift, complete the Offer Certificate according to directions. Be certain to enclose the required number of "Fashion A Whole New You" proofs of product purchase (which are found on the last page of every specially marked "Fashion A Whole New You" Harlequin or Silhouette romance novel). Requests must be received no later than December 31, 1991. Limit: four (4) gifts per name, family, group, organization or address. Items depicted are for illustrative purposes only and may not be exactly as shown. Please allow 6 to 8 weeks for receipt of order. Offer good while quantities of gifts last. In the event an ordered gift is no longer available, you will receive a free, previously unpublished Harlequin or Silhouette book for every proof of purchase you have submitted with your request, plus a refund of the postage and handling charge you have included. Offer good in the U.S. and Canada only.

HQFW-SWPR

HARLEQUIN® OFFICIAL SWEEPSTAKES ENTRY FORM

4-FWHSS-2

Complete and return this Entry Form immediately – the more entries you submit, the better your chances of winning!

- Entries must be received by December 31, 1991.
- A Random draw will take place on January 30, 1992.
- No purchase necessary.

Yes, I want to win a FASHION A WHOLE NEW YOU Classic and Romantic prize from Harlequin:

Name _____ Telephone _____ Age _____

Address _____

City _____ State _____ Zip _____

Return Entries to: **Harlequin FASHION A WHOLE NEW YOU,**
P.O. Box 9056, Buffalo, NY 14269-9056   © 1991 Harlequin Enterprises Limited

PREMIUM OFFER

To receive your free gift, send us the required number of proofs-of-purchase from any specially marked FASHION A WHOLE NEW YOU Harlequin or Silhouette Book with the Offer Certificate properly completed, plus a check or money order (do not send cash) to cover postage and handling payable to Harlequin FASHION A WHOLE NEW YOU Offer. We will send you the specified gift.

OFFER CERTIFICATE

Item	A. ROMANTIC COLLECTOR'S DOLL (Suggested Retail Price $60.00)	B. CLASSIC PICTURE FRAME (Suggested Retail Price $25.00)
# of proofs-of-purchase	18	12
Postage and Handling	$3.50	$2.95
Check one	☐	☐

Name _____

Address _____

City _____ State _____ Zip _____

Mail this certificate, designated number of proofs-of-purchase and check or money order for postage and handling to: **Harlequin FASHION A WHOLE NEW YOU Gift Offer**, P.O. Box 9057, Buffalo, NY 14269-9057. Requests must be received by December 31, 1991.

ONE PROOF-OF-PURCHASE

4-FWHSP-2

To collect your fabulous free gift you must include the necessary number of proofs-of-purchase with a properly completed Offer Certificate.

© 1991 Harlequin Enterprises Limited

See previous page for details.